BLACK WILLOW

JENNY OFFUTT

PELICAN HOUSE

For my family,

Thank you for the countless brainstorming sessions, the bottomless cup of coffee when I'm under deadline and most importantly, for your love, support and contagious enthusiasm. You make my world a beautiful place to live.

This edition published by arrangement with Pelican House Publishing.

ISBN 13: 9780998984902

Copyright 2018 by Jenny Offutt

PELICAN HOUSE

ABOUT THE AUTHOR

Jenny Offutt is a freelance author of romantic suspense. She devotes herself to providing readers with exciting, fast-paced tales of love, romance and mystery, guaranteed to keep you on the edge of your seat. She is a member of Romance Writers of America, Mystery Writers of America, Ozark's Romance Authors and Ozark's Writers League.

Jenny lives in the Midwest with her husband and their two boys, where they have a Bed and Breakfast resort on the beautiful shores of Table Rock Lake. If you would like to contact Jenny, or simply want to know more about her, please feel free to look her up at jennyoffutt.com. She always enjoys connecting with readers.

ACKNOWLEDGMENTS

A very special thank you to my editors, Caroline Tolley and Amy Knupp. Your guidance was invaluable. Also, a big thank you to Amanda Matthews at AM Design Studios.

PROLOGUE

Black Willow Farm
Marietta, Pennsylvania
1979

Run. She begged him to run to her. But he couldn't. Fear took root, sealing his little feet to the floor as flames raced across the attic, climbing the slant of the walls, licking at the curtains. Tasting, touching, devouring everything in their path.

"*Run to mommy!*" she screamed again, her voice soaring above the howl and moan of the fire.

A trace of relief swept through him. He'd thought he was alone in the house, thought everyone had left him behind. But she was there now, her voice charging through the darkness at the bottom of the stairs. She'd come back just for him.

"Mommy! I can't see you!"

A loud crash rocked the house as the support beam overhead broke free and spiraled down through the floor at the far end of the room—the floor above his mother.

"*Mommy!*"

Smoke, thick as wool, closed in on him as the fire snapped its jaws, belching black in every direction. His eyes stung, lungs burned. He had to get to her. Small hands reached out, shaking as they pushed their way into the angry wall of heat and fire separating him from his mother.

He tripped, scooting something out in front of him. *The matches*, he realized, his footsteps jerking to a halt. The ones he'd snuck from the kitchen—for the second time. The ones he wasn't supposed to have. He picked up the box, remembering how, one by one, he'd drawn each stick out, spellbound by the brilliant burst of heat and light that arced forth with every strike. But then one had escaped from his hand, sparking the quilt. He'd tried to stop it, tried with all his might.

It hit him. *What had he done?*

"Mommy!" he screamed again as loud as he could, a new kind of terror coursing through him like a river. "Please, answer me... Please!"

His grandfather had warned him never to touch the box again, or he'd be sorry. Had growled it, hot and wet against his ear. That he would personally see to it he was punished in a way he would never forget, that it would be another one of their little secrets. And his words rang true—even at seven years old, he knew it to his core. He'd had enough trips to the doctor for *accidents* since they'd moved here to keep it fresh in his mind.

Still, the lure of the tiny flickers of orange and yellow and red, his obsession with the way they danced and swayed so bright at his fingertips. The pure, raw joy of being able to create—*to control* —something with his own two little hands. It had been too much for him to deny.

Tears poured from his eyes as he took another step toward the gaping hole in the floor that now held his mother in its belly. The house groaned around him.

"Are you there, Mommy?"

He crept to the edge and leaned over, crying out as her body came into view. Fully engulfed. And then all at once, glass shattered behind him and the smoke shifted. It roared toward the sound, barreling toward the window and out into the night. *What was happening?* Someone called his name, a voice he didn't recognize, and before he knew it, large, capable arms were around him, pulling him fast. He could breathe again, his lungs sputtering as they adjusted. He was outside now. His body bobbing to and fro. Not of his own accord, but of the man who'd saved him. As the world came back into focus, a blaze of red and blue colors swirled in the distance, lighting up the night. Above him, streams of water sprayed across the house, steadily winning the cutthroat battle against flames that engulfed over half of the attic and third floor.

He stared at the scene, wild-eyed, oblivious to the sting of sleet the black sky had begun to spit at him. Fresh tears flooded down swollen, smoke-stained cheeks. He wanted his mother—wanted her more than he'd ever wanted anything in his life.

"You're out now. Everything's going to be okay," the fireman told him as he set him down. "You're safe."

But as the man turned to run back to the other side of the house, a shadow loomed just beyond—one that unleashed an inconsolable fear in his little body—and he knew he was anything but safe. A warm rush of urine wet his pajamas as he backed away.

His grandfather stared down at the box of matches still clutched in his hand. "You filthy little bastard," he hissed, tears of grief and rage pouring from dark, hollow eyes. "You will pay for this, do you hear me?" He dug his nails in deep and pulled the boy up by his hair, dragging him toward the spot where the body of his mother now lay on the ground. Black, lifeless. He shoved the boy toward her, jerked him down hard.

"Look what you've done."

The boy whimpered, pain rippling through his neck and down his back. He wanted to die. To climb down next to his mother and wrap himself in the crook of her arm and go where she went.

The grip on his neck suddenly released, startling him, and he turned to see the fireman approach again, motioning for his grandfather to follow. He watched them walk away and then collapsed next to his mother, pulling her hand into his. He held it tight, the cold grip of the ground quick to seep into his skin, crawl into his bones.

The giant house towered overhead. A monster, straight out of a nightmare, climbing up to the sky, baring its razor-sharp teeth at him. Waiting to gobble him up.

Fear paralyzed him and he tried to look away, but something caught his eye. A shadow. It moved in the window, high up on the far side of the third floor. His eyes burned. He rubbed them hard, looked again.

A woman, he realized. But it couldn't be. He could see his grandmother across the yard with his baby brother, and his mother's body still lay on the ground next to him.

He padded through the damp grass toward the house and stared up at the window, mesmerized as the figure slowly came into focus. His heart raced, blood pumping fast through him.

Long, thick waves of ebony hair, as black as the night itself, shimmered in the moonlight above, a slender pale hand reaching up to tuck one side behind her ear. She smiled down at him, lighting up the night, chasing away the monsters. The feeling wrapped around him like the warm sun on a bright summer day. It washed over him, radiated through him, comforting him in a way that only one person in this world had ever been able to.

The breath went out of him.

"*Mommy,*" he whispered.

Muddy bare feet moved swift beneath him as, unnoticed, he climbed up the front porch stairs and stepped back into the house.

Back into the arms that beckoned to him from the upstairs window. Back into the arms that now waited for him, would keep him safe.

Back into the arms of his mother.

CHAPTER ONE

Charleston, South Carolina
Present Day

Nora Bassett was late. She aimed her car into the first parking space she found, turned off the ignition and scrambled to grab her bag from the backseat. For weeks now she'd looked forward to this meeting with her agent. The three-hundred-and-fifty-page manuscript in the laptop next to her had consumed the last two months of her life, and she was beyond ready to push it from the nest and watch it fly. But as she reached for the door handle, a dark cloud moved in over her—the same dark cloud that had made its first appearance when she'd awoken out of a dead sleep late last night, only now the sense of dread began to deepen, settling low in the pit of her stomach.

She tried to convince herself that nerves were to blame—well, nerves or maybe the triple shot of espresso she'd called breakfast this morning. That, she realized, was more likely the culprit.

She pushed the car door open, greeted by an instant wave of heat and sunbaked asphalt. "Good grief," she mumbled as she climbed out, her clothing already beginning to stick. She was no stranger to South Carolina's scorchers ever since she'd moved to Charleston from her family home in Pennsylvania several years ago at the request of Jack, her brilliant attorney husband—happily brilliant attorney *ex*-husband now—but this was September, and the heat index still bordered on obscene. By the time she made it in to see her agent, she'd not only be late but would have to add *sweaty* to her growing list of flaws for the morning.

She threw her bag on her shoulder with a sigh, pressed *lock* on the key fob and merged into the trickle of busy people, politely dodging the slow ones in an attempt to make time.

Halfway there, her cell phone sprang to life.

She flipped it over in her hand, the familiar number making her grimace. Her mother. This would make the third uncomfortable call in three days addressing the fact that Nora should move back home now that she had officially cut herself loose from...*the cheater,* as her mother not-so-fondly referred to Jack.

She declined the call. *Jack.* She tried to force his image from her mind, but it crept in, lingered. She'd thought she loved him, would have done anything for him. But he'd earned the title her mother had given him—as well as a fat packet of divorce papers from a rival attorney across town—once she'd discovered that he'd taken a few tumbles between the sheets, with not one but *two* court clerks...*simultaneously.*

The vein in her forehead began to throb at the memory. She'd put her life on hold. Left everything that had ever meant anything to her behind to follow *his* dreams.

How could she have been so naïve?

Thank God she'd had her writing. It was the only thing that had kept her sane, her saving grace. She'd tackled the publishing world on her own and succeeded on her own. The wandering hands of her ex couldn't touch that.

Her phone rang again, and she declined it again. But it was no use. Her mother was a hoverer. Always had been, always would be, and there was no outrunning her. Nora's jaw tightened. A *New York Times* best-selling author of six thrillers and she couldn't escape the wrath of her own mother.

The phone rang once more and she knew she had no choice but to answer. She swiped a finger across the screen and lifted it to her ear.

"Mother, please, can this wait?"

"Nora—" her mother tried to cut in.

"I can't do this right now. I'd love to finish our conversation later, but—"

"Please, Nora—"

"I can't move home, Mom. I'm serious. I'll have to talk to you about it later. I'm running late for a meeting."

"Damn it, Nora—" Frustration exploded from her mother's voice. "*Listen to me.*"

Nora stopped. Her mom never swore. *Never.* And were those tears? The eerie combination of anger and emotion in her mother's voice stabbed a chill through Nora's core, and she was suddenly sure she wanted no part of what was about to be said.

"It's about your sister—"

Nora pressed the phone closer to her ear. "What's going on? What about Lucy?"

"Please, let me finish," her mother whispered, trying to take in enough breath to get the words out. "Nora...she died last night. Lucy's dead."

The words stung Nora's ears. "*What?* What are you talking about?"

From somewhere distant, she heard herself asking the questions, but she couldn't feel her lips moving with the words.

Her mother answered through muffled sobs. "There was an accident."

"What do you mean, an accident? Where?" She struggled to hold on, to catch her breath. She felt as if she were falling. It wasn't real. It couldn't be.

"Out at the farm—" Her mother was nearing full-blown hysterics. "Your father and I had just been with her, but there was a storm coming, and she told us to go on home before the rain hit." She gulped back tears. "Oh, God, Nora, she was all alone. If only we'd stayed—"

Nora heard her father in the background, trying to help her mother, before he pulled the phone out of her hand.

"Nora, honey—" There was a darkness in his voice. She barely recognized it. "Lucy's contractor found her on the floor in the basement of the icehouse building when he arrived at the farm for work today. We got the call from the sheriff's department just before we called you..." He slowed, struggling to get the words out. "The sheriff said she'd taken a bad fall down the stairs and that she died sometime late last night from her injuries." His voice began to crumble beneath him. "When we left your sister yesterday, she was fine. She was finished with her work and ready to turn in for the evening... I can't believe she's gone." Something in him finally broke, and his grief poured through the phone line, hitting Nora head on.

"This can't be true, Dad," she stammered. "Oh, God—it can't be. Please tell me this is all some kind of mix-up, a terrible mistake." She forced herself to stop and breathe. "I'm coming home. Right now."

"Listen to me," her father urged, his voice still trembling. "You shouldn't make the drive. Not like this. I'm going to make arrangements for an airline ticket."

She choked back her tears and tried to focus on something, anything. She could no longer feel any sensation in her body. She was a spectator watching the unthinkable unfold in front of her as she stood there in silence, unsure of what to do next.

"Nora?"

"I'm still here," she whispered.

"Call me when you get back to your place. I'll have the flight information for you. Just get some things together and come."

"Yes," she said. "I'm coming. I'm on my way." She ended the call, turned and absently walked back to her car.

Her thoughts of the book launch had vanished.

She no longer noticed the people in the streets rushing to the dentist or to lunch or to pick up their dry cleaning. No longer noticed the noisy hum of the world spinning around her. Her twin sister was dead. *Dead.* It was a mistake. It had to be. She'd just talked with Lucy a couple of days ago. She'd been a little distracted maybe, but healthy and well other than that.

Wouldn't she have known if something terrible had happened to her sister? Weren't twins supposed to feel something like that? The sense of dread that had awakened Nora the previous night— and had courted her all morning—flitted through her mind but was quickly replaced by the memory of her last conversation with Lucy.

It had been completely normal. They'd talked about Nora's book and about the upcoming meeting with her agent, but for the most part, they'd talked about Lucy's renovation of the old Victorian farmhouse she'd signed the papers on only three months before. Black Willow Farm, in Pennsylvania, not far from where they'd grown up.

The house. She closed her eyes as the image of the huge, dilapidated farmhouse flashed through her mind. It had been her sister's dream to restore it and turn it into an old-fashioned country inn. She thought of the pictures Lucy had sent her of the place, but they'd been taken at night, and all she'd been able to make out was a mammoth-sized old house that looked to be in desperate need of a wrecking ball and a bulldozer.

But Nora had never seen Lucy happier.

Grief sunk into her bones. Why hadn't she pushed pause on her own busy life to go home and help her sister? Lucy had invited her over and over, but between the nastiness with Jack and her success as an author, Nora always had an excuse at the ready.

Now it was too late. *What had she done?* Tears choked her, the

realization more than she could bear. She gripped the steering
wheel hard, her knuckles turning white as Lucy's last words
danced through her mind. She'd said she loved Nora and that they
would talk soon. But they wouldn't. No. They would never talk to
each other again. Because her twin sister was dead.

A HARD LUMP took root in Nora's throat as the stillness of her
apartment pressed in on her. She dropped her keys on the entry
table, the loud clang of metal on glass making her jump.

She needed to be with her family, needed to be home.

As she moved down the hallway to get her suitcase, the blink
of a bright red light coming from the office caught her eye.

The answering machine. She remembered noticing it when
she'd gotten in late the night before and assumed it had been her
mother. Had walked right past it.

Nora wiped at tired eyes, her finger hovering over the button.
The unsettling feeling from earlier in the morning crept back
over her. She hesitated. It was her mother...*wasn't it?* She bit the
edge of her lip. Yes, of course it was. Or maybe a friend or a
salesman or even a wrong number. Her finger trembled as she
pushed play.

"Hey, it's me," Lucy's voice chattered into the machine.

A small cry broke from the back of Nora's throat.

"I tried your cell, but it went straight to voicemail. I was
hoping to catch you before your meeting in the morning. I
wanted to talk to you about something really quick. I—" Lucy
stopped.

The uneasy tone in her sister's voice sent a chill through Nora.

"I wanted to mention it when we talked a couple days ago, but
I was afraid you'd think I was crazy." She cleared her throat. "I
haven't told anyone about this—and I'm sure it's probably noth-

ing." Lucy cleared her throat again, a habit Nora knew her sister had when she was nervous.

She leaned closer to the machine.

"I don't even really know how to explain it, but—" Lucy's voice dropped off, followed by another awkward silence. "You know what?" She clearly tried to switch gears and lighten the tone. "Never mind. I'm being ridiculous. I wish I could just delete this silly message."

There was another brief pause.

"It's no big deal. Call me later. I can't wait to hear how the meeting went. I'm so excited about your new book. I'm your biggest fan, Nor. You know it's true."

The sweet sound of her sister's laughter floated across the air in the tiny, dark apartment. Nora suddenly felt as though she would suffocate.

"Okay, I should go. Talk to you soon. I love you a ton."

There was a click on the line, and she was gone.

Hot tears streamed down Nora's face. She listened to the message again several times, then transferred it to her cell and forced herself to pack.

CHAPTER TWO

Ben Whitfield stared at the road ahead, tires thumping hard against the long stretch of highway beneath. It had been the worst day of his life, and the darkness of the day's events clung to him like a cold, wet coat. No matter how hard he tried, he couldn't escape.

He needed to drive. Just drive. It didn't matter where, as long as he had the open road ahead of him and all that had happened in the last twelve hours in his rearview mirror.

Earlier that morning he'd expected to head out to Black Willow Farm and put in another long day's work on the remodel he'd been contracted to do. The house was incredible, and he looked forward to watching it come back to life. Shining up the old and making it new again—affirming that it still had worth. It's what he loved to do more than anything. And today was supposed to be an ordinary day, just like any other. Hard work, long hours and a sore back to prove it when he was finished.

But that's not what had happened. Instead, he'd gone there and stumbled across the lifeless body of the young woman who'd hired him. Someone who'd become a close friend to him.

Someone he'd smiled with, laughed with and worked long hours beside for the better part of three months now.

He narrowed his eyes, tried his best to steel himself against the scene as it played again and again through his mind.

The storm from the night before had been one to remember. Crazy winds and hail, torrential rain. When he'd arrived that morning, he'd found Lucy's car with the driver's-side door wide open and waterlogged, but no sign of her anywhere. He'd scoured the property for her. Every inch of it. Called her name over and over. His pace quickening with each dead end.

As a last resort, he'd turned his path toward the back of the property to the old icehouse, where she'd been storing her furniture and decorations for the inn until it opened. She wouldn't be there, of course she wouldn't. At least that's what he tried to convince himself as he'd made his way across the yard, but his chest had tightened with every step toward it. And that's where he'd found her. Soaked to the bone, bleeding, broken. The memory of her body slumped at the bottom of the stairs in a stream of rainwater and muck would haunt him for a very long time.

Emotion swelled in Ben's throat, choking him.

He'd tried to revive her, called 911. Done everything humanly possible. But it was too late.

He'd spent the next several hours in a fog watching the sheriff's department comb the scene, take dozens of pictures. He'd seen them pointing and calculating, heard the murmuring. Watched them string bright yellow-and-black crime scene tape around the building—witnessed the solemn arrival of the coroner. A deputy had taken his statement, every detail meticulously jotted on a notepad.

Time of death had been estimated somewhere between ten p.m. and one a.m.

His jaw rippled as an uncomfortable flicker of blame came at him. Why hadn't Lucy listened to him about the icehouse? He'd told her several times that it was a terrible place to store things. The stairs were way too narrow, and with no windows and a single pull-string light, it was like a damn cave down there. But she'd waved him off with one of her lighthearted smiles, saying he was just like her parents. That he worried too much.

If only he'd been more convincing. If only she'd listened. If only he'd called to check on her right after the storm.

There were far too many *if onlys* banging around in his head.

The image of her body at the bottom of the stairs tried to force its way in yet again, but he drew in a long, slow breath, denied it. Instead, he let Lucy's bright smile flood through his mind, remembering the day they'd first met.

He'd just come off a string of smaller-scale jobs—bedroom additions, kitchen and basement remodels—and was hungry for something big. Something he could dive into and use the set of skills he'd honed over the years.

A few days later he'd gotten her phone call, the complete renovation of Black Willow Farm. And, his interest spiked high, he'd gone out to the property the same afternoon.

Ben closed his eyes briefly and drifted back to that day.

He'd pulled up in front of the house and stared forever. The potential the huge building had, the beauty that lay beneath layers of weather and neglect.

He'd known at that moment, no matter what, he was all in.

In fact, he'd been so taken aback imagining all he could do there that he hadn't noticed Lucy come up behind the truck to tap on his window. He'd nearly jumped out of his skin.

That was the first time he'd seen her smile, heard her laughter.

"I'm so sorry," she'd said, her eyes bright. "I didn't mean to startle you. Real nice of me to kill off the help before they even start." Then she'd offered him a firm handshake. "You must be Ben."

He'd climbed out of the truck and followed her up the front walk and into the most amazing prospect of a house he'd ever been in. The kind of place that wrapped its arms around anyone who walked through its door, pulled them in the minute they crossed the threshold—demanded their attention, their affection, their loyalty.

"Come in, come in," she'd said as she led him through.

She'd sparkled as she told him about the day she'd stumbled across the property after taking a wrong turn on her way to an estate sale near Marietta the year before. How she'd fallen in love with the old covered bridge and turned in to snap a picture. That was when she'd noticed the for-sale sign lying on the ground, lost among the weeds.

"So, what do you think?" she'd asked as they finished the tour.

"I think I can't wait to start," he'd answered.

Lucy had grabbed him, hugged him hard. Even though it was their first meeting. It was just who she was.

She'd been a breath of fresh air every day. Not only to him but to his whole crew.

And he'd been surprised by her determination, her fascination with breathing new life into Black Willow.

Ben choked back the lump in his throat as the memory continued to play out.

He'd sat with her on the porch swing for the better part of an hour while she'd rattled on—her joy contagious as she recounted her dream of running an inn and how she wanted to use her portion of an inheritance her grandmother had left her family to do something worthwhile, something life-changing. She told him the moment she'd laid eyes on Black Willow, she knew fate had led her there.

Ben smiled at the thought. He was an only child and had always wanted a little sister. She was the closest thing to it he'd ever had. She'd been a bright and beautiful light in his life, always happy, even when things were less than perfect.

His smile faded.

Today her excitement, that raw, unbridled joy, had died with her.

The eerie silence of the truck's cab closed in around him as reality crept back in, and he turned the radio on, grateful for the distraction, as the *why* of it all continued to haunt him.

THE RIDE from the airport was silent.

Even though Nora's body was there in the taxi, her mind was far away in a world where her twin sister—the other half of Nora herself—wasn't dead.

She stared through the window as the beautiful tree-lined hills and valleys of Marietta, Pennsylvania, passed by, never seeing any of it.

The world that had been bright and happy, bursting with possibility earlier in the morning, had become a giant hollow shell swallowing her into its dark void. She wanted to hear Lucy's voice, if only for a second. *God help her*. How could she make it through the next five minutes, let alone a lifetime without her sister, her best friend?

"Is this the drive, ma'am?"

The house her family had called home her entire life came into view. "Yes," she said. "This is it."

The hover of dusk had already begun to paint shadows across the yard, but a soft glow filtered out from its front windows. It looked like it always did.

Nora studied her childhood home, drawing from it both comfort and pain. She closed her eyes and imagined Lucy's laughter as she burst through the front door and down the steps to pull Nora into one of her famous "Lucy hugs," as the phrase had been coined early in their childhood. Warmth washed over her, and she smiled as she let herself be lured into the fantasy, let herself linger there.

The trunk of the taxi slammed shut behind.

Nora sucked in a sharp breath. Lucy wasn't here...would never be here again.

She felt as if she might be sick as she paid the driver and made her way up the walk.

She'd only taken time to pack a single suitcase. Still, the load felt as heavy as lead as she climbed the stairs. But just as she reached the top step, a tiny flash of light pulled her attention toward the side yard where she and Lucy had spent their childhood playing together.

Fireflies.

It was late in the season for them, and Nora stood for a long moment almost smiling as she watched them dip and dive in the coming darkness. In another time, *another world,* it would have been spectacular how they sparkled. Tiny flashes of light bobbing to and fro, each dancing to their own unique rhythm on the mild evening breeze.

Her throat tightened. How many times had she and Lucy raced across that very same yard—smiling, laughing, tumbling to collect mason jars full of fireflies?

Too many to count.

I can't do this. The words repeated in her mind, round and round like a terrible spinning carnival ride she couldn't get off.

Tears fell. She wiped them and they simply fell again.

After what seemed like a lifetime, she forced in a long, deep breath and turned back to face the house, *and the rabbit hole that awaited inside.*

NORA FOUND her mother adrift in a Xanax coma on the overstuffed leather couch in the great room, crumpled tissues strewn around her. Red, puffy eyes led down to tear-stained cheeks, flushed with the heat of unwinding anguish. She looked small and fragile and hopeless.

The living room, usually beyond immaculate, showed the same signs of emotional upheaval. She looked over to find her father sitting in the wingback chair by the fireplace, his head leaned back, eyes closed.

"Mom, Dad..."

Those were the only words she was able to get out before the floodgates opened.

Her mother rose to meet her, pulling her in as an ocean of sadness poured out between them.

Nora leaned away from the embrace long enough to hug her father, too.

"Thank God you're home safe, sweetheart," he said.

"I still can't believe any of this," Nora whispered, unable to stop her words from spilling out. "It feels like a horrible dream and I keep trying to wake up. It can't be real. I want her back. I want to see her one more time. Just once—"

"I know," her mother said, pressing her forehead to Nora's. "I know."

NORA RUBBED her eyes and pushed herself up onto the side of the bed, her feet easing down to test the cool hardwood beneath. Numbness had begun to evolve into grief, and she'd been desperate to sleep, to escape her agony, but sleep had not come. Instead, she'd tossed and turned until the cotton sheets were matted into a damp ball beneath her, as pictures of Lucy flashed through her head—her sister's smile both comforting Nora and haunting her in equal portion.

She looked at the clock on the marble nightstand. Five thirty-five a.m. It was clear that any further attempt at sleep was going to be fruitless, but coffee would at least help.

On autopilot, she moved toward the kitchen.

Traces of Lucy were everywhere. From the walls plastered with childhood photographs of the twins adorned in tufted variations of pretty bows and patent leather shoes to one of Lucy's many pairs of sunglasses still casually tossed on the entryway table. She was everywhere. Nora's heart felt as if it would burst.

"Nora?" The welcome sound of her father's voice wafted across the kitchen. "Can't sleep either?"

"Not a chance." She flipped on the light over the kitchen sink.

He pulled out a chair at the small dining table in the corner of the kitchen, offered it to her. "You hungry? Church members have been stopping in to drop off casseroles by the carload." He paused for a long moment, and she could see he was struggling to hold it together. "Everyone loved your sister."

"Just coffee," she whispered. "The world is way too upside down right now for food. I can't eat, I can't sleep."

She pulled a coffee cup off the counter and filled it to the top, breathing in the steam as she did, then turned toward him. "Something's bothering me, Dad. I keep telling myself it's the shock of Lucy's death, that it was so sudden, so unexpected. But there's something else. It sounds odd to hear myself say it out loud, but I can't get over it."

"We're all upset, honey. And we all have questions."

"I know," she echoed. "But it feels like more than that."

Lucy's last message darted through her mind as she slid down into the chair he'd offered. "Had Lucy mentioned any problems to you lately?"

His brow furrowed. "Nothing in particular that I can think of. Why?"

Nora stared into the coffee cup. "It's just that she left me a message at home, the day before yesterday, and she sounded uneasy about something."

"Well, she'd run into a few hurdles with the house, I guess. Some of the old electric was causing issues. The lights kept going off and on at random times over there, which was driving her crazy. But she never mentioned anything else of consequence."

"I don't know," Nora said, lifting the cup to her lips to test the temperature. "Maybe I read too much into it."

He sat up in his chair, leaned in toward her. "While we have a minute alone, though, there is something we need to talk about that I feel shouldn't be put off any longer. And...I don't know," he wavered, "maybe we should have mentioned it to you last night, but your mom and I couldn't bear to talk about it when you arrived."

Unease rippled through her.

Her father cleared his throat, a nervous habit he shared with Lucy.

"What is it?" Nora asked.

He drew in a deep breath and met her gaze. "Lucy called us a few weeks ago to let us know she'd made a will."

Nora sat up in her chair, the mere mention of the word *will* making her uncomfortable.

"We agreed with her that it was a good idea, that it was the responsible thing to do." He shrugged. "You know, just in case." He stopped, swallowing back a fresh round of emotion. "Of course, none of us could have known that the *just in case* would happen three weeks later."

She stared at him. Why would her sister be so quick to draw up a will? It was probably the most level-headed, premeditated thing Lucy had ever done in her life.

When her father started to speak again, his eyes took on a new seriousness that startled her.

"Nora, you need to know that Lucy told us if anything ever happened to her, she wanted you to have the farm. She listed you as the sole beneficiary."

Nora was stunned. Surely she'd heard him wrong.

"No," she stammered. "I can't do that, I—"

"It's already done." His hands dropped heavily onto the table. "It's what she wanted."

Nora searched his face. How was she supposed to make sense of any of this?

"She wanted me to have Black Willow? Why didn't she tell me? She never mentioned anything."

He reached for her hand. "I'm sure she was intending to tell you. It's just that you were on the heels of the divorce, and with your book coming out, she...didn't get the chance."

Nora shook her head. "I couldn't possibly take it, Dad. It wouldn't be right. Renovating the farm was her dream."

"That's exactly why she wanted you to have it," he said. "Because it was so very important to her. It was her final wish."

Thoughts came at her faster than she could keep up with. "How am I supposed to take on Black Willow?" she asked, her eyes wide. "I don't know anything about running an inn, and even if I could figure that out, I don't know anything about remodeling."

"It's a huge thing to process, I know. That's why I felt we needed to get this first conversation behind us. And no one expects you to decide right this minute." He squeezed her hand tight. "But you've been saying yourself that you no longer feel at home in Charleston and that you can write your books anywhere. So, if you decide you have any desire at all to take this on, your mother and I will help in every way we can."

Nora couldn't dream of such a thing right now. She closed her eyes. Most of the monumental decisions in her life thus far had involved the brainstorming and support of her twin. She'd always bounced things off Lucy, and Lucy had done the same with her.

She pulled her hand away and stood up. "I know you're going to think this sounds crazy, Dad, but I can't deal with this right now. I have to go out there. I have to see where she died for myself. I need to feel close to her."

Concern clouded his face. "I don't think you have any idea how hard that would be at this point—"

"It doesn't matter," she sat flatly. "I have to go."

"At least give it a few days. We'll all go together, but your mother's going to need a little time before she's ready to face it."

Nora had to go *now*. It was the last place Lucy had been alive.

"You stay here with Mom, she needs you. I'll be fine. It's something I have to do."

He nodded, even though his disapproval was clear. "Okay. You're a grown woman, and if it's what you feel you need to do, I'm not going to try and stop you, but please listen to me on two things."

Nora waited.

"First, don't mention this to your mother. She wouldn't want you to go alone."

She nodded.

"And my second and most important request is that you stick to the main house today. I mean it, honey. Promise me you won't go out to the icehouse. You don't need to do that alone."

It was a promise she knew she couldn't make. "I love you, Dad," she said, turning to leave the kitchen. "I hope you know that."

"I love you, too, Nora. Please just...be careful."

"I will."

CHAPTER THREE

Rain dripped down the windshield, the wipers continuing their steady march back and forth as Nora drove to Black Willow Farm. The beautiful cotton-ball clouds from earlier in the morning had vanished, replaced now by a dark blanket of gray.

She thought about the afternoon ahead, biting the edge of her lip until it hurt.

What would it be like to be in Lucy's house...*without Lucy?* Unthinkable. This was not how it was supposed to be. This long-awaited visit was supposed to be filled with the excitement and fascination of seeing her sister's dream coming true. A scene where Lucy pulled Nora from room to room of the gigantic house, brimming with happiness and blurting out every last detail of her plans, of her adventure.

She swallowed back her emotions. One day at a time, she reminded herself. One hour at a time. One minute at a time.

Ignoring the dampness in her eyes, she pushed everything out of her mind for the time being and reached down for her coffee mug. She lifted it to her lips and took a long, slow sip, letting its heat radiate through her, comfort her. When she finished, she leaned over to put it back in the drink holder, but her hand slipped and she missed, knocking it to the floor. Hot coffee splashed across her right leg, instantly breaching her thin jeans. "Damn it," she grumbled, looking down from the road for only a moment, but when she looked back up, she was over the double yellow line enough to force an oncoming truck off onto the rocky shoulder. It swerved hard as tires squealed, pelting the sides of the truck with wet gravel, gouging deep ruts in its path.

Nora screamed and yanked the wheel back to the right, the offending coffee mug flying across the floorboard and hitting the passenger-side door with a loud clang as she tried to correct her own sliding vehicle. She slammed on the brakes, skidding side-ways before the car slid to a stop.

She sat still, frozen, afraid to look across at the truck's driver —assuming that whoever it was wanted to throttle her. And deservedly so. But to her amazement, the huge black pickup eased back out onto the highway again. The windows were fogged, but she could make out the shape of a man looking in her direction. There was no doubled-up fist flailing, no obscenities mouthed. Instead, the figure waited, motioning to see if she was all right.

Her heart still pumped in overdrive, but she tried her best to smile, nodding that she was okay as he slowly pulled away. Once he'd passed, she aimed her car over to the shoulder and pressed her eyes shut tight, thankful to be alive and thankful the other driver had been kind. As she opened them again, she noticed the coffee mug on the floor. Heat filled Nora's cheeks. She'd never felt more embarrassed in her life—and was beyond grateful the poor guy in the truck had no idea who she was and that she'd never see him again. "Thank God for that," she muttered under her breath as she shifted into drive and inched back out onto the road. Hopefully the remainder of the drive would prove to be much less exciting.

SHE SLOWED on the last stretch of highway, the isolation closing in a little as the word *boonies* sprang to mind. But the drive had calmed her. It was beautiful country, there was no denying that. Every direction she looked, trees were ablaze with the vibrant golds, burnt oranges and scarlets of impending autumn. The nip of the cool, crisp rain making the colors pop dramatically against the stormy sky.

She searched for the mailbox her father had described, the now steady stream of rain splashing across the windshield making it more difficult. But just beyond the next bend, Nora's breath caught in her throat.

Off to her left was a large mailbox that read Black Willow Farm and, beside it, the covered bridge that crossed a branch of the Susquehanna River and led into the property.

Suddenly, the *why* of what she was doing out in the rainy, autumn-painted countryside hit home. Every part of her ached.

"I'm here, Lucy. I came."

She drove over the narrow bridge, the thud of tires on slatted wood making a clicking sound that reminded her of a roller coaster hoisting its cargo up a steep track, only to hurl it back down into the unknown.

Once across, she rounded a curve and stopped in front of a large rust-tinged gate.

It was now or never.

She pulled on her windbreaker, grabbed the key to the padlock and darted out into the drizzle. The weather-beaten lock took a bit of convincing on her part, but with a good, hard twist, it broke free and the gate swung open. She climbed back in the car and made her way up what seemed like an endless gravel drive.

Rounding the last curve, she slowed, her heart pounding in her chest as the three-story farmhouse loomed in front of her. Weathered, worn, *magnificent.* Shock raced through her. It was even bigger than it had looked in the pictures.

She rolled down her window enough to get a soggy glimpse.

The only hints of renovation she could see were a large construction dumpster off to the side of the house and several stacks of lumber and scaffolding that lay in the yard next to it. Other than that, there were no signs that anyone had been there in years.

It was so much to take in. The idea of it, the mere size. Thoughts raced in Nora's head, a bittersweet cocktail of happiness and overwhelming sadness unwinding in her.

"Oh, Lucy," she whispered, tears streaming as she turned off the ignition and stared up at the house.

A thick canopy of black willow trees surrounded it from behind, outlining its massive structure against the dark slate horizon. Twisted limbs reached out toward her, a few coming to rest on the roofline, while others drooped over the edge, their dying leaves left to scramble to the ground below.

On the left side of the third story, a widow's walk jutted up toward the sky, and to its right, one of several dormers peeked out, tucked just underneath the wide gable end.

Nora drank it in.

She couldn't help but love it. From the chipped white clapboard siding that marched across the house on all sides to the wind-beaten shutters. But perhaps her favorite detail so far was the sprawling storybook front porch that wrapped all the way around the house. As she glanced toward its far end, she noticed an old porch swing that hung slightly crooked. A melancholy smile pulled at the edge of her mouth as she watched it sway back and forth against the tease of wind. It looked almost wistful, as if it ached for someone to return and set it in motion once again.

She released a breath she hadn't known she'd been holding, drew in another, filling her lungs as she continued to survey the house. It oozed character even through its ramshackle seams, and she felt drawn into the dream, much as Lucy had obviously been. The only difference was that Nora dangled precariously somewhere between the joy of intrigue and the pull of drowning sorrow.

Focus, she reminded herself.

She pushed open the car door, trying to decide whether or not she was ready to go in, and quite unable to get over the fact that the three stories towering in front of her were not only breathtaking and beautiful, but also monstrous, unfamiliar.

She swallowed hard and glanced up at the widow's walk once more. She felt like a small child sitting in front of an old Victorian dollhouse. One that invited more of a charming—but equally *macabre*—feeling the longer she stared. And as she climbed out of the driver's seat, her nerves made a duly noted first appearance on the heels of the shock and awe.

She shoved the door shut behind her, a crack of lightning opening up the sky to unload another round of pouring rain. In an instant, she was soaked to the bone, changing her intended meander up the cobblestone walk into a mad dash for shelter.

Once she made it to the porch, she peeled off her jacket and shook it, cursing herself for not bringing a second set of clothes.

She found her way to the window just beyond the porch swing, where she spotted the spare key tucked safely on the top edge of the sill, just as her father had said it would be. By the look of it, she guessed the lock hadn't been changed in years. She fingered the tarnished key and gripped it tight. What she held in her hand was more precious than gold. To anyone else, it would appear to be a simple, ordinary key. Nothing more. But to Nora, it was her ticket to the inside of Lucy's world.

She walked to the front door, the tall, heavy slab of mahogany the only thing separating her from what her sister had treasured most. Nora placed her hand on the door handle, the feel of the metal ice-cold on her palm. She inserted the key and gave the door a slight shove open, immediately greeted by the not-so-subtle fragrance of must and age.

She stood motionless, a lump in her throat.

After a long moment, she searched the wall for any sign of a light switch. Once she found it, she eagerly flipped it up. Nothing.

She saw another switch at the edge of the hallway and tried it, too, but again no hint of light.

"No power. Super," she said aloud, the echo startling her. She hesitated, unsure of what to do next. But once her eyes adjusted to the darkness, her feet moved her forward, and she began to roam through the cavernous house.

The grand entryway, with its dark wainscoted walls and high vaulted ceilings, led to a large parlor off to the left and a library nook off to the right. Floor-to-ceiling fireplaces marking the center of both.

She strained in the near darkness to make out the intricate design of crown molding perched high above, and as she looked down, a river of rich, seasoned plank flooring ran beneath her feet, deep scratches and imperfections adding a layer of character to the hardwood.

A hallway straight ahead led past a wide staircase, with what appeared to be the original hand-carved wooden banister running up its length. She ran her hand over the silky smooth wood, a sad smile settling on her lips. Had Lucy's hand done the same? She felt sure it had.

At the end of the hallway, a thin door on her right piqued Nora's curiosity. She pulled the door open. A quick burst of dank, stale air jarred her, and she coughed several times before leaning in for a closer look. A cellar of sorts. She tested the cobweb-covered railing, withdrawing her hand soon after, as it easily wobbled against her touch. Tiny hairs on the back of her neck and arms stood on end as she considered going even part-way down, but the bottom was too black to see anything beyond the staircase. Another day, she told herself as she quickly closed the door and let go of the brass handle.

She turned around, more than content to leave that part of the house undiscovered.

To her left, she found a large kitchen just beyond an arched doorway. As she poked her head in, something familiar caught

Nora's eye. There on the countertop in plain sight was the set of coffee mugs she'd given Lucy for Christmas. She smiled, choosing to let it offer her happiness rather than pain.

She stepped back and studied the kitchen. Dark, dated cabinetry flowed along the walls, butting up to a deep window seat on the far end. She took a quick peek into the backyard. It was full of overgrowth and bramble and in dire need of a long-awaited afternoon of weed eating.

On the far-left side of the kitchen, two more consecutive arched doorways offered a view into the dining room and parlor, and on the right, a butler's pantry connected to a back staircase, which she could only assume had at one time been used by servants and farmhands for easy access to the kitchen area.

Nora started toward the parlor, taking a last glance around the room. *That's odd,* she thought as she walked over to the back wall and traced her fingers over the handle of an unusually shaped wooden door. She gave it a quick jiggle, and to her surprise, it squeaked open to reveal a dumbwaiter. She tugged on the pulley, and it lurched into motion. *Unbelievable,* she mused. *Just when I thought this place couldn't be any more eccentric.* She chuckled, giving it another pull, but jerked to a halt at the distinct sound of tires on gravel outside.

She moved to one of the windows, stopping cold as a large black truck pulled up out front. *The very same one she'd run off the road earlier.*

She braced herself, ready to stand her ground with whatever the scenario might bring.

The truck door swung open, and a tall man with a strong jawline and a head of dark, wavy hair—early thirties if she had to guess—climbed out. He reached back into the driver's side, grabbed something she couldn't see, and headed in her direction.

She watched him all the way, noting an easiness about him as he strode up the front steps.

Maybe one of the contracting crew?

She backed away from the window, pausing a split second to decide whether or not to answer the door. But considering she was alone in a strange house and had no idea who the man was—oh, and of course there was that little matter of running *said* man completely off the road earlier—she decided not to open it.

The tall stranger knocked.

She exhaled long and slow.

He knocked again.

"Please, just go away," she ordered under her breath.

All was silent for a moment, and she relaxed, assuming he'd given up. But the next thing she knew—though every rational part of her would deny it could be happening—the unmistakable sound of a key sliding into the lock cut crisply through the silence.

BEN PUSHED THE DOOR OPEN.

"Hello?" he called out, a hint of caution lacing the edge of his voice. "Anyone here?"

No sound returned.

"Hello," he said once more, louder. But before he could take another step, a woman appeared from the parlor.

Ben's face turned ashen.

"*Lucy.*"

Her name dropped from his mouth before he could stop it, the single word hanging in the air between them.

"No," the woman said, clearly testing the waters. "I'm Nora Bassett. Lucy is my—" She stopped. "*Was* my twin sister."

Ben's tension changed to concern, sadness.

"Of course you are," he wavered, embarrassed. "I'm so sorry. I just..."

He couldn't stop staring.

He'd known Lucy had a twin. She'd talked about her almost

every day. Even so, the sight of her standing in front of him took his breath away. Not just the fact that she shared Lucy's face—which was striking enough by itself. No, it was more. There was something in her eyes. A dark, beautiful depth. Full of knowing, tinged with sadness. He couldn't look away. He'd never experienced anything similar when he'd looked at Lucy, or any woman, for that matter, and the feeling caught him off guard in a way nothing had in a very long time. If ever.

He ran a hand through his hair and down the back of his neck, still shaken. "I hadn't expected anyone to be out here, and when I saw the car in the driveway, I thought I'd at least knock first. But then, when no one answered, I didn't know what to make of it. Again, I'm so sorry. I hope I didn't scare you."

He reached out his hand to her. "I'm Ben Whitfield. Your sister hired me to help with the renovations."

"Oh, of course," Nora said, attempting a smile as she shook his hand. "My sister told me a lot about you. I want to thank you for everything you did for her."

"I thought the world of Lucy. The whole crew did. She was an amazing woman."

Nora's eyes began to fill. "Thank you for that," she whispered.

He switched gears, giving her a moment to get her sea legs back. "Are your parents here with you?"

"No," she said. "I needed to come alone."

Ben dropped his head down onto his chest. "And here I am walking in on you. That's great. I have impeccable timing. I'll come back later, after you've had some time."

"No, no," she said. "Please...*stay.* I didn't know what to expect when I got here, and to tell you the truth, I wouldn't mind the company."

Ben opened his mouth to protest but closed it once more. It was impossible not to see that she was lost. And who could blame her?

"I'd be glad to."

The tension in her face eased for a moment. But as she looked toward the front window, he watched it return tenfold.

"So..." she said, dropping her gaze to the floor. "I'm guessing you recognized my car out front and have figured out by now that I'm the crazy person who ran you off the road earlier."

He lifted his brow, smiled. "Actually, yes. But I'd pretty much decided not to say anything at this point."

"What are the odds that it would be you?" she stammered. "I can't begin to tell you how sorry I am."

Ben stifled a chuckle. "It's all good."

"No, you're being nice. You must think I'm a complete idiot, and you'd be justified. But in my defense, I dropped my to-go mug and it splashed hot coffee up my leg which, needless to say, really hurt like—"

"Hey," he said, nudging her arm. "Honest, no harm done."

She looked up at him, and he noticed a trace of shyness moving in at his touch.

"Well," she murmured. "Thank God at least one of us was paying attention."

"I admit it was a little intense there for a minute, I'm not gonna lie. But it could have been much, much worse. I mean—" He cocked his head to the side. "You could have spilled *my* coffee. Then we would have had a real problem on our hands. That would have been a whole different ballgame."

He smiled as a tiny laugh tried to escape through her lips, but before it could fully emerge, she snuffed it out, and Ben watched as a fresh round of sadness moved back across her face.

Thunder rumbled outside, shaking the floor beneath, mimicking the mood that had once again swept in. He cleared his throat. "So, since you're standing here in the dark, I assume the power's still out."

Nora nodded. "It would seem so. I pretty much made a beeline for the light switch the minute I walked in, but no luck."

"Sorry about that. Transformer's shot from the insane storm we had."

As soon as the words tumbled out, he wished he could retract them. *Way to bring up the event that set her sister's death in motion,* he cursed himself. But she didn't crumble before him; instead, she seemed lost in her own thoughts, so he moved on quickly. "Best guess is that we'll be back up and running day after tomorrow or so."

"Oh, I see." She turned and looked up the dark staircase behind. "Guess I'll wait to see the second and third floors. This place is a monster, even if the lights were on."

Ben glanced toward the front door. "Hey, you know, I've got a flashlight out in my truck. Let me run and grab it. Then I'll walk you through the upstairs, if you'd like."

"Oh, no. I wouldn't want you to have to do that. I can wait."

"Nora, your sister was very special to me. She was a big part of my world over the last three months, and it would be my pleasure to show you what she had in mind for this place."

"Well, then," she said, "I'd actually like that very much. Thank you."

He stepped out onto the porch. "I should warn you, though," he hollered over his shoulder, "there may be excessive amounts of grueling construction mumbo-jumbo. Believe it or not, I have, on occasion, been accused of getting a little too excited about my occupation."

"I'll consider myself warned," she said as he disappeared down the front steps.

CHAPTER FOUR

Lucy was there with her as she roamed the halls.

Room after room, floor after floor. Her presence wrapped around Nora like a warm blanket, connecting them in a way she couldn't have imagined. This glimpse into her sister's world changed everything. Nora got it now. She understood the bond her sister had come to share with the property, her love for it—*her obsession*.

She also understood now, with great clarity, why Lucy had chosen Ben. Not only was he well versed in all things construction but he was sensitive and strong and kind. And although she felt a trace of guilt, she couldn't deny that he stirred a heat deep inside her that had gone cold long ago.

As they finished their tour of the third floor, Ben motioned toward one last room.

"This wraps it up," he said. "Last one. The media and game room."

Nora stepped in and walked the perimeter, ending up in front of a set of tall, narrow six-paned windows. The space was not huge, but it was quaint, cozy. "My favorite room, I think," she said.

He stepped in beside her. "Lucy's plan was to put a flat-screen television on the north wall. And she'd picked up an armoire at an antique shop in town that we were going to squeeze into that far corner. Said she was going to stock it with games and movies and —" He paused. "Your books." He shoved his hands into his jean pockets. "She was very proud of your work."

Nora looked away. She knew better than to try to respond, as it would open a floodgate she might not be able to close again. Instead, she nodded and gazed out over the giant willows and woods beyond.

"It's getting late," she finally said as she pulled herself away from the view. "A person could get lost in this gigantic place, and I've managed to forget to leave a trail of breadcrumbs on the way up."

He laughed and moved aside, letting her step back out into the hall. "As starved as I am, I probably would have eaten my way out by now, anyway."

Nora returned his laughter, surprised at how good it felt.

"You know," he said, closing the door behind them, "I've read one of your books."

Nora eyed him, curious.

"*The Darkness Beneath*, maybe? I think that was the name. Lucy gave it to me not long after we met."

She smiled. "That was my third novel. I wrote it during the beginning of my divorce. A lot of inner turmoil fueled the fire on that one."

"Well, I don't have much spare time to read, but I have to say, once I started it, I couldn't put it down. It blew me away. And I'm man enough to admit, I was even tempted to sleep with the light on for the next couple nights."

She laughed again. "I'm glad you liked it."

"I really did. Talk about intense. I never would have guessed a story like that could come from someone who looks so, well...normal."

"Ah, yes," she said with a nod. "My dark and demented alter ego. It's got some real issues."

Ben smiled. "Remind me not to get on your bad side."

As they started down the servants' staircase, Nora slowed. A cool breeze raced across her skin, lifting the edges of her hair. She turned back toward him, alarmed. "Whoa, did you feel that?"

"The cold air?" He nodded. "This place takes some getting used to, I'll admit. Old houses can have a lot of drafts." He paused. "Unusual sounds, too, according to Lucy. She called me several times about different issues. Comes with the territory, I guess. Old plumbing, old electric."

"Huh," Nora mumbled. "My dad mentioned she was having trouble with the lights going on and off."

"Yeah, we've been working on the electric lately, trying to zero in on that. It had started to bother her a lot, especially at night."

Nora tensed. Maybe that's why Lucy had been so strange during her last message. Could it have been something so simple?

She had to find out.

"Can I ask you something?" she said.

"Sure. Anything."

"Well, obviously you've spent a lot of time with my sister here in the past months." She hesitated. "And I was wondering, did she seem...okay, to you lately?"

Ben's footsteps slowed. "You know, now that you mention it, she'd been on edge lately. Almost a little jumpy. Why do you ask? Did something happen?"

Nora waited for him to join her on the next step and stopped. She thought of Lucy's message, knowing how much it would hurt to listen to it again, but slid her phone out of her pocket anyway. A second opinion would make her feel better. At least hopefully it would make her feel better, and not worse.

She lifted the phone and swiped it on. "I'm not sure," she said, "I'm probably overreacting, but she left me this."

Ben edged in close as she put her cell phone on speaker and pushed play.

Nora closed her eyes and listened with him—his affirmation of her sister's recent strangeness setting off a new alarm bell in her head.

When the message ended, he locked eyes with Nora. "Yes," he said. "She'd been nervous lately. A lot like that."

"I don't get it. Why, though? Why had she been acting like that? That was not my sister's norm at all."

"I know she'd had some dealings with the previous owner of the house recently."

Nora shifted. "What kind of dealings?"

"The strange kind," he said, starting down the steps again.

She followed, glued to his words.

"He'd gotten hold of her number somehow and called a couple times, but then he stopped by here one evening after the crew and I had gone."

Nora gaped. "What did he want?"

"The house back."

"Well, that's not creepy at all," she said, sarcasm dripping from her voice.

"No kidding," he said. "Pretty much my exact thought when she told me. She said he started to get belligerent about the whole thing. If I'd been here that night, I would have shown him the door. But like I said, he came out after the guys and I had already left."

Nora stared in disbelief.

"He told her how he'd lost the property when the market tanked, that it had been in his family for generations and by rights he should have it back. But I reminded her that his poor life choices were not her fault, and that she'd taken better care of the house in the short time she'd had it than he had in decades."

Ben motioned for Nora to take the lead toward the front door.

"Do my parents know all of this?" she asked, stepping out into the damp evening air.

"Not sure. Lucy never said."

He locked the door behind them.

Nora walked over to the railing, stood silent for a long moment. Her mind spun back and forth between all that Ben had just told her and the nagging notion that there was one other place on the property she still needed to see before she headed home. Her heart thumped hard in her chest as she turned back to Ben. "I have to see the icehouse," she said slowly. "Could you take me there?"

He eyed her, uncertain.

"Something seems off about all of this," she added. "I don't think I can rest until I see where she died. I can't explain it. I just *need* to see it."

Ben nodded. "Follow me."

She trailed him around the back of the house, remnants of mist from the rain folding in around them as a dilapidated moss-and-ivy-covered building crawled out of the darkness in the path up ahead.

Pain rose inside her, but she stood her ground.

Its roofline hung crooked above four rough and crumbling walls that looked as though they'd stood there for a thousand years—looked as if they might give up and sink down into the rocky earth below at any moment.

Nora wondered why on God's beautiful green earth Lucy would have any desire to set foot inside such a place, let alone store things for the inn inside. But whether she understood the sentiment or not, there it stood. The place her sister had drawn her last breath.

Ben stepped up to the entrance and turned back to look at her as he reached for the handle.

Nora held her breath.

The door groaned as it opened. Behind it, a wall of murky,

cold black lay waiting.

She felt as though she'd been hurled straight into the opening scene of a horror movie. *Why did I ask to come out here?* her mind pleaded. *In the dark and the damp and the fog?*

But she knew why.

BEN HADN'T BEEN SURPRISED when she'd made the request to see where her sister had died. He would have done the same and respected her for having the courage to follow through. The conditions surrounding them, though—the pitch darkness, the thunder and rain—were all too reminiscent of what Lucy's last night was sure to have been like.

"You okay?" he asked.

"Yes," she whispered, looking toward a set of concrete stairs that led down into more darkness. "That's where you found her?"

He nodded, shining the beam of his flashlight for her to see. "Door was wide open when I got here. The storm had washed rain and debris inside and down the stairs. I called her name several times and—" He stopped. "I'm sorry, maybe I shouldn't—"

"No. Please." Nora closed the distance between them. "I need to hear this. All of it."

"Sure," he said softly. "The power was out everywhere. I'd already checked the main house, so when she didn't answer up here, I grabbed the flashlight from my truck and walked down the steps to double-check."

Ben watched her, ready to stop the minute she couldn't take any more.

"When I was about halfway down, I saw her lying at the bottom of the stairs. She was so quiet and...I knew. I don't know how, but I knew she was already gone."

A lump rose up in his throat. "There were shards of broken china dishes all the way down the stairs, and the box they'd come in was upside down at her feet with the bottom ripped out. The stairs—I remember them being so slick I damn near took a dive down them myself as I raced down to her."

A small sound slipped from Nora's mouth.

Ben locked eyes with her in the dim light. "I tried so hard to help her. I swear I did." A tear breached the barrier he'd worked hard to put up. "I tried to revive her, but she'd been gone too long. I—"

"Thank you," she whispered, tears streaming down her own cheeks now. "For all you did."

"She was a beautiful person, Nora."

Nora closed her eyes and covered her face with her hands.

She tried to hold back, but Ben watched as she finally let go, her shoulders shaking as wave after wave of grief hit her. Her pain radiated through him. He'd never ached so much for another person in his life. He needed to hold her, to comfort her—make her grief turn loose. He opened his arms and pulled her in, stroking her hair. "I'm sorry," he murmured. "So very sorry."

He held her in the silence for a long, tender moment until she pulled back just far enough to meet his gaze. He felt the breath go out of him. Her eyes were beautiful, so open and unguarded. He shared her grief, her emptiness. And it was clear that she understood it. She leaned into him, and before he fully knew what he was doing, he kissed her.

The world spun. The cold, dank walls of the icehouse fell away. Thoughts of death and of loss fell away. He felt his soul touch hers in a way he hadn't known before.

Somewhere in the back of his mind, a voice urged him to stop, warned him that the moment—though breathless, sensual—was spun from raw emotion.

But he'd never felt anything like it before, and he gave in and pulled her close, kissing her harder, deeper, until he felt her breasts heave against him.

A tree limb cracked outside, yanking Ben back to reality as it crashed down on the roof above. Nora jumped and he felt her pull away.

"I'm sorry," she stammered taking a step back. "I don't know what I was thinking. I shouldn't have—"

"Nora—"

"You must think I'm terrible. My sister just died and..." A trace of guilt pulled down the corners of her mouth. "I'm so sorry."

Ben reached for her arm. "Hey, listen to me. I'm just as much to blame as you. Please don't say you're sorry."

She nodded as she wiped the remainder of dampness from her cheeks.

Ben eased her back into him. "I'm not sorry, not in the least. Quite the opposite, if I were to be completely honest."

Nora gave him a half smile.

"So," he said softly, "you about ready to get out of here?"

She looked down into the darkness below once more and then back at Ben. "Definitely," she said. "But thank you for bringing me. I had to come."

Ben gave her shoulder a squeeze. "I know you did."

NORA LOOKED at Ben as they made their way back. She knew she should regret the kiss they'd shared, but somehow, she didn't. She couldn't. It had been exactly what she'd needed in that moment.

They rounded the corner of the front porch. "Oh," she said, reaching into her jacket pocket. "I need to put the spare key back."

She ran up the stairs and tucked the key back above the windowsill as Ben waited for her. But as she walked past the parlor window, a flash of movement at the back of the room caught her eye.

Nora froze.

"Everything okay?" Ben called.

She stepped closer to the window and leaned her forehead against the glass. Everything was just as they'd left it. Nothing looked amiss.

Terrific, she thought. *Now I'm seeing things.*

"All good," she called as she rejoined him. They walked out across the yard together.

"Man, it's chilly tonight," he said.

"Agreed," she said, zipping her jacket all the way up. "I'm glad the rain finally stopped, but now this crazy fog seems to have made the air colder. What I wouldn't give for a thermos of piping hot coffee for the drive home."

He stopped to look at her. "Here we go with the hot coffee again. You know, Nora, I'm gonna go out on a limb here and venture a guess that the highways might tend to be a little safer tonight if you'd save the coffee consumption until you get back home."

It took Nora a second to realize he was making fun of her. "Oh, my gosh. Again, I'm so sorry for that," she blurted, trying not to laugh. "Like I said earlier, I swear I've never run anyone off the road before today, really, I—"

"Sticking to that story, huh?" he rattled back. "So, I'm curious, do people actually believe you when you tell them that?"

Nora narrowed her eyes playfully, appreciating the way he made her feel at ease, especially after her breakdown in the icehouse moments ago. "Why do I have the feeling you're not going to let this go any time soon?"

"Okay, I'm done now," he echoed, holding his hands up in the air. "Really I am. Scout's honor."

He chuckled again as they reached her car. But as he pulled the door open for her, Nora watched a seriousness settle in over Ben's face.

"Nora," he said. "All joking aside, I realize we just met, but I want you to know that I'm here for you, in any way you need." He tucked his hands into his pockets. "What you're going through..." He hesitated. "It's not right to have to do it alone. Anything you need, any time of the day or night, I'm here."

There was sincerity in his eyes, a sadness that once again mirrored Nora's. She slid into the driver's seat and turned back to look at him, a fresh tear pooling in the corner of her eye.

"That's very sweet," she said, wiping at the tear as it fell. "But I should warn you, I tend to shatter into a million pieces on a regular basis right now. It doesn't take much."

He knelt down next to her, reaching in to dry her cheek on the cuff of his flannel shirt. "You have every right to cry. Don't be hard on yourself. Everything's going to be okay. *You* are going to be okay."

"I know you're right. In time."

He smiled at her once more and stood back up. "Hey, would you mind if I call you out at your parents' tomorrow? You know, just to check in?"

"I'd like that," she said as she eased the car door closed.

He nodded and turned, climbing up into his truck as he threw her a wave good-bye.

Nora started the ignition and pulled out from Black Willow, stealing one last glance in the rearview mirror. The house towered behind her, slipping away into the darkness as she rounded the curve. "It's magnificent, Lu," she whispered. "It's everything you said it would be."

CHAPTER FIVE

Funeral. The word sunk to the bottom of Nora's heart and sat like a cold stone. She hated the word more than she'd ever hated anything in her life.

She leaned her head against the window of the sedan as it wound through the serene Pennsylvania Dutch countryside on the ten-mile drive to Whispering Oaks Cemetery. The procession marched solemnly behind. It was a beautiful day. Not a single cloud in a robin's egg blue sky. An odd backdrop, she thought, for a funeral.

As the brilliant colors of fall flashed by the window, Nora's mind shuffled through the details of Lucy's death. The idea that something wasn't right—that something didn't add up—had nudged her in the direction of the sheriff's department the day before, where she'd waited in the lobby for over an hour to speak to one of the officers who had been on scene the morning Lucy had been found.

An accident, the deputy—a round little man with a cherry-red face and coffee stains dried on the front of his uniform—had assured her. A sad and senseless tragedy. But no sign of foul play.

No reason to go poking around any further. *Go home*, he'd suggested. *Get some rest.*

Incompetence was the single word that sprung to Nora's mind as she thought of him.

She shifted in the car seat, uncomfortable.

The police report—she'd wept through it twice—played like a movie through her mind. Played, rewound, played again. From the horrific storm and the power outage to the steep, slick cement stairs of the icehouse, to Lucy's crumpled body in rain-soaked clothes at the bottom, the box of shattered china dishes scattered at her feet.

The report revealed that her face and arms were badly bruised and bleeding. Her neck broken. All consistent with a fall down a flight of stairs.

So why couldn't she let go? Why the hell had Lucy been out there unloading heavy boxes of china by herself in the dark? That late at night...and during such a terrible storm?

The questions clanged through her head to the point it ached. *Stop it*, she silently ordered herself. *Just get through the afternoon.*

She looked at her mother in the seat next to her, her eyes dark, void of anything but sorrow, and then on to her father. He attempted a smile but failed, his hand wound so tightly around her mother's his knuckles had lost their color.

As she turned back toward the window, Nora caught a glimpse of her own reflection in the glass. Her breath caught in her throat. It must be so hard for her parents to look at her, she realized. To look at her...and see her sister.

"A BEAUTIFUL SERVICE," she'd heard many people say. But Nora hadn't noticed. As soon as she'd smelled the aroma of fresh, over-turned earth, mingled with the heavy scent of roses, she'd gone somewhere else in her mind.

The pastor's soft, scripted words had rolled off her, lost among the sniffles and sobs and muffled crying of family and friends. She was numb. Haunted by the fact that the ground under her feet was the same ground that would now give welcome to her lovely sister, drawing her into its dark, damp chasm.

Nora's stomach churned.

For the past forty-five minutes, she'd been squeezed and touched and talked to, by an army of people. She'd become a human pinball machine—one whose player had an endless supply of quarters. She needed to get the hell away, even for a fraction of a moment, so she could breathe, or she was going to lose it—the word *postal* flashing like a bright red neon sign in her mind.

She edged around the side of the crowd and headed toward the tree line at the back of the cemetery.

"You okay?"

She spun around to see Ben walking toward her.

"Oh, hey." She squinted against the sunlight. "You startled me."

"Sorry. I saw you slip away and wanted to make sure you were all right."

"I just..." She looked down at her hands. "Need a minute. You know?"

"Then take one. Take all the time you need. If anyone asks where you are, I'll let them know. I can only imagine how hard today must be. I wish there was some way I could make this easier for you."

"You're here, and that helps more than you could understand. Thank you, Ben. Thank you for everything you've done for Lucy and my family."

"I know it doesn't feel like it now, Nora, but you will get through this...I promise." He reached for her arm, squeezed gently. "I'm going to head back over. See you in a little while."

She watched him filter back in among the clusters of attendees, then turned her face away.

Oblivious to the tickle of damp grass on her ankles, Nora walked. The property was all too familiar. It hadn't been that long ago when she'd stood on the very same plot of land, burying her grandmother. The only difference was that Lucy had been at her side then, holding her hand tight, sharing in the sadness. The idea of it was almost unbearable, and she did her best to put it out of her mind.

She made her way toward the outskirts of the graveyard, where a wrought iron fence stood guardian to the gray sea of headstones spreading out in all directions. The giant oaks above kept the grounds cool and dark, allowing only tiny glimpses of light to poke through. She stopped. Drew in a long breath, and another.

And then she wept.

Silently at first, choking sobs taking hold soon after. She let the sadness take her, *and keep her*, until there were no tears left.

Finally, she pulled a damp tissue out of the handful she'd crammed in her jacket pocket earlier.

"What happened, Lucy?" she said, wiping her eyes. "How did we get here? I miss you so much and I just don't think I can do this. I know I can't. I wish it had been me that died that night, Lu, I swear I do..."

A gentle breeze moved through Nora's hair and across her skin, lingering, leaving a trail of gooseflesh in its path. The sensation was strangely soothing, and she stood quietly for a long moment, as if something unseen held her there until she understood for the first time that healing would come. It would be a long, difficult road, but in time, she would be able to feel again, to live again. It's what Lucy would have wanted.

Nora lifted her face, let the patchy sunlight splash over her, soaking its fading warmth into her skin. She closed her eyes, hearing for the first time the soft tinkle of Indian grasses as they bobbed in the wind around her and the gentle hum of insects in the distance, the chatter of birds. It was beautiful. But then a strange and very different sensation rushed through her, and all at once, Nora was certain she was no longer alone. Her heart leapt in her chest, the much-needed fragment of peace from the moment before yanked away as she opened her eyes wide. The feeling was so strong that she half-expected to find Ben or a well-meaning friend or relative standing in front of her.

But there was no one. Even though every part of her would swear there was. A shiver crawled up her spine. She looked toward the thick wall of forest beyond, searched for any sign of what could have caused the feeling. But there was no evidence of anything out of place, no dark shadows leering. Even so, unease quickly urged her back in the direction of the group.

"Nora?" her father called as she approached. "You okay?"

She was not okay. She was anything but okay. "No, not really," she answered. She stood with him over Lucy's grave. "I can't bear the thought of leaving her here."

"I know, sweetheart. But we have no choice. It's time." He hugged her tight. "Everyone's coming back to the house now. Are you ready?"

She nodded. Even though she knew she would never be ready. She would never let go.

They began the walk back to the car, Ben arriving first to open the door.

"I'm here for you," he whispered, giving Nora's hand a squeeze.

She looked at him, tried to smile.

"You're coming by the house, aren't you, Ben?" her father asked as he pulled the sedan's door shut.

"Yes," Ben answered. "I'll be glad to help out in any way you need, so use me." He looked at Nora. "See you there, then?"

She nodded. The driver started the engine.

As they pulled away, Nora looked back one last time.

She shuddered as reality sunk its teeth in deep. This was the end. They were leaving Lucy behind beneath the beautiful, peaceful canopy of oaks. *Alone.*

Last words had been spoken, last hugs given. Everyone would now drive away from the mound of freshly overturned earth and continue on with their lives.

Everyone but Lucy.

HE STEPPED out of the woods, darkness flickering from his eyes.

A twin. *The whore had a twin.*

An irritating twist. But he'd been careful, she hadn't seen him. She wouldn't interfere with his plans. He wouldn't allow it.

He strode across the cemetery to the patch of ground where Lucy lay—the patch of ground *he'd put her in*. A smile emerged as he began to hum. The song, one his mother had crawled into his bed and sung to him a thousand times as a child. It stirred something deep inside, and he savored the feeling. It made every part of him feel alive.

Kneeling down, he grasped a handful of fresh, cool soil and lifted it toward his face. The scent of earth and grass washed over him as it oozed through his fingers.

"I warned you," he said aloud. "Didn't I? But you chose to be a pain in my ass. An obstacle. And getting rid of obstacles is sometimes necessary. Wouldn't you agree?"

His pupils thinned to tiny pinpoints. "I guess the long and short of it, dear, sweet Lucy, is that you screwed with me and got what you deserved...*just like the others.*"

He turned and stared out across the graveyard for a long moment, losing himself in his thoughts. "Don't worry, mother," he whispered beneath his breath. "I'll be home soon and we'll finally be together again. I know what I have to do." He pushed up from the ground, a new darkness slithering out from somewhere deep inside him as he tossed the last bit of dirt onto Lucy's grave. "And no one is going to stop me."

CHAPTER SIX

The moving truck crept up the hill toward Black Willow, its transmission slipping several times as Nora's father struggled to make the top. She followed behind in her car, attempting to summon patience as her mother fretted in the passenger seat next to her.

Three and a half weeks had flashed by since she decided to make the move. Three and a half long, crazy, exhausting weeks, tying up loose ends in South Carolina, packing and preparing to make the leap to innkeeper. But she'd somehow managed to pull it off, and had even squeezed in a long weekend midway to attend an innkeepers seminar that Lucy had planned to attend in Lancaster. One, she realized afterward, that taught her more than she could have dreamed about the new venture she was embracing. An *Innkeeping for Dummies* sort of weekend. She'd walked away with a wealth of ideas, contacts and vendors. No doubt there would still be a fair amount of stumbling along the way, but she was armed with a much better grasp of the whole concept now. She had actually enjoyed herself. Lucy would have been pleased.

Lucy. Nora blinked back the sting in her eyes. She'd promised herself she wouldn't allow emotions to drive her. Not today. As the weeks passed, the gaping wound in her heart had begun to heal. Painstakingly slow, yes, but she could breathe again now.

Ben had helped her with that more than she'd known possible. His face flashed through her mind.

They'd called and texted and video chatted more times than she could count. Ben checking on her, keeping her abreast of the progress at Black Willow. And she'd come to look forward to his calls. She'd dreamed of him on more than one occasion—dreamed of the heat during that mind-blowing kiss they'd shared the first night they met. Dreamed of kissing him again, only this time without the darkness, the guilt. It hadn't taken her long to realize how much she wanted to see him in person. *Needed* to see him.

Gears sputtered as the truck ahead slowed down, forcing Nora's mind back to the task at hand. She pulled in a quick breath, nerves making a brief appearance. *This is it*, she thought to herself. *For better or worse.*

She'd gone back and forth and back again about the decision to take this on. Wondering if it was really what she wanted. Could one person step into and carry out another's dream? Make it their own? A host of tearful middle-of-the-night debates with herself led to the conclusion that she could. After all, it wasn't just anyone's dream. It was Lucy's. And so she *would*.

As they pulled around the final curve, she noticed her mother wringing her hands. She eyed Nora like a hawk.

"I wish you'd stay with us tonight," she pushed. "You just got back and now you're spending your first night out here. Alone."

Nora wished, for the umpteenth time, that she had a pair of industrial earplugs.

"I'm serious, honey. We'll unload everything and then you'll come back home tonight."

"Mother, I'll be fine. We talked about this, remember?"

"I know, but Dad and I thought you'd stay with us for a little while until you get your feet wet out here. At least let us stay out here with you tonight."

"You guys helped talk me into this, and now it seems like you're the ones with cold feet."

"I'm sorry, honey. I can't help but worry."

Her mother meant well, of course she did. But if Nora was going to do this, she was going to do it right. That meant being there as the gate first swung open. She would live it, breathe it, be a part of it. And she wouldn't be alone—would never be alone there. Lucy would be with her. *Always*. She believed it with all her heart.

The caravan crawled to a stop in front of the massive house.

Nora stretched her legs, her aching back, while her mother walked up to meet her dad.

She faced the house and took a long look at the exterior, her eyes climbing high. How could it be so much larger than she remembered?

A jab of uncertainty danced just beyond reach in the back of her mind. Breathe, she reminded herself. Just breathe.

The front door opened and a sunny smile beamed down toward her. A new feeling moved into the pit of Nora's stomach as the ruggedly handsome figure she'd so longed to see again— longed for so much that it caught her off guard—emerged and strode down the steps toward her. Ben smiled, the feeling in her stomach deepening.

"Glad you made it." He pulled her into him, the embrace tempting every part of her. "Welcome home, Miss Nora."

"Thank you," she echoed, letting the word *home* sink in as the warmth of strong, capable arms wrapped tighter around her, drew her close. She breathed him in, intoxicated by the faint fragrance of wood and spice.

"Ben," her father said as he shook his hand. "Glad to see you again."

"Great to see you all, too," he said, giving Nora's mother a quick hug.

Her father moved to the back of the truck and hoisted the

door up. "I can't tell you how much we appreciate your offer to help out here today. You sure you're up for this?"

Ben peered inside the truck, frowned. "Whoa, how many people are we moving in here today? Half the population of South Carolina? I'd assumed it was just you, Nora."

Nora smirked. "Very funny."

Ben winked at her and rubbed a hand across his chin. "You do realize I get paid by the hour."

She shot him a crooked smile. "The check's in the mail."

"Yeah, I'll bet it is," he laughed. "I'll bet it is."

BEN LOADED himself up with boxes and headed toward the porch. Behind him, Nora surveyed the front of the house, a look of happiness, tinged with another emotion—one he couldn't quite read—played across her face.

He'd been pleased to see a glimmer of happiness in her eyes when she'd arrived, even though he knew that today, the day that Nora would officially take over Black Willow, must be filled with unimaginable pain, too. That was part of the reason he'd come. To be here for her.

He set the boxes down inside the parlor, meeting Nora as he started back out.

She opened the door for him, scooting to the side so he could pass. "Hey," she said as Ben caught her gaze. "I hope you know how much it means to me that you're here today. To help with the unloading and lifting, yes, but..." She hesitated. "For other reasons, too."

Ben soaked in the sight of her, wanting to show her how much he'd missed her right then and there. How much she'd begun to mean to him. She was breathtaking. Smart and sexy with just a hint of shyness. How could this incredible woman be divorced? What man in his right mind wouldn't fight to keep her? To hold on to her, to love her fiercely... He couldn't imagine.

"Ben?" Nora said, her voice luring him back. "You okay? You were a world away there for a second."

"Sorry," he said with a smile.

She smiled back. "Well, anyway, I want you to know how grateful I am."

"I'm glad to be here with you. I mean that."

She nodded and joined him as he walked back down into the yard.

"So, you never had a chance to say much about the conference. How was it?" he asked.

"Actually, pretty amazing," she said. "I at least have an inkling of what I'm doing now."

"Glad to hear it. Any favorite seminars?"

"Definitely not the cooking sessions. I steered clear of those. I'm planning to leave the cuisine end of things to the professionals. Whenever I find some, that is."

"Yeah, there is that issue." Ben tilted his head to the side. "I heard from a fairly reliable source that cooking isn't your strong suit."

Nora rolled her eyes. "Leave it to my mother to air all of my dirty laundry to anyone who will listen. As much as I'd like to deny it, though, she's pretty much spot on."

"Come on, it can't be that bad."

"Trust me. Imagine it that bad, and then imagine it a little bit worse." She laughed. "That's one thing I have to work on before any and all other things. Hiring someone to run the kitchen. If the breakfasts here are left up to yours truly, there will be a serious shortage of Pop-Tarts and cereal at the market in town."

"I bet you aren't giving yourself enough credit. Anyone can scramble eggs and fry bacon."

"You'd be surprised."

He handed Nora a box and she propped it onto her hip. "Oh,

Ben, I meant to tell you thanks a million for getting the power situation straightened out. The house is amazing, but I'd prefer to have electricity all the same."

"No problem at all. They put a new pole in and, of course, the new transformer. I went ahead and had them up the amps to two hundred, so you should be fine. I wanted to get up to code on that particular issue. It'll save us a lot of time later. The guys ran some new wiring this past week for temp lighting, so you should have plenty of light until we can get the permanent fixtures in. It's all good to go."

"Super."

"And," he said, snapping his fingers, "before I forget..." He pulled two keys out of his pocket and handed them to Nora.

"Yeah, I guess these might come in handy. But you should go ahead and keep the one you had, in case you need in and I'm not here."

"Probably not a bad idea." He took a key back and put it in his pocket, then climbed up into the truck. "Now I better finish getting this furniture unloaded so you're not up all night long."

"I'm sure I will be anyway," she hollered back as she carried her box inside.

NORA DROPPED off the box of books in the library.

The late afternoon sun shone through the window, illuminating the tiny dust particles she'd disrupted, making them dance in the shimmering light. The room was just as beautiful and intriguing as she remembered. The entire house was.

Now that she had a minute alone, she did another walk-through of the first floor, ending up in front of the deep mahogany staircase. She looked up into the darkness above, the absolute silence, and wondered what her first night would be like.

The moment she'd walked over the threshold earlier, she'd

felt a sense of peace. She'd made the right decision, she was sure. But the peace, she now realized, was courted by another feeling. One that had become increasingly familiar. It flirted with the far corners of her mind, making a trickle of uncertainty—*of caution*—inch up her spine. But what was it? And why?

She rubbed her eyes, reminding herself that the luster of the day was overcast by her sister's death. Surely that had something to do with it. What else would it be? Nothing, she decided. Absolutely nothing. Lucy's death was more than enough to bring on the hover of ominous feelings.

She shook it off and painted on a smile as she walked back outside, deciding to take a quick detour to her car for the bottle of water she'd left in the front seat. But as she reached the car door, the trickle of uncertainty crept back into her belly. She turned around and looked up at the house for a long moment, unable to look away. It was as if the giant house looked back at her. It held her gaze, challenged her. Refusing to let go. As if it had a heartbeat, *a soul.*

It stood before Nora, tall and wide and grand. But beneath its grandeur, a melancholy lingered. A haunting blend of beauty and darkness. She could almost feel the hum of its history coursing through weary veins. There was a story there, Nora felt it in her gut. A story that lay hidden deep within its walls.

Her creative wheels began to spin, the writer in her refusing to be ignored.

And she decided that after the dusting off of a few thousand cobwebs, she would be there, pen in hand, to flesh it all out. She would let the ink drain until every last detail was laid to paper. Every last secret uncovered.

~

BEN STACKED the last of the boxes in the parlor and went in

search of Nora. They'd been so busy, he felt like he'd barely seen her all afternoon.

He poked his head inside the library, an easy smile pulling up the edges of his mouth as he saw her in the far corner of the room.

Unable to look away, he stared quietly. Waves of thick, dark hair slipped down over her shoulders as she knelt over a large box marked *Books*, sorting and stacking them into piles, readying them for the floor-to-ceiling shelves near the fireplace.

Ben's heart beat hard in his chest. He thought of the night they'd first met, that brief moment in the icehouse—the kiss he knew they'd both felt a trace of guilt for sharing at such a time. He remembered the heat, the honey-sweet taste of her lips, savored the feeling. *Was he in over his head?* But he already knew the answer.

"Guess that's about it," he finally said.

She spun around, a smile lighting up her face. "Oh, hey."

"You have a finished bedroom to sleep in, and most, if not all, boxes have been deposited in their designated rooms, ma'am."

"Oh, great."

"Your dad told me he's leaving the moving truck out here for the night, and then you'll be taking it back tomorrow, so I'll run your parents home here shortly."

"You don't have to do that. It's a long drive. I can take them."

"Too late. I already offered and they accepted. This way you'll have some time to get settled."

"How can I argue with that? Thank you so much."

He shrugged. "Like I told you, anything you need."

"Well, I owe you dinner sometime this week," she said with a firm nod. "I'm not taking no for an answer. Your choice."

He glanced toward the kitchen and opened his mouth to speak, but Nora quickly cut him off.

"Dinner *out*. Not in," she laughed. "Trust me on that. I don't want to scare you away with my culinary challenges."

She joined him in the doorway, her skin lightly grazing his as she stepped up beside him.

She was so close. A rush of heat pulsed through Ben as his eyes locked on hers, the look on her face telling him she felt it, too. "Have I told you how nice it is to see you?" he asked.

"I wouldn't mind hearing it again," she answered with a sexy smile he could hardly take. He leaned closer, his lips brushing hers in a soft kiss that quickly deepened.

He pulled her in, ready to kiss her the way he'd wanted to since the first night they'd met.

"Nora?"

She pulled back as her mother's voice wafted down the staircase.

"Sorry," she whispered.

Ben smiled. "I'll take a rain check."

"I guess we're ready any time you are, Ben," her father said, walking into the library. "We sure got a lot done today, didn't we? Hope we didn't ruin your back."

Ben chuckled. "Nothing a hot shower and a few hours of sleep won't cure."

Nora's mother hugged Ben's neck. "You are a Godsend. I vote we keep you around."

Her tone changed as she faced Nora. "And you... I wish you'd reconsider coming with us tonight." Her eyes dampened as she pulled Nora into a long, clingy hug.

"My bed is here, Mom. I'll be fine. I promise. Now get Dad home and make him rest. You guys worked like Trojans today. I can't have him keeling over because of me."

"Give us a quick call first thing in the morning, okay, Nora?" her dad said as he ushered her mother out onto the front porch. "Try to get some sleep, kiddo."

Ben smiled, enjoying the fact that even though Nora was in her early thirties, her father still called her *kiddo*.

"I know, I know," she mumbled toward Ben's ear. "He'll still be calling me that when I'm sixty."

Ben stifled a chuckle. "Hey, I didn't say a word."

"You didn't have to."

He followed Nora out onto the front porch and watched her parents head down toward his pickup truck. "It was a long day. Go settle in."

She lifted a hand to rub her eyes. "I would love to have at least offered you a quick glass of wine, but I don't have the first clue where to find a glass or the corkscrew...*or the wine*."

He laughed.

"Oh, boy," she said. "And I just realized that I don't know where my coffeemaker is." She closed her eyes and sighed. "Oh, that's really bad news for you and your crew tomorrow morning. I don't function very well—more like not at all, really, if we're being honest—if I don't have caffeine by first light."

Ben chuckled again. "Thanks for the warning."

She shrugged. "It's the least I can do. Didn't want you to stumble into this thing blind."

He watched Nora yawn. "Go. Sleep."

"Yeah, I think I'll hit the shower, followed closely by the mattress," she agreed. "But if I can get through most of those kitchen boxes in the morning, maybe tomorrow night I can be more hospitable and offer you an actual glass to drink from. And if you're really lucky, maybe I'll even find some wine to fill it with."

"I'm in." He winked at her.

"Well, then, sounds like a plan."

He hugged her tight, wishing it were followed by a long, slow kiss.

As he made his way down the steps, he looked back. "I think everything's pretty well in order with the electric now, but call me —makes no difference how late—if anything worries you. Anything at all. I'm only ten minutes away."

"I will."

He looked at her, skeptical.

"I promise I will. So, I guess I'll see you bright and early then? What time will the crew be here?"

"Seven a.m. sharp. I run a tight ship. They're terrified of me," he joked as he loaded his toolbox into the bed of the truck. "Hey, you should head back inside while we're still here."

She nodded. "Well, good night then. See you tomorrow."

"I look forward to it," he said. "Good night."

CHAPTER SEVEN

Nora watched the truck's headlights drift off into the night, carrying Ben and her parents away, leaving her behind. Alone. Exactly as she'd commanded.

She let out a long sigh. "Well, big, beautiful, spooky house, I guess this is it. Just you and me now." But even as she said the words, she remembered that she wasn't alone. Lucy was there. And the thought brought her immense comfort as she shut off the lights and headed up the long staircase.

As she reached her bedroom, a soft rattle from the rear staircase halted her footsteps. But by the time she was able to focus her attention in that direction, all was silent once more. She stood still, the hair on the back of her neck rising high.

After what felt like an eternity, she dismissed the noise. Perhaps a mouse that thought the house was his domain? Could be, she decided. Whatever the case, she was wide awake now.

Nora swapped her clothes for a nightshirt before dropping into the comfy armchair she'd positioned near the window. She sighed as taut muscles sank into its broad belly. She'd looked forward to crawling into her bed and getting a good night's sleep, but that idea had skirted off with the furry little villain who'd startled her.

She would write for a few minutes.

She opened her laptop, setting her fingers ablaze to its keys. The peace of the house—minus the four-legged intruder—was bliss. No bickering of neighbors above or below, no sirens firing through the night. Not so much as a passing car to interrupt her concentration.

As if on cue, the sound rattled again from the direction of the back stairwell. Her fingers froze. She put down the computer, padding to the doorway to listen.

Once again, the noise ceased.

She forced her muscles to unclench and reverted to the mouse theory. "You know," she hollered into the darkness, "you'll need to relocate when this place is up and running. I'm not too crazy about the idea of guests watching you scamper up and down the hallway."

Nora pushed the door closed. Maybe bed sounded good after all. If she was asleep, there would be no scampering. At least she wouldn't notice it anyway. She shut off the lights and climbed into the cool, crisp sheets, tucking the comforter all the way up snugly under her chin. The house around her was silent once more, with the exception of a slight breeze moving through the willows outside.

Much better than the scratching of tiny claws.

She grimaced, pushing the thought from her mind, and focused instead on the gentle scrape and sway of branches against the window, letting them lull her to sleep.

~

"Nora."

Had someone called her name?

Nora's heartbeat quickened.

The voice called to her again.

"*Nora...*"

Just a whisper at first, tugging at her subconscious. Then desperate, urgent. It seemed to get farther away the harder she tried to focus, to clear her head of the remnants of sleep.

Nora drew in a sharp breath, surprised at how cold and damp the air around her suddenly felt. Its chill biting painfully into her skin. She forced her eyes open and looked down in disbelief to find her bare feet submerged in an icy puddle, slick with leaves and muck. A small cry broke from the back of her throat.

She was outside. But how did she get there?

All at once the wind picked up in every direction. Twisting her, turning her. Nora cried out again as bony, vine-covered limbs thrashed toward her, clawing her clothing, tasting her flesh. She drew herself in tight against the razor-sharp branches as they scraped at her arms and face, bringing the sting of fresh wounds.

What the hell was happening?

She rushed up the path that lay before her, stumbling over jagged outcroppings of rock, commanding her legs to move faster. She wanted to run, to get back to the house somehow. But the dream pulled her into its quicksand trap, and the harder she tried to make any kind of headway, the slower her steps became.

"*Nora...*"

The voice floated on the air, whispering to her, *pleading* to her. It led her down another path to a small building, its own island in a pool of ashen moonlight. Nora felt herself moving toward it— not of her own accord anymore but by the terrifying hand of an unknown puppet master. It forced her toward the murky black of an open door.

The icehouse.

She blinked hard, realizing she was now inside its crumbling walls, the air so stagnant she struggled to breath.

"*Nora...*"

She turned to face the voice as it wafted up from somewhere

down below, her eyes widening as she recognized who the voice belonged to now. *It was Lucy.*

"Oh, God, Lucy!" All of Nora's senses snapped into focus. She had to find her sister. "I'm coming!"

But then a strange sound shot up from the abyss below. A sickening sound, like the crack of bone against rock. All the blood drained from Nora's face, and she screamed down into the pit below. "*Lucy!*" Only silence drifted back up to greet her.

She tried to jump down inside, but the dream tethered her where she was. "God help me, Lucy!" she screamed. "Say something...*anything!*"

Again, nothing returned as her eyes scoured the void beneath, frantic.

When Nora looked up again, she froze. In the darkness ahead, something waited. A shadowed figure. It pulled her on an invisible string away from the icehouse. *Away from her sister.*

She looked around, now aware that she was no longer inside the building. "No!" she shrieked. "I won't leave her." But it was no use.

She plunged toward the figure, ready to fight with every last bit of strength she had left. But all at once the air was filled with a piercing, metallic noise. It jolted her, cutting through the night and bringing everything to a screeching halt.

Nora bolted up in bed, out of breath as the alarm on her cell phone continued its blaring chime.

She scanned the room, forcing her pounding heart to slow. The bed sheets bunched around her, damp with sweat.

A dream. It had been a damn dream. She rubbed her eyes as fragments of the dream skittered through her mind.

"What in the world?" she said aloud, trying hard to remember what she'd dreamed of, what had been so terrifying.

Then tears came. *Lucy*. She had dreamed of Lucy.

CHAPTER EIGHT

The doorbell echoed through the entryway and into the kitchen at seven a.m.

Nora shrugged off the weariness the nightmare had left behind and shoved several boxes out of her way, dismayed she still hadn't been able to locate the coffeemaker.

"Morning, sunshine," Ben said as she pulled open the front door. "A little housewarming gift." He lifted a steaming to-go cup and a small brown bakery box toward her. "Marietta's best bagels and coffee."

Nora stared at him. It was all she could do to keep from kissing him. She took the cup, reveling in its warmth against her palms. "There are no words to describe how much I needed this."

He smiled. "You're welcome. Cream and sugar are in the box. Wasn't sure how you take it."

"Two creams, usually, but this morning I'm desperate enough to have taken it black. Maybe even cold and black." She paused. "Who am I kidding? I would have guzzled down *yesterday's,* cold and black."

"And I thought I was bad. That's pretty hardcore."

She lifted the cup to her lips, blowing on it. "It's been that kind of morning so far. Thanks again."

"There is one condition, though," he said.

"Hmm, okay. I'm almost afraid to ask."

"No driving while drinking the coffee. The good people out and about on the streets of Marietta this morning will thank you, trust me."

"Really?" she barreled back, eyes flashing defiantly. "I thought we'd moved past that whole me-running-you-off-the-road business. How long do you intend to hold this over my head? So I know what to expect."

"That's the last time, I swear," he said, trying to keep a straight face. "Well... maybe, anyway."

"You're very funny," Nora said, feigning irritation. "Honestly, you are. But let's leave comedian off your resume for now, shall we? Maybe stick to carpentry."

The doorbell sounded again.

"Ah, saved by the bell," Ben said with a laugh. "My guess is that's Mitch. He's usually the first one in and the last to leave."

Nora opened the door, greeted by a tall, broad man loaded down with a tool belt and a small cooler. A tall but slighter-built man standing just behind him.

"Name's Mitch," the first man said, reaching out his free hand to shake hers. "Nice to meet you."

She smiled and shook his hand, her eyes shifting to the second man, who'd stepped up beside him.

"And this is Ethan," Ben added. "He's only been with us a few weeks, but he has a strong back and knows how to swing a hammer."

Ethan stared at her for a long moment before his gaze dropped to the floor.

Nora swallowed hard, a bit uncomfortable. It was obvious he'd been filled in on what had happened to her sister and had no idea what to say.

And she couldn't blame him, or any of Ben's crew for that matter, for not knowing what to say to her.

Relief swept through her at the thought of getting the first meeting over with.

"Really nice to meet you both," she said.

Ben looked at his watch. "I sent Carlos into town for more lumber. You'll appreciate him," he said with a wink. "He's the closest thing we have to normal."

Mitch grunted. "Your version of normal and mine must be different then, Ben, my boy."

Nora laughed, their banter putting her at ease. The morning had gotten off to a rough start, but she had higher hopes for the rest of the day.

"Well," Ben said. "It's about that time. I guess we all know where to start."

Mitch nodded and walked down the back hallway. Ethan followed.

"What can I do?" Nora asked.

"Well, Miss Nora," Ben said, "what's your strong suit?"

"Writing books," she said flatly.

He laughed. "Hmm, well then, maybe just start with a little painting, and we'll see how it goes from there."

He motioned her into the parlor.

NORA STOOD over the sink scrubbing the last stubborn remnants of paint from her hands. The morning had flown by. She'd spackled, sanded and painted until her arms were sore, but it had been good to lose herself in the work.

"Might as well leave it. There will be more joining it later."

She turned to see Ben in the doorway.

"If you're lucky," she said curtly, drying her hands on a kitchen towel. "I haven't decided if I'm signing up for more of your shenanigans after lunch or not."

"I see," he said. "Were we really all that bad?"

"Actually, I had a lot of fun. I love the guys. They were more than patient with me. I haven't felt that useful and appreciated in a long time."

"Well, you are." A sexy smile pulled up the corners of his mouth. "Useful and appreciated, I mean." He walked slowly toward her. "Very much so. In fact, I'd like to show you just how appreciated you are."

Nora's senses heightened, her appetite growing for what she hoped would be a much awaited—and uninterrupted—kiss.

"Ben?" Ethan's voice cut in between them.

Ben turned around. "Yeah. What's up, Ethan?"

"Can I see you for a few minutes? Got some questions."

Ben shot Nora a hopeful smile. "To be continued?"

She nibbled the edge of her lip, giving him a look that would make sure he came back in search of her later, a look that was meant for his eyes only. But as she turned, Ethan's gaze was on her again, making her just as uncomfortable as it had earlier in the day.

NORA PULLED OUT HER SANDWICH, taking a bite as she eased down onto the top step of the front porch. She let her head fall back, soaking in the afternoon sun.

"That took a lot longer than I expected. Sorry."

She opened her eyes to find Ben standing beside her, cooler in hand.

"This seat taken?" he asked.

She sighed, patted the spot next to her. "All yours."

He sat down and opened the cooler. "You okay? You look a little tired today."

Nora grunted. "Uh, thanks."

He laughed. "Still insanely gorgeous—let me clarify that—but maybe a little fatigued."

"You do have a way with words."

Ben shrugged. "All the ladies seem to think so." He chuckled again. "In all seriousness, did you sleep okay last night?"

"Yeah, I guess. For the most part, anyway."

"You don't sound so sure about that."

She glanced over at him. "I'm sure it was nothing, but I did hear some odd sounds coming from the servants' stairs on the second floor. Wondering if we might have had our first guest."

Ben's brow lifted.

"Of the furry persuasion, I mean," she laughed. "No big deal, but the scratching did make me a little nuts after a while."

"Lucy mentioned the same problem several times, so we had an exterminator come out and take a look."

"And?"

"Nothing." He shrugged. "Nothing at all. In fact, she had him double-check and put out traps on every floor. She was pretty determined. But they came up empty."

A pang of unease moved through Nora, and she tried her best to brush it off. "Well, the furry little buggers must have outwitted him. Either that or I've lost my mind." She paused. "Option two may be a real possibility at this point."

She lifted her sandwich again, but her voracious appetite from before had faded.

BEN FINISHED off his sub and crumpled up the wax paper wrapper. "What an incredible afternoon," he said, admiring the way the fall foliage popped against the crisp backdrop of bright blue sky.

"It is," Nora nodded. "Autumn is my favorite."

"Agreed." He lifted his soda can and took a long drink. "Hey," he said as he turned to face her. "I wanted to run something by you."

"What is it?"

"My buddy Mark and his wife own Bradley Farms."

"Isn't that the place with the giant corn maze? I saw a billboard for them when I was in town the other day. Looks like a neat place."

"Yeah, a big hit with everybody here and for miles around. Anyway, every year they close up early on Halloween and have a bunch of us out there for a party. They'll have a huge bonfire, tons of food."

"Sounds fun," she said.

"I'm glad you think so, because I was thinking you might want to head out there with me. Meet some neighbors."

"Oh, really?"

"No pressure," he said, holding up his hands. "But it'll be a great time. I should warn you, though, that costumes are involved."

"I'd love to go. Between heading off to college straight out of high school and then the move to Charleston, I don't really know many people around here anymore. It would be great to meet some of your friends. And maybe get the goods on you while I'm at it."

He grinned. "And who's going to give me the goods on you?"

Nora stood up, brushing a few stray crumbs from her lap. "You're out of luck. My secrets are safe."

Ben grabbed for her but missed as she stepped back out of reach. "Gonna have to try harder than that," she added with a laugh. "Hey, I need to run down and check the mail real fast. I'll catch up with you in a little bit."

"Sure, but I didn't mean to scare you off," he hollered as she took off toward the driveway.

He watched her go, unable to take his eyes off of her. The way she walked, those thick, loose waves of dark hair swaying gently at her shoulders, the smile she threw back to him. It made Ben tremble. She tempted him like no one had before. *No one.*

There'd been other women before, yes, especially in college. Though not as many as he could have had. He'd never been *that* guy. Most of his college years he'd been too focused, too driven to enter into a lengthy relationship. The fact that he'd left his home in West Haven, Connecticut—and a good job at his parents' custom furniture business—to accept a full-ride scholarship in drafting and design engineering at a top Pennsylvania university, had fueled his love affair with a high GPA. He'd left a solid thing behind to follow his dream, which meant failure, or even mediocrity, had not been an option.

There had only been one woman he'd ever considered getting down on one knee for. An art major named Kate. He'd loved her, or thought he had. But after nearly a year and a half together, she'd announced that she'd signed up for a summer exchange program in southern Europe. To spread her wings and see the world before they settled down. Which would have been fine, if she'd ever come back.

Instead, she'd called late one night and dropped the bombshell on Ben that settling down and having a family was just not something she was *into* anymore. He'd tried to convince her to come home. To give them a fighting chance. Only to find that the reality of the situation was that she'd met someone at a hostel in Italy who shared her carefree, live-in-the-moment notions. She'd had no intention of returning to the States at all.

From that night on, Ben had thrown himself into finishing his degree and building the bones of a successful contracting career. For years, he'd shied away from any kind of serious relationship. He'd been incapable of letting down his guard, opening his heart again.

Until now.

He watched Nora disappear around the bend, staring at the

empty road. His feelings for her surprised him. Deep, emotional, physical. And his willpower was waning, closing in on him to the point of no return.

He ached to hold her, to feel the rise and fall of her breasts against his body as she breathed him in. Ached to feel the velvet touch of her hair on his chest as he skimmed hungry fingertips down the small of her back and below.

God help him.

He wanted her but had forced himself to wait for the right timing. Out of respect for her sister, respect for her. But he was ready now to show her how he felt. He wouldn't be able to hold back much longer.

Not much longer at all.

~

NORA'S MIND spun as she walked. She felt happy for the first time in way too long. She loved the time she and Ben shared. Loved the laughter. Loved the promise of intimacy yet to come. She could feel the winds shift inside her. Being with him felt the way she'd always dreamed she'd feel with the right person. The polar opposite of how she'd felt with Jack. But those dark and disappointing days were behind her.

And a night out was just what she needed. A chance to let her hair down and reclaim herself. The Halloween party was a fantastic idea.

She started across the covered bridge lost in her thoughts, jerking to a stop as a truck pulled up, loaded with wood.

"You must be Nora," a man with dark skin and even darker brown eyes hollered, throwing her a friendly wave. "I'm Carlos, one of Ben's crew."

"Oh, yes," she said. "Great to meet you."

Another truck slowed to a stop behind him, and he waved and moved on across the bridge.

Busy place, Nora mused. A woman that looked to be in her early thirties hopped out of the driver's side of the second truck.

"Hello," Nora hollered. "Can I help you with something?"

"So sorry to pop by like this," the woman said, taking several steps toward her. "But I've been wanting to meet you, and when I saw you out, well, I couldn't help myself. My name's Elizabeth Ellis; everyone calls me Liz. I'm one of your neighbors."

Nora brightened, pleased to find someone so cheerful and of similar age living close by.

"Our property adjoins yours," Liz bubbled on. "About a half mile or so down, I guess."

"Oh, of course," Nora nodded. "I wondered who owned that place. Beautiful house."

"Thanks. We love it. And what about this place?" she said, gesturing up to Black Willow. "I got a sneak peek a while back, and I couldn't believe how amazing that old house is. And what your sister was doing with it, I—" Her voice cut out. "I hope I'm not overstepping, but I was so sorry to hear about what happened. I only knew Lucy for a short time, but she was very sweet." She looked up the hill again, her face clouding. "I worried about her being up there in that huge place by herself every night, but she seemed more than up for the challenge."

Nora's stomach twisted.

"I can't tell you how wonderful I think it is that you're stepping in for her like this," Liz added. "My heart goes out to you and your family."

"Thank you," Nora said, brushing over the condolence. It was not the time or the place for the emotional dam to spring a leak. She offered her hand. "I'm Nora Bassett. It's great to meet you."

Liz gave her hand a quick squeeze. "My husband, Scott, and I are friends with your contractor."

"Oh, you know Ben?" Nora's eyes lit up.

"We do. What a great guy. We met him a couple years ago when we bought our house. We were looking for a contractor to add on a nursery, and everyone we met told us Ben was the best. We spent the next few weeks together with him and his crew while he lived up to his reputation." She glanced back toward her truck. "Speaking of the nursery, my youngest is sound asleep in the truck. We have two boys. Henry's five and Noah's almost two. I should probably get him home now, I'd intended to just say a very quick hello when I saw you, but I'm a talker." She chuckled. "Once I start, I can't seem to stop. My husband would be the first to agree."

Nora smiled and looked over her shoulder. "Ben and the guys are working away up there."

"So, is Mitch still working for him?"

Nora nodded. "Yes, Mitch, and Carlos—he's the one who just pulled up the hill. And then there's Ethan."

"I know Mitch a little, and I've heard Ben mention the name Carlos a few times, but I'm not familiar with Ethan."

"Yeah, not sure where Ben found him. Kind of quiet, but I know Ben's glad to have every one of them right now. We're trying to make a December deadline."

"That's coming up. I can't imagine how busy you must be. I'm sure there's a lot to starting up an inn."

"A ton," Nora agreed. "My sister already had a website started, which is huge. And I signed with a booking agency a couple weeks ago. They're ready to start taking reservations. So, in other words, I'm counting on Ben big time."

"If anyone can do it, Ben can. He's the kind of guy a girl can count on." She leaned in to Nora. "Not too hard on the eyes, either," she laughed. "But seriously, I think the inn is a fantastic idea. From what little time I spent with Lucy, I could tell it meant the world to her. I'm glad you're here."

"Thanks. Being here makes me feel closer to her. And after getting to know the property, I feel very at home here already."

"Well, I better get Noah home," Liz said. "My cranky husband is going to be even crankier if I don't get back." She chuckled, heading toward her truck, turning back at the last second. "Oh, hey, did I hear right? Are you an author?"

Nora smiled. "I've written a book or two..."

"Wow, a celebrity in the neighborhood. That's so exciting. I'm a huge reader. Romance, mostly, but I like all genres."

"Mine are a bit on the darker side. I mainly write suspense. I've got plenty of copies up at the house. Feel free to come up and grab one any time."

"You said the magic words," Liz echoed, smiling. "I can't wait." She climbed in the truck, pulled the door closed and rolled the window halfway down. "Oh, and if you need an extra set of hands before opening," she whispered, careful not to wake her son, "have Ben call us. We'd love to help."

"I may just do that. Thanks so much." Nora waved as Liz pulled away, then stepped through the weeds, taking a shortcut to the mailbox.

Her smile faded. *Empty again.* This would make the second day in a row.

Lucy's attorney had left a message several days ago telling her he'd mailed information concerning the deed to the house and to make sure and watch for it.

Something wasn't right. It should have been here by now, without question.

She turned to head back up to the house, making a mental note to follow up with him immediately.

CHAPTER NINE

B en stood at the edge of the veranda watching Nora as she brushed the last few strokes of paint on the shutters. He'd been so busy after lunch he'd barely seen her the rest of the afternoon, and he found himself missing her company to the point he couldn't concentrate any longer.

He smiled as she surveyed her work, giving herself a small nod of approval as she wiped her hands on the front of the oversized coveralls.

"Wanna ride into town with me really quick?"

She whipped around.

"We're running low on trim and I thought you might like to take a break from painting. We could grab some early dinner, too, maybe?"

"Say no more. I'm in." She started down the ladder. "Every time I close my eyes, all I can see are brushstrokes."

Ben laughed. "Is that a hint that maybe I should release you from your painting duties tomorrow?"

"Gosh, no. I was just whining a little."

"Then I'll meet you at my truck in five? I have to get my keys."

"I'll be there in four," Nora said, giving him a flirtatious half-smile as she shimmied out of her coveralls.

He swallowed hard. Picking up more trim was suddenly the last thing on his mind.

He hurried back inside and grabbed his keys from the counter, unable to stop thinking about Nora.

By the time he made it to the truck, she was waiting for him.

Ben opened the door for her and then climbed in himself. He pulled down the hill, slowing as they neared the covered bridge.

Nora scooted up in her seat. "Oh, hey, mind if I jump out and check the mail again? Lucy's attorney said to watch for some important paperwork, and so far, it's a no-show. I called him after lunch and he said it should have been here days ago. Guessing maybe I checked the box a little too early today. I haven't figured out the mailman's routine yet."

"No problem."

Ben shifted the truck into park halfway across the bridge and hopped out before Nora could stop him. "I'll check for you."

"No, no—" Nora scrambled out after him. "I didn't mean for you to have to do it. I just thought while we were here, I—"

"Empty," he hollered back.

"That's crazy," she muttered. "Okay then, thanks for trying."

She turned back toward the truck, but stopped and walked to the edge of the bridge to look at the river.

"Peaceful, isn't it?" Ben said as he stepped up beside her.

"Very much so."

They stood together for a long moment watching the ebb and flow of the dark water as it tumbled through the riverbed beneath.

He caught the subtle fragrance of her perfume. It was intoxicating. *She* was intoxicating. She was so close he could feel the warmth radiating from her skin. She turned to look at him, his heart pumping harder in his chest as he saw the look in her eyes. It was more than he could take. He hesitated, then leaned down, Nora moving in to meet him, her lips parting to welcome his.

Time stood still. It was a kiss to rival any other kiss he'd had in his life. He breathed her in, diving deeper and deeper.

Her fingers tightened on his shoulders, inviting him to touch her. And he obliged, smoothing his hands down over her breasts and around to the small of her back, the soft curve of her hips, readying every part of him. Leaving him wanting more. Needing more.

His mouth eagerly traced across the nape of her neck, leaving a trail of hot kisses. Nora quivered beneath his touch, pressing in as close to him as she could. Her heart beating against him.

But out of nowhere, she stopped. Ben caught his breath. "Nora?"

She pulled back, the smile draining from her face. He watched as sadness rushed in to take its place.

She stepped back, letting her hands fall away.

He searched her face. "What is it?"

She cleared her throat. "I..."

"What's wrong?" Ben's concern bled through the edges of his voice.

"I can't do this. I...I'm so sorry." Her voice trailed off, leaving an uncomfortable silence between them as she took another step back.

Confusion drowned out the moment they'd shared as Ben cursed himself silently, assuming he'd overstepped somehow. Moved too fast. He should have waited, given her more time. "All right, then," he said, unable to hide his bewilderment.

She tried to smile, failed. "If it's okay with you, I think I may stay here and finish up some things instead of going into town. I..."

Her pain was undeniable, and though he couldn't begin to understand, Ben nodded. "Yeah, sure. No problem. I'm sorry if I did something to—"

She held up a hand to stop him. "Please don't think that. It's not you, I swear. I just...need time." She turned and started back up the drive.

"At least let me take you back up," he echoed after her.

"No, really. It's fine. I'll see you a little later."

Ben watched her disappear around the bend, then stood for a moment, blindsided. He wanted to jump in the truck and follow her, make her explain to him what had just happened. What it was that he'd done wrong. But he would give her the space she needed.

Nora's hands tightened on the steering wheel as she drove into town to mail out a packet to her editor. An hour had passed since she'd made a fool of herself in front of Ben—worse yet, she'd *hurt* him. But even now, all she could see was the look she'd put on his face as she'd pulled away from the warmth of his embrace, from the most incredible, sensual kiss of her life. She'd wanted to make love to him right then and there. Give him every part of her. Hold nothing back.

She swallowed the hard lump that formed in her throat as she continued to remember the moments from earlier. There she'd stood on the banks of her sister's lovely river, happier than she'd ever been, falling in love with a wonderful, perfect man...less than six weeks after Lucy died.

What kind of person did that?

A selfish one, she convinced herself. The moment she'd truly opened herself to Ben, invited his mouth to hers, she'd felt as if she were somehow betraying Lucy.

Her heart ached. She forced the image of Ben's face completely from her mind, focusing instead on the drive into Marietta.

The autumn leaves were even more picturesque than her first

trip to the farm. And now with the festive addition of bright orange pumpkins and smiling scarecrows on every street corner, it was like a beautiful page torn from a fairy-tale book. Nora soaked it in. She knew without doubt that she would never tire of the warm, open arms of small-town life. She was happy to be back where she felt so at home.

She pulled up in front of the tiny post office and sighed as she read the *Closed* sign hanging on the front door. She started to back up, but stopped as she noticed an antique store on the opposite side of the street in the rearview mirror.

Bella's Treasures.

Memories of the many treasure hunts she'd gone on with Lucy and her mother rushed back in. *What she wouldn't give for one more of those stolen afternoons.*

Nora considered going in. There were still countless pieces of furniture and decor she needed for the inn before it opened less than two months away. A perfect excuse to shop, so she turned off the ignition and headed toward Bella's.

As she came to the shop window, her footsteps slowed. There, beautifully framed in rich, distressed mahogany, a large familiar picture hung over an antique desk.

She couldn't believe her eyes.

"It can't be," she said under her breath. But as impossible as it seemed, it was the very same picture she and Lucy had fallen in love with in a small antique shop in Amish country, near Bedford. Nora had been crushed when she'd found the *Display Only* tag on its side. She pressed a hand to the glass, leaned in closer. On the right-hand corner of the frame was the same deep scratch she remembered from the first time she'd seen it.

The sounds of passing cars and chattering shoppers faded as she stood in front of the picture. The scene reached out and drew her into its deep woods, where the angry twist and churn of an impending storm hovered in charcoal clouds above. Off to the right, a pair of twin girls stood at the edge of a winding path that would lead them into the dark tangle of forest beyond. Long golden-brown pigtails, tied up with yellow ribbons, swirled in the coming wind as the two moved forward as one.

The first child held a tin pail spilling over with ripe, bulging blackberries, while the second dangled a fistful of daisies, each grasping the free hand of the other as they walked shoulder to shoulder into the darkness. The look on their faces was half of what held the enormous intrigue. Where there should have been a grimace of panic, of fear, there was only calm. The look of strength and reassurance uniting the sisters. They held each other's hand as they forged ahead, into the frightening unknown.

Tears slid down her cheeks as Nora remembered Lucy's words. "Remind you of anyone, Nor?" Lucy had smiled at her, with that sunny smile she'd always been known for. "It's strange. They don't look the least bit afraid, do they?" Then she'd hooked her arm in Nora's. "But I guess there's nothing to be afraid of, as long as they're facing the big, dark, spooky woods *together*. Right?"

She'd given Nora another quick smile and followed it up by asking the owner of the shop if she knew where they could find another copy of the picture. The owner had been quick to apologize, explaining that she'd never come across anything similar, hence the reason it was not for sale.

Nora forgot about the post office and the packet for her editor and the kiss she'd run from just an hour before. She wanted the painting. She took a deep breath and opened the door to Bella's, fully prepared for a battle. Pleading, begging, boxing. Whatever it took to leave the shop with that picture in her hand.

She followed a friendly voice to the rear of the store, where she found a well-dressed woman in her late fifties or so, wearing a pleasant but busy smile. She was on the phone but covered the receiver long enough to whisper in Nora's direction. "Hi, sweetie, feel free to take a look around. I'll only be a minute."

Nora didn't want to start off on the wrong foot, so she smiled and nodded, stepping over to a basket of antique postcards.

Bella, Nora could only assume, ended the call and crossed over to her with a curious smile. "Sorry about that. Welcome to Bella's, who, incidentally, happens to be yours truly." She laughed, her eyes shining. "So, how can I help you, sweetie? You have the look of someone on a mission."

Nora looked toward the front window. "I guess you could say that. I have a question for you. The picture, the one in the front window—"

"Ah, the painting of the twins. Isn't it interesting? I bought that from a friend of mine who closed her shop. She loved it and had a hard time parting with it. But her husband had a stroke and she had to shut down."

Nora braced herself, ready to roll up her sleeves. "Is it for sale?"

"You know, I've had it a little over two months, and you are the second person to inquire about that particular picture. Funny thing is, the first customer actually paid for it but never came back to pick it up. Isn't that strange?" Bella rattled on as she walked up toward the display window. "I put a sold sign on it and left it hanging there for several weeks, but the woman paid in cash and never came back. I would have called her about it if my husband hadn't misplaced her contact info." She rolled her eyes.

Nora followed her up to the front, listening as Bella continued.

"Thought it was the craziest thing, to tell you the truth. I was out of the shop the day she'd come in, and my husband was running the store. He said she was such a nice young woman, and she'd told him she had a twin sister herself and was thrilled to have found that particular painting." She shrugged. "So, why in blazes would she pay full price and never come back?"

A knot began to form in the pit of Nora's stomach.

"She bought several other lovely items, too. Apparently, she'd been out shopping for some sort of B and B or an inn or something."

The color drained from Nora's face.

"Anyhow, she paid for everything and told my husband she'd be back the next day to pick it all up." Bella shook her head. "It was really a shame that she never came back, too, since she said it was going to be a surprise Christmas gift for her sister, who lives somewhere down south. I just don't understand people these days, I—"

Nora opened her mouth to speak, but no words came out.

Bella looked at her, concerned. "You all right, honey? You don't look so well."

"This can't be happening," she rasped. "I..." Those were the only words Nora got out before her legs buckled.

NORA DRIED the last of her tears. After the lengthy explanation of what had happened to her sister—why Lucy had never come back for the gift, along with the rest of her items—she was mentally spent. Bella made her a cup of steaming hot ginger tea and sat with her for a few minutes before wrapping up the picture and helping her load it into the back of her car.

"You sure you're okay to drive now?" she asked, walking back toward the front entrance of the store. "Got your sea legs?"

"Yes. I'm much better. It was just such a shock."

"I know, sweetie, I know." She rubbed Nora's shoulder.

"The tea helped a lot. Thank you."

"My pleasure. You call me and we'll make arrangements to get the rest of your sister's purchases out to you whenever you're ready. And again, I'm so sorry to hear about all of this. My husband and I certainly didn't expect this kind of end to our mystery." Bella gave Nora a tight squeeze.

"Thank you so much for giving me the picture," Nora said.

"Well, *as we now know,* it was intended to be yours to begin with, dear."

"Yeah, I guess it was." Nora reached for the car door handle, turned back. "I will treasure it. Always."

BY THE TIME SHE RETURNED, the crew had gone for the night and the house was quiet. Almost a little too quiet.

Nora climbed the stairs to Black Willow's third floor, picture in hand. She knew just where to hang it. According to Ben, the media and game room had been Lucy's favorite nook in the house, and that's where it belonged, she was certain.

The whole day had been an emotional roller coaster, and she was ready to get off the ride and let a long, steamy shower wash away the residual melancholy clinging to her.

But as she propped the picture against the wall outside the media room, the panic alarm on her car blared from the front yard.

"Great," she muttered, realizing she must have bumped her key fob. She ran a hand over her jeans pockets. No key fob. She did a quick search of the floor and the hallway, then walked back downstairs to figure out what in the world had sparked the alarm.

There were her keys on the credenza, in plain sight. She jabbed a finger at the panic button, halting the blaring out front. Confused, she shrugged it off and started back upstairs.

The slam of a door above stopped her in her tracks.

What the hell?

Nora froze, suspended between the first and second floor, unsure of what to do next.

After several minutes of silence, she gingerly started back up the steps. She had to check it out, of course she did. Her house, her job.

She leaned over the rail and looked up as much of the stairwell as she could.

"Hello?" Her voice echoed through the silence.

She started up again, but the closer she got to the second floor, the slower her footsteps became.

"Hello?"

She inched down the hallway, peering into each room as she did, and then all at once, a whiff of something sweet washed over her. She sniffed the air, took a few steps, sniffed again. Lilacs. Yes, lilac perfume if she had to guess. But she was here alone.

Her mouth went dry. As she lifted her foot to take another step, the clamor of the doorbell yanked her attention downstairs.

She looked down at her watch. It was nearing eight p.m.

Her feet moved her swiftly back down the stairs, grateful to whomever it was for the distraction.

She reached for the front door, glancing out the side window before she pulled it open.

Ben.

At some point in the evening, she'd realized how much she regretted the way she'd acted earlier. He was the best thing to happen to her in a very long time.

Nora unlocked the door. "Hey."

He stepped inside and took off his ball cap. "I hope it's okay that I came by."

Nora swallowed hard, preparing to attempt some sort of apology. "Of course it is, Ben. I'm—"

Before she could finish, he cut her off.

"I could make up some excuse about coming out tonight because I forgot something, or maybe that I needed to check on something from earlier today, but I'm just going to be honest, Nora."

She watched him, listening.

"I cared a lot about your sister. Lucy was an amazing person. And I care a lot about you too, but in a very *different* way."

He looked down, running his fingers over the cap in his hand. "I upset you somehow this afternoon, and I wanted to say that

I'm so sorry. I hope you can forgive me. Upsetting you is the last thing in the world I would ever want to do."

Nora was surprised by how serious he was.

He lifted his gaze to meet hers directly, and she saw the worry in his eyes. She felt terrible. She knew full well that *she* was the one who had in fact been the guilty party earlier, not him.

"Ben, I'm the one who should be apologizing. You did nothing wrong. In fact, this afternoon was amazing. *You* are amazing."

She sat down on the bottom of the staircase. "I just got...well, scared."

"What do you mean?"

"Of my feelings for you." The words were out of her mouth, and she couldn't take them back. Not that she wanted to. It felt good, the weight of guilt lifting.

Silence settled between them as Ben sat next to her on the stairs, the crease above his brow lifting. "I thought I'd somehow done the wrong thing, said the wrong thing—"

"I couldn't be sorrier." She shifted toward him. "You've been nothing but wonderful to me and to my family. I let guilt creep in to the point I felt I couldn't breathe."

She could see he was absorbing every word she spoke, not just nodding along, but really *listening.*

"As strange as it might sound," she went on, "it hurts that I'm here in this beautiful place. That I'm taking over the life my sister dreamed of. And on top of that, I feel guilty that it's truly becoming *my dream,* too. I love everything about Black Willow. Not to mention the fact that I'm alive and falling for an incredible, wonderful man when she's..." Nora stopped short of finishing the sentence. She refused to let the terrible word cross her lips.

Ben took her hand in his.

Every part of her trembled from complete mental exhaustion.

"Nora. Listen to me."

The smooth, soft velvet of his voice eased her down from the emotional high wire she dangled from. He brushed several loose strands of hair out of her eyes. "Take a deep breath. It may take more time, but everything's going to be okay, I promise."

She wiped at her cheeks for what felt like the thousandth time in the past weeks. "I know. It's just that it doesn't seem fair that she's gone and I'm here."

"Lucy would want you to be happy." He tilted her chin toward him. "I think deep down you know that better than anyone. If the tables were turned, if it had been you who died that day, you would have wanted Lucy to go on and live her life fully and without guilt, too. Her happiness would have meant everything to you. It's a fact. Think about it."

She soaked in his words.

"And I want you to know that I will wait for you. No matter how long you need. I'm not going anywhere."

Ben tightened his grip on her hand.

"You are the strongest woman I've ever known. You *will* get through this. And if you'll let me, I'll go through it with you. The good days and the hard days. All of it."

Nora held his gaze, unable to look away. His eyes were deep and full of understanding, of compassion. They saw her need, and had come to her rescue.

She let herself fall into him. His arms opened wide, pulling her close.

She lay nuzzled against him for a long moment, losing herself in the peace she felt, until the picture she'd found at Bella's darted through her mind.

She sat up. "I have to tell you what happened to me earlier. I still can't believe it myself."

"Yeah? Let's hear it."

She stood, pulling him up with her. "And since I stumbled across my wine glasses last night, I can offer you a glass while I tell you the story."

He followed her down the hall. "Best idea I've heard in a very long time. I'm in."

CHAPTER TEN

Nora laughed as she stared at her reflection in the mirror. "Ben is going to have a field day with this. Are you sure I look okay?"

"I'm sure," Liz echoed. "That costume fits you perfectly in all the right places. I only wish it had ever fit me like that."

Nora smiled. "Thanks for the loan. I'm glad you called. You saved me a ton of stress."

"Just wait until you see what we gave Ben to wear. He's probably cursing Scott and me as we speak. We thought you guys should complement each other, somewhat." She chuckled and glanced down at her watch. "Okay, I have to run now, but I'll see you tonight."

Nora smiled as she walked Liz to the front door. She was ready for an evening away, a mental break from the daily grind of unpacking and painting and phone calls to newspapers and vendors as they continued the steady march toward opening.

"Thanks again, Liz," she hollered, watching her leave.

She pushed the door shut and climbed the stairs in search of her purse, but slowed in front of her bedroom. She drew in a breath, certain she smelled smoke. *Oh, God*, she thought, instantly fearing a fire somewhere in the house. She scoured the hallway, her heart in her throat. But as she breathed in again, she recognized the sweet, heavy smell. A smell she'd spent many holidays and long summer weekends submerged in when they'd visited her dad's parents in upstate New York as a child. She would recognize it anywhere. *Cigar smoke.* Subtle, yes, but there, all the same.

Impossible. No one was in the house but her. She sniffed again, trying to figure out which way it had come from. But almost as soon as she'd smelled it, it vanished.

Not knowing what to make of it, she did a quick walk-through of the second and third floors to be sure there weren't any obvious problems with construction or the electrical wiring, even though there was very little doubt in her mind of the scent.

She thought of the perfume from the night before. Was she losing her mind? Nothing looked unusual or out of place.

Ben would arrive any minute and she didn't want him to think she was crazy. She decided not to mention it. The evening was supposed to be lighthearted and fun. A night out that she desperately needed. Maybe she was getting a sinus infection. Fall was well known for bringing them on, and they could affect the sense of smell. Yes, she would go with that for now.

She made her way back downstairs and took a quick look in the mirror in the entryway just in time to see his truck pull in.

When she opened the door, Nora gave Ben a quick study, trying not to laugh.

He stood before her, clad in a black-and-white striped prison uniform, topped off with a tight little cap that looked at least two sizes too small. But the best part was the ridiculous oversized ball and chain attached to his ankle.

She couldn't hold it in any longer and laughed. Hard.

"Go on, yuk it up... I can take it."

"Ah, come on," she said, planting her hands on her hips. "You have to admit, it is *kinda* funny."

He gave her a once-over. "What I want to know," he said,

pointing to Nora's outfit, "is why did you get to be the cop and I'm stuck being the robber? I'd rather wear that costume."

"Well, first of all, seeing as this happens to be a policewoman's costume—*woman,* being the operative word here—I'm not sure how to feel about the fact that you would want to wear it. And secondly," she said, narrowing her eyes, "I've never looked good in stripes, so you're plain out of luck."

Ben glared at her. "Go ahead and have your fun at my expense. I exist solely for your entertainment pleasure, Ms. Bassett."

"That's *Officer* Bassett to you, fella."

"Wow," Ben muttered. "I have a feeling this is gonna be a rough evening." He smiled at her as they walked out the door. "By the way, does that costume come with handcuffs?"

"Wouldn't you like to know," she shot back, the edge of her lips curling up.

"Oh, I would," he said. "You have no idea."

THE TREES above sparkled with the glow of a thousand twinkling lights as Ben led Nora around the side of the sprawling country home at Bradley Farms, a long, winding path of ghosts in mid-flight and flickering jack-o'-lanterns leading their way.

"It's beautiful," she whispered.

He eased an arm around her as they walked. "I told you it would be amazing."

Behind the house an enormous bonfire lit up the night, its roaring crackle accompanied by the crisp snap of sparks as they rocketed up into the wide-open sky.

"There's the corn maze." Ben nodded toward the far side of the property.

"I'd love to see it later."

"Then see it you shall."

He caught the delicious fragrance of smoldering firewood and hot dogs on the breeze. "Hungry?"

She nodded. "Starving. That smells amazing. There's something about a fire on a chilly night, isn't there? It's one of my favorite things. Someday I would love to use the fireplaces at the house, but I haven't had a chance to get the chimneys swept yet."

Just then, a friendly voice called to them from the back porch of the house.

"Hey, you two."

Ben saw Liz and Scott heading their way.

"When did you guys sneak in?" she asked.

"We just got here," Ben said, giving her costume a look. "Who are you guys supposed to be? Tarzan and Jane?"

Scott glared at his wife. "I told you no one was going to get this whole Adam and Eve thing."

Ben tried to contain a laugh. "My bad. Sorry, Liz."

Liz rolled her eyes in Ben's direction and gave Nora a hug.

"Nora, this is my dashing husband, Scott."

He reached out to shake her hand. "Nice to meet someone who can hold their own with this guy," he said, motioning toward Ben.

Liz threw Ben a mischievous grin and grabbed Nora's arm. "I'm borrowing her for a few minutes. I want her to meet some people. Don't worry, she'll be back." She paused. "Maybe, that is. If I can't find anyone to convince her otherwise."

Ben reached for Nora but missed as Liz pulled her away. "Don't listen to a word that woman says, Nora. She's a compulsive liar."

NORA WAS STUFFED. She took the last sip of hard cider and leaned back in the lounge chair. She soaked in the warmth of the bonfire, its heat, along with the slight buzz, flushing her cheeks.

She glanced at her watch, unable to believe almost three hours had flown by, but she was grateful she'd made the decision to come and grateful for new friends who somehow felt like old. Especially Liz.

"Well," Ben said, reaching for her hand. "I should help clean up a little, and then how about that quick stroll through the maze before we head home?"

"Yeah, sounds great. But I'll help, too."

"No, you relax. I made a lot more of this mess than you did. As you can see, my s'more-making skills are limited. As Liz so kindly pointed out to everyone within a half-mile radius before they left."

Nora tossed her head back and laughed.

"So," he said, hoisting himself out of the chair. "It's settled. You relax and I'm gonna go help out a bit and then run out to the truck for a flashlight."

"Afraid of the dark, are you?" she teased.

"No," he said back. "I have you to hold on to." He leaned into her, softened his voice. "And believe me, I intend to do just that if you'll allow me."

He lifted her hand to his mouth, grazed it with his lips.

A rush of heat pulsed through Nora.

"Now, as much as I hate to leave you, I'd better get going if we're gonna have enough time to see the maze. They have ten acres of it back there. That's a lot of corn."

She watched him walk away, enjoying the view.

"Hey," he hollered back. "If you get tired of waiting for me, you can head on over and I'll meet you at the entrance."

She pushed out of her chair and looked around for some way to help, but all of the dishes had been taken in and the trash already bagged. She grabbed her jacket and turned to face the silent cornfield.

The corn jutted up, rising majestically against the black sky.

She made it to the entrance and glanced back over her

shoulder to look for Ben, spotting him talking to Mark on the back porch of the house.

He waved to her and hollered something she couldn't make out.

She took a few steps, hesitated. Then took a few more. She would just grab a quick peek.

The moon shone bright as Nora entered the tufts of corn, splashing its brilliant silver glow across the trail ahead. As she looked up, she was surprised at how small she felt beneath the massive stalks. She listened to the rustle of the cool autumn breeze as it moved, slow and gentle, through the pathway, reminding her of ocean waves lapping against the seashore. She closed her eyes, soaking in the sound.

As she opened her eyes again, the maze spread out into three different directions before her. She stepped up to the center pathway. Off to her left and right were smaller paths that led to even more paths—or in some cases, a dead end.

Her intention was to take a quick look and stay up toward the front until Ben arrived. But as her thoughts wandered, so did her feet, and before she knew it, she was lost.

She tried to remember which path would lead her back to where she'd started, but the corn walls were thick, almost solid. And by the light of the moon, everything started to look the same. She tried several different directions, but every turn led her to a new and different path.

She stopped, hoping to hear a sign of Ben's arrival. But the sway of corn was all that greeted her. She wasn't afraid. She felt at peace in the solitude of the corn patch under the gorgeous moon.

Until she heard the footsteps.

Off to her left, without warning, the jarring rustle of heavy feet plowed through the corn. The merciless crushing of stalks and ground pierced her ears as the footsteps headed straight for her.

A pair of doves joined in her terror, cooing wildly as they shot up from the safety of their nest somewhere just beyond.

Nora froze, her legs like slabs of concrete, her heart lodged in her throat. Now she was scared.

"Ben?" He must be playing a joke on her. When he didn't answer, she called out again, keeping her voice as calm and steady as she could. "Ha, ha. Now who thinks they're funny." She swallowed hard. "*Ben?*"

The corn tops stopped swaying and the air fell silent. As if nothing had happened, as if no one was there. But Nora sensed someone on the other side. Sensed it to her core. And she knew without doubt someone *was* there, with only darkness and a simple wall of stalks separating them.

She held her breath as she waited for another burst of life from the surrounding stalks. Halfway expecting to jump out of her skin as Ben dove through, laughing at a well-played practical joke.

But there was no sound. Nothing at all. Just the intense sensation that eyes were on her. Eyes that didn't belong there. And the longer she stood in the eerie silence, the more the tall stalks became prison bars, trapping her on every side.

She backed up against the opposite side of the path, as far away as she could. "Come on, Ben," she called, her voice quivering. "It was funny at first. But it's getting less funny by the minute."

Her legs threatened to give way as she took one more step back. Then she heard it. Breathing. From *behind* her. She turned as that side of the corn, too, jolted into motion. She tried to scream, but no sound came out.

Run, her mind commanded. And she obeyed. Before she knew it, she was in another row of corn, and then another. *Oh, God, where was she?* She tried to turn back, to remember where to go, but the world spun around her, tangling her feet, and she tripped, coming down hard on her knees.

She could hear the wild snapping of stalks in the distance, headed straight for her, closing in fast. Her heart pounded as she tried to stand. Please let it be Ben playing the world's worst joke, her mind pleaded.

As if on cue, from the opposite direction of the property, Ben's voice called to her from the distance.

It hadn't been him.

Nora's stomach roiled, threatening to empty. "Ben, I'm over here," she screamed. "This way!"

"Nora? What's wrong? Where are you?"

She pushed herself up, knees throbbing, and aimed her footsteps toward his voice.

Relief washed over her as the beam from his flashlight poured across the path in front of her.

"Are you okay? What happened?"

She tried to calm herself. "No, I'm not. What the hell was that?" she breathed.

"What are you talking about?" Ben said, worry darkening his face.

"Someone was in there with me."

"What? Who?"

"I don't know, but they were chasing me, I—"

He flashed the light through the stalks. "Could it have been an animal, maybe? A deer or coyote?"

"No." She looked out over the corn, its thick, dark labyrinth now haunting her. "It was definitely *someone*."

"I'm going to take a look around. You stay put for a second."

"No—" she said a little too fast, her hands darting over to his arm. "Don't go. Let's get out of here, if that's okay with you."

"You sure? I'd like to find the son of a bitch and have a little chat with him."

"No. I'm good now." She forced an awkward laugh. "Probably just some teenagers pulling a prank. It is Halloween, after all."

He hesitated. "If you're sure."

She nodded. She was very sure. The lovely corn wasn't so lovely anymore, and she wanted to get as far away from it as possible.

Ben handed her the flashlight and put his arm around her shoulders, pulling her close. "You're shaking like crazy."

She scooted into him. "I'm good now."

She watched Ben take a last look around. All was peaceful, silent.

"I sure would like to find the bastard who did this to you. Teenage prank or not. They had no right."

She shook her head. "I'd rather just go."

"You're the boss. You ready then?"

The muscles in her dry, knotted throat began to unclench as his smile brought her back down to earth. "Yes," she whispered. "A thousand times, yes."

HE MOVED through the shadows beyond the house, his breath coming hot and fast as anger surged through his body, pushing him nearly beyond his limits. But he had to wait. It couldn't happen this soon. Someone would suspect.

His jaw hardened.

A different direction would have to be taken with this one, and he'd already begun to plan.

He'd followed them tonight. It was a dangerous chance to take. But curiosity had won the battle inside him.

He'd watched them laughing as they sat by the fire in the midst of all the ridiculous festivities. Their flirtation—nails on an endless row of chalkboards.

He had enjoyed his time alone with Nora tonight, however. *Immensely.* He'd been there among the cornstalks, and she'd known it. The smell of her fear was exhilarating. It had taken all of the willpower he had not to teach that smug little whore a lesson, right then and there. And he commended himself for the control he'd summoned.

She was exactly like her sister, and the sight of her burned him to his core. He'd thought he'd taken care of the problem the night he'd given Lucy a generous taste of why she shouldn't screw with him. Had assumed that was the end of it, that everything would fall into place.

It had been like the sting of acid splashing into a raw wound to see an exact replica of her arrive at the house. *His house*.

But he would take care of her, too. He had to bide his time. Patience was key, as well as planning. It was all in the details, and Nora was going to bring him even more satisfaction than her sister had.

CHAPTER ELEVEN

Nora stared at the blank laptop screen. It mocked her, holding the words—which normally spilled onto the pages with little effort—hostage.

She'd been at it since nine a.m. and it was now nearing noon. Write, delete, repeat, her mantra for the day. If she were to be perfectly honest with herself, it had been her mantra for the entire week since the Halloween party.

She shut the laptop, leaned back in the chair and rubbed her eyes for the thousandth time. Thank God she had a little leeway before her next deadline.

She sat there until the scrape of branches against the window pane drew her attention. The weather had taken a bleak turn for the worse, bringing cold, dark, overcast skies. It mimicked her mood. And as much as she hated to admit it, the incident in the maze remained responsible.

The terror of the experience still nibbled away at her nerves, fraying them a little more each time she recounted it. She'd been so frightened, felt so helpless—*a feeling she despised*. It bothered her to her core that she'd allowed herself to run, to be intimidated that way. She'd like to think that if she could turn back the clock, she would react differently. Would call the bastard out, to show himself instead of getting his jollies preying on her from beyond the veil of corn.

And who had it been?

That was the question that plagued her more than anything else. Who would go to that extreme to rattle her...and why? And what might have happened if Ben hadn't come when he had?

She pushed back from the desk and stood.

She was getting nothing worthwhile done on the new book, and there was a list a mile long of things that needed to be addressed with the inn. Starting with a supply run.

She walked downstairs to find Ethan changing out electrical outlets in the entryway. He turned to look at her, not speaking a word, as was his usual way—especially when there was no one else around as a buffer.

"Hey," she said, walking toward the kitchen. "How's it going down here?"

"Storms coming," he muttered. "Just trying to finish."

"I thought it wasn't due to hit until day after tomorrow. They must have moved it up."

He nodded but kept working until she'd passed him.

Nora turned back for a split second, noticing his eyes dart away from her and back to the outlet in front of him.

Not my favorite of the crew, she thought to herself, and then instantly felt bad for it.

The back door swung open. Ben stepped inside and pulled off his coat.

"Man, it's frigid out there, and I'm starting not to like the look of that sky. Snow's coming."

"I should make a quick supply run then," Nora said. "Talk about a blunt transition from fall to winter."

Ben unhooked his tool belt and propped it on the floor next to the credenza. "It's happened before. My senior year of college we got fourteen inches overnight in early November. Shut the town down. Snow like that is nasty business. By the way, Ethan and I brought the generator over from the shed and put it on the back porch. Started up fine. Wanted to make sure it was in good shape, just in case."

"Thanks for wanting to keep me warm," she said with a wink and a sexy smile.

He reached for her arm and pulled her toward him. "Trust me when I tell you it's my pleasure."

Nora started to laugh, but it was cut short.

"Outlets are done," Ethan said, walking toward them. He turned to face Nora. "I couldn't help but overhear you say you need to go into town. I'm headed there now to get gas for the generators. I can give you a lift to the store if you need one."

Nora was surprised at the offer, considering how short Ethan usually was with her, how uncomfortable he appeared on a regular basis. Her stomach knotted. Time alone in a truck with that particular member of Ben's team was not something she was at all interested in.

"I appreciate the offer," she began, "but my list is long, and I couldn't do that to you. Thank you, though."

"Suit yourself," he said, grabbing his coat. "I'll be back, Ben."

Once he'd gone, Nora nibbled the edge of her lip, looked at Ben. "I hope I didn't offend him. It's just—"

Ben waved her off with a smile. "Don't worry about it. He's a little different. Mitch said he's got a pretty hefty chip on his shoulder. Guess he's been through some stuff. I don't know the details, but I don't think he'll be with us much longer anyway. Guys like that, unless they bond pretty tight with the rest of the crew, they tend to move on quickly."

She nodded and plucked her keys from the kitchen counter, then walked to the front door with Ben.

He pulled her coat off the rack, helped her into it. Then looped her scarf around her neck and eased her to his chest. "Again, just me wanting to make you warm," he murmured.

Nora's eyes flashed as she allowed him to draw her close, press his lips to hers.

"Hey, now," Mitch hollered as he pushed through the back door. "No time for that. Storm's on its way. It's almost here. I can feel it in my tired old bones."

Nora's heart sank. She wanted more of Ben, craved time alone with him. Just the two of them.

She reached for her purse. "Okay, I'm off."

Ben shot her a knowing look, kissed her cheek. "Please be careful, and make sure you're back before nightfall. They keep upping the amount of snow, as well as its arrival time. Every time I check my phone, they've changed the damn forecast."

"I'm just running by the gas station and grocery store. Oh," she said, snapping her fingers. "And Bella's Treasures for a couple minutes. I'd called her to ask if she would keep an eye out for a canopy bed for that last room on the third floor, and she called this morning and said she has one now. I'd like to take a peek at it before it's gone."

"Well, I'm going to let everybody here head out a little early this afternoon. Just in case."

"Yes. Sooner rather than later. Sure hope it doesn't do all that they are saying."

"If it does, things could get pretty dicey."

Nora swung the door open, the cold air biting at her cheeks. "You weren't kidding. This is crazy."

"Be safe," he said firmly, stepping out onto the porch behind her.

"I will, thanks."

She made it down the front steps but looked back over her shoulder as she started across the yard. "See you a little later then, if you're still here by the time I get back, that is."

And she desperately hoped he was.

～

BELLA HELD the door for Nora as she carried a large box out to her car.

"Thank you so much for calling me about the bed. I'll be out next week to pick it up."

Bella smiled. "We can deliver if you need. I'm glad it worked for you. And that you found a few other things to round out your décor. I'll have to come out and see your inn when you're all finished."

Nora closed the car door. "I would love that. We're getting close now. I think we have a real shot at finishing ahead of schedule." She looked up. "If the weather cooperates, that is."

"I'm afraid we're in for it, my dear. I'm about to close up and head home. You should do the same."

"I hope I didn't keep you too long."

"Goodness no. I only live a couple of streets over. I'm worried about you getting home before it starts."

"I hit the market on the way here and loaded up with enough food to last a few days. So, you're my last stop, besides the gas station. Don't want to head home in this on half a tank."

"Oh," Bella rattled. "I almost forgot. Are you looking for any employees to help out when you're up and running?"

"Yes, I will be very soon. Do you have someone in mind?"

"Well, my niece moved here not long ago and might be interested in helping part-time. You know, with cleaning or various odds and ends. She's twenty-three and a sweet girl, hard worker."

"Send her my way. I'd love to talk to her."

Bella grinned. "It's as good as done. You be careful out there, sweetie."

Nora climbed in the car and started the engine.

As she pulled away, the first snowflakes emerged from the sea of gray above. Hard and fast. And by the time she pulled into the gas station, traffic had slowed to a crawl, the line at least four vehicles deep at every pump. She cursed herself for having stayed so long at Bella's.

When it was finally her turn, she topped off her car, then headed in to pay.

Another mile-long line.

She grabbed a coffee and a bag of ice melt and took her place at the back, watching customers skitter through the aisles, depleting the little station of bread and milk and most everything else. People were nervous.

Nora tried to tune out the string of uneasy predictions regarding the storm's magnitude, in addition to the exhumation of horror stories from winters past, each one trumping the last. By the time she paid and made it back to the car, she wanted nothing more than to be tucked into the cozy halls of Black Willow. Strange smells, scratching mice and all.

She made her way down the highway as eerie layers of silence upon darkness snuffed out the previous buzz and hum of the outside world.

She thought of Ben, wondered if he'd gone already. Felt a little guilty for hoping he hadn't. Road conditions had deteriorated at an alarming rate with the asphalt now glazed over, and she knew he would need to get back to his own place to check on things before the weather opened fire on Marietta.

The wall of white beyond thickened, forcing Nora to lean forward on the edge of her seat as the headlights finally poured across Black Willow's covered bridge.

She breathed a small sigh of relief as she inched across its length. A beacon in the wintry night.

She'd made it back safe...and mostly sound.

At the top of the hill, she looked around. No cars. Ben had gone.

She looked up at the giant, dark house, nerves crawling into her belly as she contemplated riding out the storm alone. And who knew? Possibly with no power, minus a single generator.

She sighed and swung the car door open, the burst of damp,

icy air only making things worse. Now, the unloading, she thought. *This should be fun.*

She inched her way to the trunk, wedged it open and leaned inside to get the first load when the crunch of frozen footsteps jerked her to a halt.

Nora's heart slammed in her chest as the terror in the corn maze sprang into her mind, front and center. She angled her face toward the sound to see a figure approaching in the darkness. Her eyes opened wide.

"Thank God you made it, Nora. I was getting worried."

Nora let her lungs fill with air. It was Ben.

"You okay? I didn't mean to startle you."

"I thought you'd gone," she said, forcing her pulse to slow. "Where's your truck?"

He pulled her into his arms and hugged her tight. "I ran into town for a few minutes after you left earlier, and when I got back, I parked behind the house. I'm glad you're okay. I tried your phone, but it went straight to voicemail."

"It did? I'm so sorry. My battery was on its way out earlier, and I was in such a hurry to get everything done, I guess I forgot to charge it."

"That would explain it." He reached in for the bags. "No big deal. Now get yourself inside before you catch pneumonia. There's a blizzard going on out here, in case you hadn't noticed."

She and Ben laughed like children as the snow fell heavier by the moment. Nora's heart soared. He'd stayed. And the prospect of sharing the quiet, snowy wee hours with him left her so warm inside that no amount of sleet or wind or ice could take that away.

They reached the front steps and Ben motioned for Nora to take the lead. "Hope you don't mind that I stayed. I couldn't stand the thought of you stranded out here in this mess by yourself."

"Just try and leave," she said, shaking the dusting of white off. "I dare you. Honestly, I'm very happy you stayed." She reached for the door handle but stopped. "I could swear I smell firewood burning, but that's impossible. I—"

She opened the door and walked into the entryway. The house was dark and quiet and warm. A lovely amber glow seeped out from the now finished library, accompanied by the unmistakable nutty smell of burning firewood.

She stepped closer and looked inside.

Words escaped her.

On the floor was a plaid blanket spread out in front of a crackling fire. A bucket of champagne, two long-stem glasses and a plate of cheese and fruit rested next to it.

She turned to look at him. "I don't know what to say. How did—"

"I know how much you love these fireplaces, so I had a guy come out and sweep them this week while you were out. My gift to you." He paused. "And there's plenty of wood on the back porch to last at least a few days."

"I..." She stopped, overcome. "How beautiful and thoughtful. I love it. Thank you, Ben. Thank you so very much."

"My pleasure. I hoped you'd be pleased," he said, slipping out to take the bags into the kitchen.

Nora stood in silence, soaking in the romance, the sweetness. He'd stayed to make sure she was all right during the storm, and had paid close enough attention to her daily ramblings to learn of something that would mean a great deal to her, and had made it happen. But perhaps the most caring and gentle thing he'd done for her since they'd met, was that he'd given her the time she needed to heal, respected her wish to take things slowly. Why had she waited so long to show him how she truly felt?

The time had come.

She slid off her coat and walked to the kitchen with tears in her eyes.

Ben looked up as she walked in. "Hey, what's wrong? That was supposed to make you happy, not—"

Nora closed the space between them, lifted her finger to Ben's lips, halting his words. She took his hand and silently led him back to the library.

THE WORDS BEN had started to speak drifted a world away. Nothing mattered, or even existed, except the two of them as Nora lifted her face to him. The look in her eyes, telling him all he needed to know.

He drew her down onto the blanket in front of the fire, breathed in the scent of her, delicate and sweet. He'd come to care more about her than any other woman in his life. Ever. And now he would finally show her.

"You are so beautiful, Nora," he murmured. "I've wanted this for a long time. Being here with you...like this."

He brushed her lips with a soft kiss. A gentle moan stirred in her, and she melted into him, parting her lips. He kissed her again, deeper. The kiss lingered between them, a tender, breathless moment he'd waited for, *longed for*.

Ben pulled her in tight against him, his arms enveloping her, the need to feel her close—as close as two people could be—something he could no longer ignore.

He eased his hands down her back as his mouth reclaimed hers again and again, her breath coming faster as the heat between them ignited. He could feel the pounding of her heartbeat as she opened herself to him, her hips pressing into his. She pulled back just enough to guide his hands to the front of her shirt, her eyes never leaving his. He obliged, slipping the buttons open one by one, his body awakening more with the release of each. She slid her shirt off, her skin shimmering like silk in the flickering light.

She was breathtaking.

He kissed her mouth again slowly, then let his lips wander

down over her neck before laying her back onto the blanket. She reached for his shoulders, gripping, her fingers rippling over his muscles as she arched her back, urging his hands, *rugged, splintered,* to drink in the soft suppleness of her breasts. His mouth joined them, then eased downward to the curve of her belly. She quivered beneath his touch at the glimpse of what was to come.

Slow and steady, he touched, tasted, *tempted* every part of her, until he felt her buck against him, her body wrapping around him tightly as she let go.

"Ben," she cried beneath gasps of breath. She pulled him back up toward her face and kissed him hard, this time with an urgency that took his breath away, a carnal need.

He leaned back briefly, reaching for his wallet from the back pocket of his jeans. "Just a sec," he whispered, tearing open the small silver packet he'd always thought it smart to carry but hadn't had any need for in as long as he could remember.

She sat up behind him, her hair spilling down over his back as she laid her cheek against him. "You mean the world to me," she said softly, her lips working their way across the blades of his shoulders. "I hope you know that."

He shifted back to her, sliding her hair from her forehead. "I do," he answered, running his fingertip down the length of her arm. "Now, let me show you how much you mean to me." He eased her down onto the blanket once more and took her face into his hands. Beautiful, dark eyes brimming with desire, invited him. And when he couldn't wait any longer, he lowered himself toward her. Careful to go slow. Nora's body welcomed his, a small sensual cry sounding from the back of her throat. And by the light of the fire, Ben's soul wrapped around Nora's as they moved together as one.

∽

SNOW CONTINUED to fall into the night, covering Black Willow in an endless blanket of cold, crisp white.

Ben watched Nora sleep as she lay nestled in the crook of his arm. The fire down to embers, he should have felt the bite of the cool hardwood beneath him or the chill of the draft coming in from the crack at the base of the front door—the one he still had yet to fix. But he felt warm to his core, the most content he'd ever been in his life. And he knew that it was all due to the breathtaking woman lying next to him.

He pulled her in close, trying his best not to wake her, but she stirred against his touch.

"Sorry," he whispered. "I didn't mean to wake you."

"I'm glad you did," she echoed softly.

She reached for him, kissing his fingers one by one, inviting him to her once again.

He slid the blanket back far enough to see the silhouette of her breasts in the faint moonlight. Taking his time, he caressed them, feeling her body come alive beneath him. He guided his mouth to hers, tasted her again, *made love to her again* until the last traces of firelight died, draping the house around them in darkness, silence.

CHAPTER TWELVE

The aroma of rich Colombian coffee wafted into the library.

"Good morning, beautiful."

Nora rolled over onto her side to find Ben standing in the doorway, a steaming cup in his hand.

"It *is* a good morning," she replied. "The very best of mornings, I would say." She pushed up to a sitting position to take the cup he offered.

He stoked the remaining coals in the fireplace, added another log. "You hungry? I rounded up the ingredients for pancakes."

"You might just be the perfect man."

"Might?" Ben laughed. "Come on, dream woman, let's get you fed. You will very likely need your energy later." He winked at her and offered his hand.

Nora smiled, grabbing the shirt she'd worn the night before and pulled it on as she padded into the kitchen behind Ben.

"How beautiful," she said, walking to the window. The world beyond was white and clean and perfect.

Ben cracked an egg into a bowl. "Snowed all night long. Must be a couple feet."

"Unbelievable." She pulled herself away from the snowy scene with a yawn. "I think I may need a shower to wake up. I don't usually stay up quite that late."

"Yeah, well, I would say I'm sorry about that, but I'd be lying, so..."

He shot her a sexy morning-after smile, making her want to skip breakfast altogether.

"Go on up and shower," he said, "I'll call you when it's ready."

Nora lifted the coffee pot and walked toward him. "Now, what kind of girl would I be, taking advantage of you all night long, only to follow it up with having you cook me breakfast all by yourself the next morning?" She topped off his coffee cup and kissed him lightly on the cheek.

Ben stopped whisking and took the pot out of her hands, set it on the counter. Then smiled at her and pulled her to him. "Let me do this for you. Please. Go on up and enjoy a hot shower."

She sighed. "Why do I find it so hard to say no to you?"

"I'm just that charming," he answered.

"Fine, you win. I'll go," she said. "But I'm at least doing the dishes afterward. I insist." She started out of the kitchen but turned back. "Wait, we are using paper plates, right?"

He laughed and hurled a hand towel at her as she darted out of the doorway.

"You're too good to me," she said, her words filtering down the hallway after her.

BREAKFAST EATEN, dishes done and too much coffee consumed, Nora bundled in layers, ready to embrace her inner child.

Ben pulled on his gloves. "So, how's your aim?"

Nora scrambled down the front porch steps to grab a handful of snow, sculpting it into a ball as fast as she could. "Guess you're about to find out!"

She pelted the ball of snow toward him, hitting Ben square in the chest, then retreated to a nearby cluster of bushes to reload.

He grunted, swooping down to retaliate. "So, this is how you treat the man who allows your advances all night long and then makes you breakfast?"

"Yep. What are you going to do about it," she squealed out from the fortress of evergreen.

"Just remember, you asked for this." He hunkered down, raking up an armful of snow, and opened fire.

Another squeal rang out through the cold midday air as Nora bolted around toward the back of the house to hide. But the fun screeched to a dead halt as she saw what lay imbedded in the drifts of white in front of her.

Footprints.

Good-sized ones, too. She scanned the yard, trying to wrap her mind around what she was seeing. The prints led to the library window and around to the back door, then disappeared out toward the river. She wondered when Ben would have had time to go outside earlier that morning and why he'd been at the window.

She stood for a moment, sifting back through the morning in her mind. Maybe while she was in the shower?

Ben finally caught up to her.

He pulled her into him and leaned to kiss her cheek, but stopped when she didn't reciprocate. He took a step back. "What's wrong?" He followed her gaze, seeing the problem.

Nora looked at him, hopeful. "Were you out here this morning?"

"Who the hell?" Ben's jaw hardened as he saw the tracks, his eyes surveying the property around them. "No. It wasn't me."

"Could one of the crew have come out for something early this morning?"

Nora already knew the answer but asked the question anyway.

"Considering I don't see any vehicle tracks, it's doubtful." He paused. "I would say Liz or maybe Scott, but again, no tire marks, and I doubt either of them would have come over in this weather."

"No, Liz would have called if they needed something."

"I don't know who they belong to, Nora. But I intend to find out."

A shudder ran through her as she wondered at what point the onlooker had been at the window, unbeknownst to her and Ben. Their intimacy had been open and unguarded. She felt the beginnings of a knot form in her stomach. "Well, I guess they got their money's worth, anyway," she tried to joke.

She watched as the question of timing hit him, too.

"Don't panic," he said. "We don't know at what point they happened by."

He took her hand and led her back toward the front of the house. "You know, it could have been someone just drifting through, looking for an empty place to escape the cold for the night."

Nora stared at him, her mouth falling open.

"Okay," Ben said, shrugging, "so that doesn't sound too great, either. Sorry. Maybe someone with car trouble? Who knows, maybe they ended up over at Liz's place."

"Yeah, I guess so."

"If anyone is on the property who shouldn't be, and I find them, we'll call the police. Although, it might take them a while to get out here on a day like this."

She nodded as he walked her up the steps and opened the front door. "Why don't you run in and call Liz, just to be sure it wasn't them. I'm gonna take a quick look around up here. I need to bring more firewood around anyway."

"If you promise you're not going to go rogue and follow those tracks down toward the river without me. I don't want you to go alone."

He leaned in and kissed her. "You worry too much. Has anyone ever told you that?"

"Just you," she said as she turned in search of her cell, spotting it on the coffee table in the parlor.

"I'm locking the door behind me," Ben hollered, "and I don't have my key."

"I'll listen for you."

"Okay, I'll be back."

Nora heard him close the front door and dialed Liz. "Come on. Pick up, pick up," she mumbled as voicemail kicked on.

She swiped the off button and slipped the phone in her sweater pocket as she walked into the kitchen. She wandered over to the bay window and studied the backyard hoping to find some piece of evidence to link the footsteps to friend rather than foe. But there was nothing. Nothing but the hush of a vast ocean of white.

She nibbled the edge of her lip as she considered the reasons there would be tracks beneath the library window. None of them made her feel any better. Finally she turned her path upstairs to look for her laptop, deciding a few minutes with her manuscript would be a welcome distraction.

In her bedroom the phone buzzed, and she pulled it out and looked down at the screen to see Liz's name.

She quickly answered. "Hey, Liz."

"Nora, I saw that I missed your call a few minutes ago. I was out front with the boys putting the finishing touches on the most hideous attempt at a snowman—in the history of all snowmen, I'm pretty sure." She laughed. "I was going to call and check on you this morning, but you beat me to it. Can you believe this weather? The boys are loving it."

Nora sat down by the window, absently looking across the yard again. "Yeah, it's really something."

"Hey, you know what? Scott and I are planning to throw on a pot of chili a little later. You should come over. We have an old tractor out back that will drive in anything. I could have Scott pick you up."

"That sounds really great, but Ben is here and I just needed to ask you a quick question."

"Oh, Ben's there with you?"

Nora could almost hear Liz's wheels spinning.

"He stayed out there with you last night?" she asked, a hint of excitement in her voice.

"Yes, he's outside right now. Which brings me to why I called."

"Sure. What's up?"

"Well, Ben and I were out earlier and noticed footprints leading up to the house."

"Who was out in this weather?"

Liz sounded as surprised as Nora herself had been.

"Judging by your reaction, you've just given me the answer to my question. We wondered if by chance you had come by looking for us and we didn't hear you knock, which is apparently not the case."

"Sorry. It wasn't us."

"It was worth a try. I guess no one showed up over there at your place, either..."

"No, we haven't seen anyone at all."

Even though Nora had known it would be a long shot, she was disappointed. "No big deal. Sorry to bother you."

"Nora, you're never a bother. Call anytime. I'm sorry not to be of help. I wish I could tell you it was one of us, ease your mind a little."

"I do, too. More than you know."

Liz brightened her tone. "Talk to Ben about the chili. We'll drag out the cards if you can make it. You and I can give the guys a run for their money. Take your mind off whoever was lurking around last night."

Nora shrank back into the chair as the image of a dark figure hovering at the window paraded through her mind again. "I'd be lying if I said this isn't completely unnerving."

"Agreed. Just the thought creeps me out, too. Hope you get some answers. We'll help any way we can. Call me later."

"I will. Talk to you soon."

Nora ended the call and tossed the phone on the nightstand, disappointed. She looked down at her watch and then out the bedroom window again, hoping to catch a glimpse of Ben. When she didn't see him, she leaned her head back and closed her eyes until the phone rang again.

She hoisted herself up and reached for it. *Dad cell* flashed across the front as she swiped it on.

"Dad..."

"Hi, honey. Just checking in."

Nora smiled. "I'm glad you called," she said, dropping heavily into the chair once more.

EVERY MUSCLE in Ben's body tightened as he trudged through the snow. He hadn't wanted to upset Nora before—hadn't wanted to ruin the incredible night they'd shared, but he'd noticed the prints were not those of someone who had just come up to the window for a quick scan of the room. The snow around the tracks had melted and was packed down hard, telling Ben the stranger had lingered. But even worse, the telltale sign had been the ashes he'd seen at the edge of Nora's foot. Someone had taken quite a few drags off something while they'd hunkered down for the show.

He pulled his phone from his coat pocket and snapped several pictures of the tracks beneath the window and in the direction they led in case the situation escalated.

Anger coursed through him. He wouldn't have allowed Nora to know how upset he was, but whoever had helped himself to a look at the two of them—either in passion or in sleep or whatever they'd seen—would certainly know, as soon as he found him.

And if he was still on the property...*he would find him.*

He knew he didn't have much time, or Nora would come looking for him, so he moved fast. He followed the prints around the back of the house.

Before he knew it, he'd gone farther than he intended, irritation and confusion driving his steps. He'd followed the prints all the way to the river, where they vanished into nothing.

What the hell?

His mind couldn't wrap around it, and it drove him crazy not to have any clue of who the unwelcome visitor had been. But just as he was about to give up and turn around, he saw a flash of red farther up the road.

He took a few more steps and hunkered down.

A good half mile up, the red paint of an old pickup truck stood out against the white backdrop of snow. It was turned sideways off in the ditch, not a soul in the cab or anywhere to be seen.

Ben moved toward it, neither hearing nor seeing anything of consequence. He eased up to the passenger door and cupped his hands against the frosty glass, scanning the front seat.

Relief swept over him as he took inventory of a backpack, tennis shoes and a calculus book, along with an assortment of empty chip bags and candy bar wrappers.

A teenager's truck.

The knots in Ben's gut began to relax as he realized the poor kid probably slid off into the ditch, panicked, and walked up to the first house he could find for help. And chances were good that if the kid had seen him and Nora making love, number one, he probably had a hard time looking away, and second, he was likely too embarrassed to knock on the door and interrupt. But one thing did bother him. What teenage kid in this day and age didn't have their own cell phone to call for help? An irresponsible one, he decided.

Ben turned and looked down the road. He could make out the outline of additional tracks the fresh snowfall had attempted to fill.

There were a few other houses around the bend past Liz's, and he was willing to bet that the kid had gone on down until he found a house where the inhabitants weren't completely naked and in the throes of passion.

It still irritated him, though, that a stranger—even one with a wrecked truck and raging hormones—had seen more of Nora than he should have. But as he began the long hike back up to the house, Ben reminded himself that he had been a teenager once, too, and he made a mental note to call the authorities and report the truck, just in case the kid was still out there somewhere and needed assistance. No harm had been done, and besides, he was more than a little relieved to have uncovered a reasonable explanation that would put Nora a bit more at ease.

NORA CLIMBED out of the chair as her father said good-bye. She glanced out the window again, frowning as she caught a tiny glimpse of Ben through the trees coming up the river path.

She knew it. He'd gone to the river without her.

She lifted the window in an attempt to razz him about it, the cold air nipping her cheeks, but he was too far away to hear. She closed the window once more and stood in the quiet, letting her eyes wander over the snow-covered willows. The outside world felt as though it were a million miles away.

She pulled back from the window and walked toward the hallway intending to go downstairs, as the muffled squeak of a door creaking open high above shattered the silence.

She stopped. Had she imagined it? Of course she had, she was alone in the house. She took another step, but the same door above now swung shut—and this time it was accompanied by what sounded like the scuff of slow, deliberate footsteps.

"Ben?" Panic began its descent over her. It wasn't Ben and she knew it. She'd just seen him outside. She struggled to find her voice once more. "Who's up there?" she called, truly not knowing whether to hope for a response from the third floor or not. Definitely *not*, she decided.

She looked toward the stairwell as another door overhead creaked open, followed by more footsteps. Then everything stopped.

What was happening?

She rushed back to the bedroom window, her heart lodging in her throat as she saw Ben continuing up the path. She reached for the cell, her fingers trembling as she dialed him.

He answered on the first ring. "I'm almost back," he said before she could speak. "And I've got good news."

"Ben, listen to me," Nora cut in. "I know this sounds crazy, but someone's in the house."

"What? Wait, Nora, slow down. What's going on?"

Her words spilled out faster than she could keep up with. "Someone is upstairs walking around. I know it sounds insane, and I don't know who it is or how they got in, but I'm telling you *someone is upstairs in this house right now*. I heard them—"

"I believe you," Ben said, his voice laced with worry. "Where are you right now?"

"I'm in my bedroom, but I'm going back out to check it—"

"You're not going anywhere. Stay put. I'm coming to you," he ordered, then stopped. "Damn it, I don't have the key."

She remembered their earlier conversation about the key. "I'll meet you," she said, keeping her voice low. "The noise is coming from up on the third floor. I can make it down to the front door." She hesitated. "I can't imagine who the hell it is."

There was a long pause on the other end of the phone. "Ben? Hello?" She looked down at the screen. *Call dropped.* "Are you freaking kidding me?"

She dialed him again. Voicemail.

She hated this damsel-in-distress routine. She couldn't stand the thought of him viewing her as needy or weak, unable to look after herself. At this point, she grew angry. She walked to the bedroom door and waited what felt like an eternity. The house was calm, silent. Too silent.

Nora raced down the stairs and yanked open the front door. Ben hadn't made it there yet, so she headed across the front yard. With the distance at least offering the facade of safety, she turned and faced the house as the flutter of curtains from a third-floor window caught her eye.

Something had moved.

But then she wasn't sure. Nora's jaw clenched into a hard knot. Had she actually even heard the noises?

Doubt began to tug at the corners of her mind as Ben emerged from the side of the house.

He moved to her, holding her tight against him.

"You okay? I was so worried when we got disconnected."

"I'm all right, just a little freaked out. I'd be lying if I said I wasn't."

"You have every right to be spooked." He turned his attention to the house. "What in the world happened?"

"I have no idea. I walked into the hallway on the second floor, and either I'm completely certifiable or noises started coming down from the third floor. Footsteps, or at least they sounded like it. Doors opened and then shut again. I don't know. You don't think it's the same person who left the prints, do you?" Nora felt sick. She hated coming off as vulnerable but didn't know how to be anything else at the moment.

Ben squeezed her hand. "I think I may have an explanation for that, so I doubt it. But you wait out here. I'm going in to check it out."

"Not without me."

"I'll be fine. I promise."

"You can't promise something like that."

"Nora..."

She could see that he wouldn't budge. "Fine, but at least

promise me that if you hear or see anything, you'll come back out and we'll call the police. No heroics, okay?"

"You have my word."

She followed him up onto the porch and waited just inside the door, until it dawned on her that when she'd hurried down the stairs earlier, she'd had to unlock the door to get out. It had still been locked, just as Ben had left it.

Nora crept down the hall toward the back door, curiosity thwarting her attempt to remain in the safety of the entryway.

That door was still locked, too. Exactly as she'd left it earlier in the day.

How could someone have gotten in if all the doors had been locked the entire time?

A new thought entered her mind. She tried to shut it down. But it came at her again. What if it hadn't been someone, but rather some...*thing.* The thought sounded absurd in her head. She didn't believe in the supernatural, never had. But what then?

"All clear," Ben hollered as he came back down. "No sign of anyone at all and nothing's out of place, that I can see."

Nora met him at the bottom of the stairs.

"Well, thank God." She tried to smile even though inside she was conflicted as to whether that was good news or not. "I swear I heard something up there. I wouldn't have called you if I hadn't."

Ben nodded. "Of course you heard something. I believe you did. I've heard some strange things in here myself. But my guess is that it was the contraction and expansion of these old pipes since it's so cold outside. Like I said before, old houses can make some crazy sounds. Even more so when temps drop below freezing outside."

Nora tried to push the echo of footsteps out of her mind, choosing to believe Ben's explanation, even though uncertainty still churned in her. "Well, since the doors were all still locked and you didn't find anyone prowling around, I guess you're right."

"Now onto more good news," he said with a smile. "I found a truck off in the ditch a little way up the road and it had teenage boy written all over it, so I'd be willing to guess our visitor was someone who slid off the road and was looking for help. Probably got embarrassed when he looked in the window."

"Really?" She knew she should be relieved but somehow wasn't. "That's good news." She looked down at Ben's soaked pants as she helped him out of his coat. "But I thought we agreed you weren't going to go off without me."

"Just felt like taking a little walk, that's all."

She frowned. "Ben—"

"I know, I know. But I felt like I needed to get to the bottom of it. I'm sorry you were frightened while I was gone. Can you forgive me?" He nuzzled her neck.

"Especially since the mysteries have been put to bed now and all is well again?"

"I may need a minute to think it over," she teased. "I'll let you know." She reached to kiss him, but stopped. "Oh, I almost forgot. When I called Liz, she invited us for chili later."

"Hmm, I've had Liz's chili, and though it's tempting..." His eyes darkened. "It doesn't hold a candle to the idea of another evening here, with you all to myself."

She smiled. "I'll text her in a little bit."

He kissed her. "I'm sorry I left you alone earlier."

"Well," she sighed, "I guess you could try to make it up to me."

Ben smiled as he nibbled the edge of her ear, making his way toward her mouth. "I can do better than try if you'll let me."

"Let you?" she whispered. "I insist."

She kissed him harder, urging him toward the stairs, shedding layers of clothing as she did. The fear from earlier melted away as they made their way to the bedroom.

CHAPTER THIRTEEN

Nora wondered what had awakened her. She could feel the warmth of Ben's body wrapped around her from behind, the rhythm of his breathing confirming that he was sound asleep.

All was peaceful and well. So why didn't it feel that way? What had flicked her eyes wide open in the middle of the night? Her mind combed back through the incidents from the day before, and no matter how hard she tried, she couldn't shake the feeling that something was off. From the unexplainable scent of smoke wafting through the corridors to the phantom footprints beneath the window, and the eerie sounds that echoed through the house at all hours. Something wasn't right.

Ben had offered clear and believable explanations for everything, but the longer she lay there, the more her mind zeroed in on the footsteps she'd sworn she heard upstairs.

It had been easy—a little too easy—to shrug them off in the sunny fresh air with Ben safe at her side. But in that terrifying moment, when she'd been alone and vulnerable, the sound of footsteps above had been enough to bring her to her knees.

Could it have been so trivial as a fluctuation in the pipes?

Could she have overreacted that much? No, it had been more than that. But what?

A thought from earlier resurfaced in her mind, twisted her stomach. She tried to deny it, but the idea circled like a hungry shark in deep, dark water.

What if her experiences had been caused by something *paranormal?*

It couldn't be...could it? *No*, she silently scoffed at herself. *You're losing it, Nora.* It was a ridiculous notion, crazy. She thought back to the time when she and Lucy were kids and how Lucy had gone through a ghost-hunting phase, how she'd tried desperately to convince Nora that spirits were real, that houses could be haunted. Nora had made fun of her, had never taken the bait. And she had no intention of taking it now, either. No, she would be much more likely to believe that it had been a person lurking upstairs in the house yesterday—a fairly good-sized man, from the sound of it. But, she remembered...*the doors were all locked.* She frowned. Yes, there was that.

She drew in a deep breath, tried closing her eyes once again. But it was no use, sleep was not going to revisit any time soon. She gave up and inched out from under Ben's arms in search of her laptop. Once she found it, she pulled the bedroom door shut behind her and walked downstairs.

The comfort of a fire suddenly sounded good.

Nora flipped on the kitchen light and started a pot of coffee, then stepped outside to bring in firewood from the back porch.

The moon overhead was nearly full, making the ground sparkle like diamonds as flurries continued to filter down. She tilted her head back to look at the endless sky, letting them dot her cheeks. So peaceful, she thought. It felt as if she'd been painted into a beautiful wintery scene, every shimmering flake meticulously appointed to the perfect canvas.

She gazed into the thick white woods beyond, savoring the brief moment of solitude, until she could no longer feel her feet.

Then she loaded her arms with wood and went back inside to start the fire.

THE COFFEEPOT BEEPED in the distance, and Nora pushed up from the hearth, hating to leave the warmth of the fireplace but desperate for a hot cup of coffee.

As she entered the kitchen, floorboards creaked above. She reached for another cup from the cabinet, realizing she must have woken Ben. The clock on the wall read five forty a.m.

She filled both cups, made her way back to the library and climbed into the overstuffed leather chair to wait for him to make an appearance.

But minutes passed with no sign of him.

Nora rose from her chair and moved toward the stairs.

"Ben?" When he didn't answer, she climbed them toward the landing.

The hallway light above flipped on, splashing shards of light across the top steps as floorboards groaned again. This time she could tell it came from the far end of the hallway near the bathroom.

A door swung shut.

"Sorry, I woke you," she hollered as she stepped up onto the last step. "I couldn't sleep, but I made coffee if you want some."

The hallway was quiet as she made her way toward the bathroom. Eerily quiet. And, she realized, if Ben had just gone into the bathroom, there would be light coming from beneath the door.

"Ben?"

Nora hesitated, the certainty she'd woken him fading. A chill skittered up the back of her neck.

She'd just seen the hallway light flick on—seen it herself. There was no imagining that. She stopped and turned back toward her bedroom door, now afraid that Ben might not be in the bathroom at all. That instead, he might still be in bed. *Asleep.*

Nora eased the door open. She froze. There was Ben snoring softly in the same exact position she'd left him in earlier.

The chill she'd felt at the back of her neck now splintered and ran down both arms. She looked down the hall toward the bathroom door that had just swung shut, unsure of what to think or do.

For the first time, Nora felt as if she might really be losing it.

Who was it? And what was she supposed to do about it? Wake Ben and have him think she was ready for a luxury suite at the nut house? No way. Not after yesterday. After all, what kind of intruder would stop to use the facilities on their way to murder her, use them rather loudly, at that.

Nora stiffened and made her way to the bathroom door. As she took the last couple steps, she halted. *No time like the present.* Her hand trembled as she turned the door handle and pushed it open.

Empty.

No psychopaths washing up in preparation for an assault. No masked thieves lying in wait behind the glass shower door.

The longer she stood there, the more her childhood debates with Lucy began to swirl in her mind, equal parts of fear and intrigue settling in.

What if...

She stopped herself. *Don't go there,* her mind warned. But the thought crept back in, demanding to be courted further, demanding to be considered. She added up the string of strange occurrences over the past weeks.

The farm had been around for a very long time and was certain to have a colorful history. What if something *had* happened there? What if there was more going on inside the house than she'd been willing to admit?

It was either that or she was going mad.

She'd never been one to leave many stones unturned, which had served her well in her writing career, so she would do what she did best.

Nora aimed her path back to the library and stoked the fire, wrapping a cashmere throw around her shoulders. She opened her laptop and braced herself for what she hoped would prove to be a very enlightening remainder of the night.

BEN TOOK THE SERVANTS' stairs down to the kitchen in search of Nora. He'd awoken just past eight a.m. to an empty bed and a quiet house, wondering what had become of her.

The strong smell of coffee had given him a clue as to her whereabouts, but as he followed it, he was dismayed to find that she was not there.

"Nora?" he called as he made his way down the hall toward the front door.

"In here," she hollered, a strange lilt in her voice.

He found her in the library. "Hey. Missed you this morning."

"Sorry, I couldn't sleep and didn't want to wake you." She wrapped her arms around him, greeting him with a soft kiss. "I was going to do a little research, but the Internet went down almost as soon as I started, much to my great dismay. Must be from the weather."

"Ah. Middle-of-the-night brainstorming session on the new book?"

"More often than not, my answer would be yes, but not this time...exactly," she hedged.

Ben raised an eyebrow.

"I was going to look into the history of the house and property," she said.

"The house?"

"Yes, just looking into things. Curiosity is eating me alive. But like I said, no Internet, so I ended up dozing by the fire. By the way, I made coffee, but it was several hours ago. I should probably make more."

"No worries," he said. "I'm on it. I make better coffee than you do anyway." He winked at her and left the room.

As he waited for the fresh pot, he heard Nora talking to some-one. Telling them she was thrilled they'd answered the phone, and that with all the snow, she hadn't expected it. He poked his head back into the library, the look on her face stopping him.

"You can't be serious," she said, her mouth falling open. "No, I had no idea. I'm sure no one here does. At least no one has mentioned it at all."

Ben cocked his head to the side, wondering what was so intriguing on the other end of the line.

"Unbelievable," Nora went on. "I will look into it, for sure. And if my Internet doesn't shape up, I may come in and do a little digging."

He watched her pace back and forth between the desk and the window, enthralled in the conversation. "Yes," she said. "Any idea of the location? This may actually explain a lot. I just wish I had connected with you sooner."

The coffeepot beeped and Ben headed back toward the kitchen.

"I'll talk to you soon," he heard Nora say as she followed him.

"Okay, thank you so very much." She ended the call and turned to Ben, her eyes bright with surprise.

"That was Mrs. Krenshaw, the librarian from Marietta. You are never going to believe what she just told me. She sounded like she was about a hundred years old, which would make perfect sense as to why she might know something about the house, that we don't."

Ben handed Nora a steaming cup, pulled out a chair and sat. "Careful, it's hot. So, what about the house?"

"Well," she continued, "I decided to call and see if the library might be open today so I could chase down some odds and ends about the property. And I figured they could tell me if the roads were decent in town."

He nodded. "I'm sure they're better today."

"Yes, that's exactly what Mrs. Krenshaw said. But anyway, when I told her where I was coming from, she recognized the farm's name and asked if I knew this house was once a part of the Underground Railroad."

"What?"

"I know, it's crazy," Nora said. "I had no idea, either. She said it was over a century ago, and that it's not common knowledge anymore."

"But, if that was true, don't you think we would have found some sort of indication by now?"

"That was my reaction, too, at first. But Mrs. Krenshaw said she'd heard rumors the access to the secret passages had been sealed off after a deadly fire in the house a little more than thirty years ago. According to her, the owners were terribly eccentric. It was their daughter, only in her late twenties, who died in the fire."

Ben leaned forward as Nora rushed on, trying to absorb the extent of what she was telling him.

"After the daughter died, I guess the father lost it, mentally. Mrs. Krenshaw said he was never the same, and that the family became even more reclusive. Oddly so. She said this house has seen its share of other hardships, too. As if the daughter's death wasn't enough." Nora paused. "I can't believe Lucy didn't mention any of this, I would have thought she'd have told me something like this."

"For sure," Ben stammered.

"So, my sister never brought up the history of the house to you either?"

"No. Never. I don't think she'd taken the time to find any of it out."

"Well, Mrs. Krenshaw told me there was a list of things

demanding her attention this morning, but if I could give her a little time to jog her memory, she would try to make some notes for me, round up some of the history. Sounded like she may be able to tell me quite a bit I won't find with an Internet search."

Ben sat back in his chair once more. "Wow."

"I know. I can't believe I'll have the opportunity to actually sit down face-to-face with someone who can shed some light on this place. She told me I should stop by the library first of next week and ask for her."

Secret passageways, Ben thought. He ran a hand across the back of his neck, a prickle of concern nudging him as he thought of Nora's absolute certainty that she'd heard strange noises in the house—footsteps, in particular. He didn't want to frighten her, but all the same, it was his duty to make sure that no one had unknown access to the house or to Nora. "Did she mention where the original entrance was?"

"She said she'd heard talk of a corner wall in the attic that led to a secret room wedged in between the second and third floors. Beyond that she was unsure. But she knew for certain that Black Willow Farm was a well-known hub many years ago. Can you believe that? This is the stuff bestsellers are made of."

Ben set his cup down and straightened. "I don't know what to make of it, but I'd like to have a look up there now that we know there's something to look for. Interested?"

"Just try and stop me."

He pushed up from the chair. "Let me grab my hammer and a flashlight. It's pretty dark up there."

Nora took one last swig of her coffee. "I haven't gone over to the far part of the attic much at all. Most of my boxes are stored right at the top of the stairs."

"Well, we may not find anything," he said, handing her one of two flashlights he'd pulled from under the kitchen sink. "But it's worth having a look."

He tucked the hammer into the edge of his belt and let Nora

take the lead up to the third floor, then reached around her to push the door open that led up to the attic.

She tugged the pull-string light. "I wish she'd given us more to go on. Maybe it's not even true, who knows."

Ben followed her up the narrow staircase and shined the light into the far corners under the eaves. "If there is any evidence here, I promise you we'll find it."

Nora split from him and walked toward the far-left side. "I'm not even sure what to look for."

"Inconsistencies in the thickness of the walls would be the main thing," he hollered, tapping along the far wall with the wooden handle of his hammer.

He heard her cough as she shuffled through the dust and cobwebs to the back of the large room.

The floor beneath grumbled under Ben's weight. Where the hell would someone hide an entrance? At this point, he was beyond determined to find it and make sure it was sealed off. It would set his mind at ease to know for certain that Nora had been hearing the normal sounds that went along with a hundred-and-fifty-year-old house and not something of the human persuasion.

He could see the bob of Nora's light through the support beams as he continued to tap on section after section of wall, but as he was about to give up and move to another area, the echo of Ben's hammer strike thickened.

He hit it again, harder.

"Nora," he called. "I may have something."

"No way. Really?"

"A good chance."

He moved over a few feet, tapping the walls again as she watched. "Listen to the difference. You hear it?"

Nora nodded, her eyes wide. "That's a completely different sound. What now?"

"It's your call. I'd be glad to take a look behind the wall. Up to you."

"Rip it out. I'm up for it. No one comes up here anyway."

Ben nodded. "If you're sure. Might want to step back a little. I don't want anything to hit you."

"Here, let me hold the light for you."

He wedged the claw of his hammer behind the top board and pried. The board moved, but not enough. Ben tried again, picking up speed as the corner cracked and popped free. He moved down to the next board, and the next.

Nora gasped as the top row of a brick-and-mortar archway came into view.

There it was. A wave of adrenaline rushed through Ben. "Son of a bitch, she was right."

Nora stared at him, her mouth hanging open. "We have to tear off the rest, Ben. *We have to*. Do you have a second hammer? I can help."

"I've got this." He assaulted the next section. Shards of splintered wood filled the air as he cracked board after board. Beads of sweat dampening his shirt as he worked.

He stepped back again when he was halfway down. "Looks like she was right about it being sealed off, too. Solid brick all the way to the floor."

"But hey," Nora sighed, "at least we found it." She leaned in. "Do you see that?" She moved the flashlight in close to the wall as Ben took a second to catch his breath.

"See what?"

"I'm not sure." Nora crouched to her knees, shining the beam of light even closer. "Look at this, Ben." She rubbed dust from a row of bricks.

"What is it?" he asked, walking to her.

"*Mother*," she whispered into the silence, running a finger across the eerie message. "That's what it says here. Look. It's scratched into the brick over and over."

Ben lowered himself down next to her, leaning in to dust off more of the wall below.

Nora drew in a sharp breath as additional bricks came into clearer view.

He turned to look at her. "It's gotta be written there several dozen times," he said. "I don't know whether to say that's incredible...or a little creepy."

"No kidding," Nora echoed. She pulled out her cell and snapped several pictures of the wall. "I'm not sure, either, but I'm leaning pretty hard toward creepy."

He helped Nora up and they stared at the wall for a long moment. "Strange, to say the very least. Would you like me to finish tearing off the rest even though the entrance is closed? Just so it's finished?"

Nora nodded. "I can take a turn. I might as well help."

"No, it won't take me but a few minutes."

"Well, how about I at least run down and get you a cold drink. Iced tea, maybe?"

"I wouldn't turn that down. It's a sauna up here," he said as she turned to leave. "And hey, I'm sorry this didn't pan out better."

"Yeah, me, too. But thank you so much for tearing the boards out. At least now we know an entrance was there, even though it's bricked off. The not knowing would have eaten me alive. I don't think I could have slept a wink until we checked it out." She smiled at him and started down the stairs.

NORA FILLED a tall glass with ice and reached into the fridge for the pitcher of tea, the question of who had written the word *mother* on the wall, swirling relentlessly in her mind.

Likely a child, she realized. But who? And why?

The fashion in which the words were carved into the brick—

so determined, so tireless, over and over. She'd felt a sense of pain when she'd read them, of anguish. She couldn't shake the feeling.

She'd been so excited to find out the house had been part of the Underground Railroad that she'd forgotten why she'd called the Marietta library in the first place. That there was more to the house than met the eye.

Nora shuddered.

What secrets lay hidden behind the brick and mortar? She knew two things for certain. Number one, she had to speak to Mrs. Krenshaw as soon as possible. And number two, she wanted to know what was beyond that sealed-off wall.

Nora looked up as Ben walked through the door.

"Sorry, I was just about to bring your tea up."

He set the hammer and flashlights on the table. "It didn't take that long. I stacked the wood over in the corner for now." He showed her a picture of the wall's lower half on his phone, then dropped onto a barstool as she handed him the glass.

"More words?" she asked, staring at the picture.

"The word *mother* must have been scrawled there more than a hundred times." He drained the glass. "Something feels a little off there, Nora. Like I said, creepy."

"I don't know about you," she echoed, "but I would really like to know more."

He raised his brow. "Now that we know for certain this house was used for the Underground Railroad, I'd be willing to bet there are more hidden tunnels underneath, or deep inside the walls. Didn't the librarian say she wasn't sure whether or not the attic was the only access? Just that it was the only one she'd heard of?"

"Yes, I'm sure that's what she said. I'll try to get all the information I can when I meet with her. If the farm was as big of a hub as she suggested, there's got to be more information on it somewhere."

"I know the inn's opening is coming up, but if you have any desire at all to break through the wall up there, I'll make it happen. I think it would be worth checking into. And if there are more hidden passages, maybe even open them up and incorporate them into the inn. People love places of historic value. Could be a big draw for clients."

Nora kissed him hard. "You're incredible," she beamed. "I was just thinking how much I wanted to get behind that wall. Dig into the history of this place. Feels like there's something there. Doesn't it?"

"I say we find out," he agreed. "I'll talk to the guys first thing when they're back. We're in the final stretch with the house, so maybe Mitch and Carlos can take over a few things from my punch list so I can break away and do a little sniffing around. I've already thought about the locations that would make the most sense structurally. That would grant travel from the attic all the way down. Some original blueprints would be helpful, though I have yet to see any."

"I'll see what I can do when I head into town. I'm desperate to have the Internet up and going again. I can track down some of this stuff myself."

"Let me see if I can reboot the router. If not, the cable company may have to hook up a new one. The one I have at my house is on the fritz half the time. But I'll at least take a look at it. Remind me later tonight."

"How did I get so lucky? Thank you for today." She offered him more tea.

"You are more than welcome," he said, raising his glass toward her. "I'm in this with you. If there's anything there, we're going to find it. You ought to know what it is or isn't. I'll make it my personal mission."

He looked toward the bay window. "Man, I lost track of time up there."

Nora checked the digital clock on the microwave. "Yeah, me, too. It's almost one. Hey, since you're the one who swung the hammer most of the morning, I'll throw some sandwiches together for lunch."

Ben reached for her hand, squeezing it gently as he stood up. "Sounds good. I'm starving. But at least let me help."

HIS HEART RACED to the point of pain as he measured his steps, back and forth across the small, dark space. He'd suspected that Ben had the potential to become a real problem but had sorely underestimated to what extent. He'd worked too hard for this, come too far—sacrificed too much—to have some asshole with a hero complex get in the way now.

He struggled to calm himself as the heat of pure raw hatred coursed through him, gripping him from the inside out, refusing to release its hold. "Enough," he said into the silence. "Time for you to go."

He stared at the wall, letting one idea surface and then another, until he homed in on the most suitable, the fastest, the easiest to carry out under the shifting circumstances. He closed his eyes, let it begin to take shape.

The sound of Nora's laughter filtered through the vent.

You won't be laughing much longer, he thought to himself. He'd done his share of research over the past weeks. The new plan would work. He was sure of it.

He calmed.

She laughed again, and this time he allowed her image to take center stage, his lips curling up into a smile as he once again replayed the scene at the library window in his mind. She'd been oblivious while he'd partaken of every inch of her. And though he'd come to despise her, Nora *was* beautiful...and he was, after all, a man. He'd hardened as his eyes roamed every inch of her curves, her back arching in the firelight to show him full, round breasts. He slowed the images, lingering on long, sculpted legs and perfect hips that led to the soft velvet of her inner thighs. He'd craved release like never before.

He took a step backward and lowered himself onto a stool.

The footprints in the snow had been an afterthought, but a brilliant one. He'd assumed Ben would need to be the great protector, racing out to prove that he was the alpha and could keep her safe. Yes, he'd danced like a marionette on a string. It was, however, pure luck that Nora hadn't gone with Ben. That had been the best part. *Oh, how he loved toying with her.* But how long would she play the game with him before she'd had enough?

It would be much easier to kill her now and be done with it. But he'd never been one to take the path of least resistance. Where was the fun in that? Caution at this point was key, as was patience. Additional attention brought to the house would set off too many alarms. The last thing he needed was to have to duck into the shadows during any more investigations. His luck in that department had been pushed to its very limits.

"Nora, Nora, Nora," he whispered, his head pressed hard against the inside of the false wall beneath the staircase. "I've enjoyed our time together, but time is running out. Much like it did for your sister." He smiled at the thought. "Lucy was brave, though, I will give her that. *Right up until the night I gave her what she deserved.*"

He stood and turned to leave. "How brave will you be, Nora? When Ben isn't around to protect you?"

CHAPTER FOURTEEN

T he knock at the front door came early. Nora opened her
eyes to find Ben climbing out of bed.

"Good morning," he said, pulling on his jeans.

She smiled at him. "Who in the world is that?"

"Who knows, maybe it's Liz or Scott or one of the guys. You
stay in bed. I'll go."

He leaned down, kissing her forehead.

"Be right back."

"I'm counting on it." Nora closed her eyes, basking in the
glory of waking up next to an incredible man who was willing to
go down and answer her door at the crack of dawn and—if she
knew him as well as she thought she did—bring her coffee on the
way back up.

She rolled over, savoring his scent on the pillow next to her.

But no coffee returned. Only Ben, and by the look on his face,
Nora knew something was wrong. She sat up in bed. "What is it?"

"That was Mitch. He said he's been trying to call me for over
an hour. It's my dad." His words were coming fast. "There was
some sort of attack."

"A heart attack?" Nora stammered.

"No, *he was attacked*."

"What?" She threw back the comforter and stood, watching the color drain from Ben's face.

"Oh, Ben..."

"I guess it was late last night. Mitch didn't know the details. He said my mom's been trying to get me and finally called him at home to get the message to me. I must have left my damn cell phone downstairs."

"I'm so sorry. Let me help you. What can I do?"

"I have to call my mom. I bet my cell's in my coveralls from yesterday."

"I'll get dressed and be right down. Whatever you need, just tell me."

A worried smile creased his strong features. "Whisper a little prayer for my parents, if you will."

She squeezed his hand tight. "Done."

BY THE TIME Nora made it down, Ben was rushing from room to room collecting his things.

"My mom sounds terrible. She's at the hospital. They're taking my dad into surgery. Whoever did it, beat the shit out of him and left him for dead."

Disbelief planted Nora where she was.

Ben's shirt hung open, unlaced boots dangling at his side. His eyes brimmed with uncertainty. "Look at me," he said, "I'm a damn mess. Who would want to hurt my dad? He is the nicest guy you'll ever meet. I don't understand this at all."

She took his boots, helped him button his shirt. "I'll go with you. I could drive."

"No, no. You have to oversee things here. Who knows how long I'll be gone. I'll let you know more once I get to the hospital."

She knew he was right.

"This whole thing is just crazy. My dad called my mom just after dark last night to let her know he had a flat and that he'd be a little late. Then when she didn't hear from him for over an hour, she started calling him and finally drove out to his office."

Ben scrambled to toss the remainder of his things in a bag. He took a breath, trying to regain his composure. "She said she found his truck parked where it always was but propped up on the jack. When she went to look for him, she found him lying on the ground behind it." He hesitated. "The insane part is they didn't take anything. His wallet, keys, over one hundred dollars in cash, all of it still on him. So, what the hell?"

Nora could see Ben's veins pulsing near the surface of his temple as he continued.

"It almost sounds like some maniac punctured his tire on purpose. And then waited for him. I don't know what's going on, but I intend to find out. And when I catch up with the bastard, I swear I'll—"

"Oh, Ben."

"It sounds bad, Nora. He still hadn't regained consciousness when they took him to surgery. My mom said they don't know if he'll even..."

His voice crumbled, fear darkening his face. "I have to go."

She wrapped her arms around him, *willing everything to be okay*. "Of course you do. Let's get you on the road. I can help you finish packing or make you some coffee. I'm so sorry."

"I'd be eternally grateful for a quick coffee for the road. It's frigid out there."

"I'll make it right now."

She rushed toward the kitchen, worry sinking to the bottom of her stomach like a rock as she filled the glass carafe with water. She loaded the coffee filter and pushed the brew button, her hands shaking.

As she hurried back down the hall to help Ben finish, he

caught her arm and held her for a brief moment, taking her face into his hands. "I cannot begin to tell you how much I hate leaving you like this. It's killing me. You'll be okay?"

"Don't worry about anything here. The remodel is so close to being done. The guys and I can handle it. Just go. *Please*."

"Nora," he said again. "I—"

"*Go*. Call me when you know something. I promise I won't stop praying."

Ben followed her back into the kitchen and waited as she filled a to-go cup.

"Please be careful," she said, handing him the coffee as they made their way toward the front door.

"I will." He grabbed his duffle bag, stopping to collect her into his arms one last time. "Nora..." His voice was tender yet laced with urgency. "I love you."

Her eyes filled with tears as his words washed over her. "You *have* to know that I love you, too. I have for a long time now."

His lips joined hers in a kiss so tender, so deep and full of love, that neither fear nor haste could touch it.

Nora breathed him in, knowing it would have to last until he could hold her again. And she had no idea how long that might be.

Her heart broke as she watched him leave, disappearing down the cold, white drive. Away from Black Willow, away from her.

DEEP within the belly of Black Willow, a melody floated across the dank, cool air. He hummed the familiar song, letting it soothe him as he went over every detail of the plan again.

Nora paced back and forth in the kitchen above. He could sense the tension, even through the floor that separated them. His heart pounded as he imagined her anguish, her concern for

Ben, the isolation she must have felt as he'd left her behind. "Don't worry, lovely Nora," he whispered. *"You're not alone."*

Reaching down into his pocket, he pulled out a small silver charm bracelet and held it up in the light. He smoothed a finger over the tiny hearts that dangled from its chain, smiling as he recalled the night he'd plucked it from Lucy's wrist at the bottom of the icehouse stairs—the night he'd watched her draw in her last breath.

He'd taken care of one sister, and soon he'd finish off the other. The coming weeks would bring results and he would get what he wanted without anyone being the wiser. Like he always did.

Darkness poured from his eyes as he tossed the bracelet onto the table and turned to leave. There was work to be done.

CHAPTER FIFTEEN

"Any idea where I set that box of bath towels? I swear ever since my uterus started popping out babies, my brain has pretty much been a regular no-show."

Nora smiled at the sarcasm in Liz's voice. "Possibly." She turned from the sink and poked through a stack of boxes in the corner. "Voila," she said motioning to Liz. "Ask and ye shall receive."

"Well, at least now your guests can shower."

Nora laughed. "That's always a good thing."

"So, did your crew leave?" Liz asked as she moved into the dining room and sat down at the table. "I didn't realize I was up on the third floor that long."

Nora dropped into the seat across from her. "Yeah, Mitch left before you came back down, he was the last one out. He told me poor Ethan just got word that his grandmother died. I guess he won't be back for a while."

"Oh, no," Liz echoed.

"I feel terrible admitting it," Nora said, "but he's not my favorite person. Isn't that awful of me to say? There's something about him that makes me…I don't know, uneasy. Still, I hated to hear about his grandmother."

"Well, that's not good for you either. Trying to get the inn up and running with Ben away, and now down another guy."

"As they say, when it rains…" Nora ran her hands over the smooth dark wood of the table. "Thank you so much for coming over today and for helping with all the bedding and linens. You're a lifesaver. It seems like before Ben had to race out of here, we were ahead of schedule, with time to spare. Now it feels like the whole bottom is falling out. Is Scott going to be upset with you for being gone so long?"

"No, actually, he offered to make dinner for the kids and give them their baths tonight."

Nora lifted her brow.

"I know, right?" Liz shrugged. "You have the same look on your face that I did when he offered. He'll want something in return. And I have a feeling I know what that will be." She rolled her eyes. "Pretty sure I feel a headache coming on…"

Nora laughed out loud. "Well, at least have a glass of wine, then."

"Music to my ears."

"We got a ton accomplished today," Nora said standing up to head into the kitchen. "Thank you, again."

"No problem." Liz waited for Nora to return and then followed her into the parlor, plopping down onto the sofa. "Glad to help."

Nora filled two glasses with wine. "Want me to heat up a frozen pizza?"

"Oh, gosh, no. I'm quite happy to drink my dinner," Liz said, reaching for the wine, "…and my dessert." She pointed to the half-empty bottle. "It'll help me get through Scott's part of this deal later." She tossed her head back and guffawed.

Nora joined her laughter, setting the bottle on the coffee table. "This is really great wine, too. Ben picked up several bottles before the storm. I've gotten in the habit of having a glass—or two, if we're being completely honest here—every night before bed. Who needs actual food for dinner anyway?"

"Totally overrated, I say." Liz raised her glass in cheers. "Speaking of food, Thanksgiving's coming up fast. Any plans?"

"Not really. My parents were invited up to my uncle's place in Maine." She settled in next to Liz on the sofa, tucked one foot up under her. "They want me to go with them, but I need to stay here. Can't afford to be gone even a couple of days at this point."

"Then come to our place. My in-laws will be there, too."

"No, no. I couldn't. Not if Scott's family is visiting."

"All the more reason for you to come over and keep me from flipping on the gas and shoving my head in the oven," Liz said dryly, then winked at Nora and laughed.

Nora returned the laughter, then fell silent.

"Hey, you okay?" Liz asked.

"Yeah, I just can't stop worrying about Ben, about his family."

"Oh, I know. Have you talked to him since he texted you earlier?"

"No. He's staying at the hospital again tonight."

"Anything new with the investigation?"

Nora ran a finger absently around the rim of her glass. "They looked into the security footage from his dad's office building, and it showed a man puncturing his dad's tire hours before the attack. He was wearing a hood, so unfortunately they couldn't get a look at his face. Ben said the same man reappeared later and jumped his dad as he started to change the tire. Beat him unconscious."

Liz stared at her. "I don't even know what to say. Did they see the guy's car in the video? Maybe get a plate number? Anything?"

"No. He was very careful."

"That's crazy."

"I know," Nora said, a deep frown pulling at the corner of her mouth. "I couldn't agree more. Why would anyone puncture his tire, jump him and then not take anything? *Nothing at all.* It doesn't make any sense."

Liz swallowed the last of her wine and reached for the bottle, topping off Nora's glass before refilling her own. "No, it doesn't."

"I just can't stop thinking about it. Maybe it's the author in me. I do have a track record of digging into things pretty deep. Too deep, some might say."

"But that's why you're so good at what you do."

Nora attempted a smile but fell short. "And I miss Ben so much. It's killing me. I know he had to go, of course he did. But every time I talk to him, he sounds beat. He's on overload."

"Could Scott and I fill in for you here so you can go see him for a couple of days? You know we'll do whatever we can to help."

"I want to go to him, I do. But I can't leave right now. I've got several meetings coming up next week and I'm nervous about the final inspection walk-through. It's still up in the air. Ben said the fire chief tends to spring those on you at his leisure, without a lot of warning." Nora rubbed her eyes. "Oh, and then there's the not-so-little matter of needing a chef."

"I thought you were going to put an ad in the paper for that."

"I was. I mean, I am. I haven't had time yet and today's Saturday, so I won't be able to do anything about it until the first of the week. But Monday, for sure." She sighed. "If I don't find someone soon, it's going to delay everything, which wouldn't be good for business. Especially an inn trying to get off the ground."

"Sounds like you may have to dust off your cookbooks and roll up your sleeves."

Nora grimaced. "Good grief, this place wouldn't make it twenty-four hours if I had to throw on an apron."

Liz laughed out loud. "That bad, huh? I wish I knew someone."

"You and me, both. At some point I'll need an extra set of hands to help with housekeeping, too. Bella, from the little antique store on the square in town, said she would be sending someone out, but no one has contacted me yet. Guess I'll run by her shop next week and follow up on that."

"Well, like I said," Liz added with a smile, "I'll be glad to help out as much as I can until you get all this sorted out."

"I might have to take you up on that. The answering service I'm using already has several guests checking in starting mid-December. So, we open in just over three weeks. *Whether or not.*"

AFTER WALKING LIZ OUT, Nora poured herself another glass of wine and threw together a plate of cheese and crackers to nibble on. She kicked off her shoes at the bottom of the stairs, her mouth stretching into a wide yawn as she headed up to find her computer.

She needed to get a few chapters in. The house wasn't the only thing that was falling behind. How had she believed that she could complete a novel at the same time as opening an inn? *Because I'm a delusional idiot with a serious lack of time management skills,* she reminded herself.

She found the laptop and continued on up to the media room. A favorite spot of hers, just as it had been her sister's. Her eyes briefly traveled over the assortment of prints and oils hanging from the walls. She loved them all, but her most cherished piece in the room—in the entire house, for that matter—was her picture from Lucy.

Nora had hung it over the sofa, making it the first thing anyone would see upon walking into the room. She set the wine and cheese on the coffee table and took a long look at the picture, letting the sentiment behind it comfort her. It was beautiful. The dark, rich colors, the dramatic scene. It accented the leather furniture in the room perfectly. Its very best attribute though, was that she felt Lucy there with her each time she looked at it.

She lowered herself onto the sofa and opened the laptop,

trying the Internet again, though she didn't set her hopes too high. No luck. Her thoughts turned to Mrs. Krenshaw and the bricked-off tunnel above her—the word *mother* scratched onto the wall. Nora's stomach twisted. She'd called the library number twice the day before, but Mrs. Krenshaw hadn't been there either time.

She pushed the situation from her mind the best she could and clicked on the file that contained her neglected manuscript. Before long, the soft click of the keys was the only sound in the house. One sentence became two, two became three, until she looked up at the clock on the wall and realized that almost two hours had passed.

Two hours that felt more like two minutes.

She lost track of time that way. Writing was as familiar to her as breathing. It felt good. When the words were flowing, she had no concept of time or space, allowing herself to become engulfed in ideas and scenarios as they made their way to the page. The marriage between character and plot, conflict and resolution. It was like peeling back the layers of an onion. Every aspect, every new dimension fascinated her.

It was who she was, and writing had done well for her.

Nora closed the laptop, flipped the lights off and headed toward the back stairwell, stopping abruptly as a draft raced across her skin. Goose bumps rose up from weary flesh as she stared into the darkness. She would swear she was no longer alone —that someone was there with her, watching. The sensation was overwhelming.

But as she waited, nothing happened.

Irritated with herself, she made it back to her room and shut the door, then laid the laptop down on the dresser.

All of the recent oddities in conjunction with too many late, sleepless, nights were getting to her. She climbed into bed and turned off the bedside lamp.

As she rolled over, she put a hand on the pillow next to her, longing for Ben. "Soon," she whispered into the darkness and closed her eyes.

A door slammed in the distance. Nora's heart leapt in her throat, her eyes shooting back open. There was no mistaking the sound. It echoed through the house. Not as if perhaps the draft she'd felt earlier had nudged a door closed somewhere, but the door had slammed shut with undeniable hostility. *Fury* was more like it.

She lay silent, sealed to the mattress. Her first instinct was to yank her cell off the nightstand and dial the police, but the memory of Ben's recent search of the house when she'd *sworn* she'd heard someone—and how he'd come up empty—snuffed out the idea. She would not be known around town as the crazy lady of Black Willow Farm, who made a perpetual habit of crying wolf.

But what *should she do?* Run out into the hallway swinging her laptop, not knowing what she might find? Or pull the covers over her head like a child hiding from the boogeyman in the creepy dark closet?

Fear continued its reign over her, holding her there, frozen— half expecting to hear footsteps heading toward her, or worse yet, the terrifying click of a twisting doorknob across the room.

After several minutes passed, she padded over to the doorway. All was quiet.

Muscles wound tight, she opened the door and flipped on the hallway light, a trace of comfort washing over her as its bright glow snuffed out the shadows down the long corridor.

She inched down the hall. Each door she walked by was open, just as she'd left it moments ago. Until she made it back up to the media room. Nora's face darkened. The media room's door was now sealed tight, the exact *opposite* of how she'd left it. She reached for the handle, but instantly jerked back as the sound of muffled voices echoed from within.

She was losing her mind.

The trauma of Lucy's death had broken something inside her

and she was going mad—and the reality of that particular thought scared her more than the notion of some ghastly apparition.

She had to hold on to what was left of her sanity, which was getting more difficult as of late. Nora braced herself and shoved the door open, completely unprepared for who, *or what,* awaited her.

She burst in, her body rigid. And it took her a moment to zero in on the fact that no one was there. The lights and television were on, though. And not just one light but *all of them.* The side table lamps, the overheads, even the track lighting.

Every single light in the room.

How it had happened, she had absolutely no idea.

The only light she had used earlier, she was certain she'd turned off when she'd gone down to bed.

And she'd never turned the television on. Period.

Her eyes raided every corner of the room. She was alone.

Suddenly, she whirled around, making sure that nothing dreaded had crept up behind, while she'd been distracted. But there was only silence.

Absolutely nothing else.

Nora cursed under her breath. She liked explanations, facts—cold, hard ones. But there were none to be had, not a single scrap. Nothing to grab hold of.

She swallowed hard.

Sure, she loved a good mystery, as every fiction author should. Murder, mayhem, chaos. The intrigue of all the exciting details, life hanging in the balance. Not knowing what happened or who was responsible for it until the very end. That was the life of a writer. But she preferred to *write* the mystery, not be written into it.

Uncertainty wore her thin as she turned everything off once again.

She pulled her robe in tight against her body and walked back out into the hallway. As she did, the light above flickered briefly, stopped, flickered again. Her feet slowed beneath her as she stared up at the fixture.

Could it really be that simple? Could the whole thing have been caused by some sort of power surge? It was possible, right? Of course it was. Old house, old wiring. Ben had rewired a great deal of it, but maybe there were still issues. She remembered him mentioning Lucy'd had similar complaints. It made sense.

She turned and gave the offending room another long, hard look. But old wiring hadn't slammed the door shut.

She checked the rest of the house, knowing she'd be unable to sleep unless she did.

All appeared well as she made her way down the hall, her nerves easing up a bit. And as she moved into the last guest room, she noticed a window cracked open. Left that way, she assumed, by Mitch or Carlos.

She sighed. No wonder the door had slammed shut. "Come on, guys," she muttered, pushing it closed. "Well, at least I haven't completely lost it. Not yet, anyway."

She felt the tension ease out of her shoulders. The world had righted itself for the moment and all she wanted to do was crawl back into bed and shut everything else out.

As she walked into her room, Nora tossed back the comforter, noticing she'd gotten a text on her cell. She reached for it, her heart instantly overflowing as she read the message from Ben:

Hey. Thought it was worth a shot to see if you might still be up working. I can't stop thinking about you. Hope you know that if I were there, I'd make sure work was the very last thing on your mind tonight. Being apart this long is killing me. Hope you get some rest. I love you.

BEN POURED lukewarm coffee into a Styrofoam cup as he stood in the snack room, on his father's floor of the hospital. He'd been there for four days. The first two of which he'd spent pacing the hallways waiting for his father to wake from the medically induced coma the doctor had put him in until his brain could heal from the trauma.

He took a quick swig from his cup, grimacing. Hospital coffee was bad enough, but add in the fact that it was a good five hours old and it packed quite a punch. He forced down another sip as his phone vibrated. Smiling, he swiped it on.

"Please tell me my text didn't wake you," he said before Nora had time to speak.

"No, no," she said. "But it wouldn't have mattered anyway. I'm glad you texted. So glad. You have no idea."

"Oh man, it's good to hear your voice. I miss you more than I knew possible."

"Me, too. How's your dad tonight? Any change?"

"Pretty much the same as this morning. But at least it's an improvement from when they first brought him in. It's great to be able to talk to him now that he's conscious again. They're keeping a close eye on his brain, though. Worst-case scenario, they may have to operate again and relieve more of the pressure. Really hoping it doesn't come to that."

"Is your mom okay? I can't imagine what you're both going through."

"I made her go home tonight. She needs to sleep. The recliner in my dad's room leaves a lot to be desired. She looked so washed out earlier, and the last thing I need right now is her collapsing, too."

"And how are you holding up?" she asked. "You sound exhausted."

"No, I'm good. Like I said, just miss you like crazy. How are things there? Mitch called earlier and told me about Ethan."

"Yeah, his leaving was a surprise. But we'll be fine. It'll all work out. Liz spent the afternoon over here today. She said she and Scott will do all they can to help."

"I'm sorry that our little expedition is on hold. I keep thinking about the attic. I haven't mentioned it to anyone yet. Have you?"

"No," she said. "I'm waiting until you get back. I think we'll be lucky just to get the inn finished enough to open at this point."

"Well, if my dad does as well as we hope, I'll be back in time to look around a little before opening. If not, I promise you we'll do it the first chunk of downtime we get between guest bookings. We just need to get our hands on an original set of blueprints." He leaned against the counter, set his coffee down. "Did you ever meet up with the librarian?"

"Not yet. I called, but she wasn't in. She still hasn't gotten back to me. I'm desperate to sit down with her even for a minute. There's so much I'd like to ask her." She sighed. "Between her absence from the library and the mass chaos I've got going on here, I swear I'm starting to feel like I'll never catch her. And the Internet is still useless, so—"

"*Damn it*," he said. "I am so sorry I forgot to work on that. With everything that happened, it slipped my mind."

"Are you kidding me? Don't you dare apologize. My Internet issues are the last thing you should be worrying about. Besides, I rebooted it myself after you left. No luck, but I called and they said they'll send someone out."

Ben moved to a chair and sat down. He hated being so far away and hated that she was having to handle everything by herself. "You sure you're okay? You sound upset."

"I'll be fine, just a long day. You focus on your dad and get him well."

Ben looked up to see his father's nurse motion him toward the doorway.

"Nora, I'm sorry but I have to go. They need me for something."

"Yes, go. I'll talk to you soon. Hang in there."

"I'll call you tomorrow," he said, then swiped the phone off as he headed out into the hallway.

The sound of Nora's voice echoed through his mind as he followed the nurse down the long, quiet corridor. What he wouldn't give to be with her, even for one brief moment.

CHAPTER SIXTEEN

Nora stood at the window in the parlor, confusion and anger bubbling up inside her as the woman on the other end of the line at the cable company told her that no one was coming out to fix the Internet issue, that her request for a workman had been cancelled.

"Cancelled? No, I never cancelled anything. I called days ago to set this up."

"I'm sorry, ma'am, but a gentleman called shortly after you did. He told us that your Internet was working again and there was no longer a need for us to send anyone out."

Nora paced into the dining room. "You've got to be kidding me. I can't imagine who would do that."

"He said he was Black Willow's owner, if that helps."

Nora cleared her throat, buying a moment to collect her cool. "That's impossible, because *I'm* the owner. And as you can tell, I'm a woman, not a man. I'm not sure what miscommunication has occurred, but my Internet service is very definitely not working, and I need it fixed."

"I'm sorry, Ms. Bassett. I spoke with the man myself, and he stated that he was indeed the owner. I see now that he wasn't. I have no idea how I could have misunderstood, but I will get a workman out there today. You have my word."

"Thank you very much. I hope I didn't come across as rude. I'm just ready to have it going again."

"No problem at all, ma'am. I'm going to dispatch someone out to you. Please call us if you have any further problems."

As soon as Nora hung up, she dialed Ben. Maybe he knew something about the mix-up, although she doubted it.

No answer.

She slipped her phone into her pocket. Whatever had happened, she was grateful it would be fixed by day's end. The evening ahead would be dedicated to catching up on email and social media, and perhaps the most important thing, a little digging into Black Willow's past.

She started toward the kitchen, but decided to make a run down to the mailbox instead. She pulled on her jacket and opened the front door, the burst of fresh air washing away any residual irritation with the cable company.

The snow had melted and the sun had once again climbed back out from behind the clouds. She wondered if she would have the good fortune of finding any mail in the box this time. Black Willow's mail system, in her opinion, left a great deal to be desired. At least she'd started getting junk mail. Even so, several items of importance had failed to arrive, with no resolution. It was as if they'd vanished into thin air—including the papers from Lucy's attorney—which bothered Nora to no end. After two attempts on the attorney's part, she'd requested he make duplicates and FedEx them out to her, which had finally resulted in success.

As she stepped off the bridge, a vehicle rounded the curve. Nora threw Liz a wave as she slowed to a stop next to her.

Liz rolled down the window. "Hey, just the lady I was looking for."

"Oh?"

"Yeah, I just came from town and I think I might have good news for you. Maybe. Crossing my fingers."

Nora's face brightened. "Unless you're hiding Ben in the backseat of your truck, I can't imagine..."

Liz frowned. "Uh, not quite that good, but I still think it could be something to get excited about."

"Well, you definitely have my attention," Nora said, lifting a hand to shade her eyes from the sun's bright glare.

"So, I was at the market in town picking up a few things since Scott and the boys ate us out of house and home during all the crazy weather. Anyway, when I got in line to pay, I heard this guy on his phone behind me."

Nora nodded as Liz continued.

"He was telling someone on the other end that he'd heard back from one of the hotels in Lancaster where he'd put an application in and that they offered him a job. This is where it gets interesting. He told the person he'd decided that he'd really rather find something closer to Marietta since he had family planning to move here next month."

Nora hoped she knew where this was going.

"Long story short," Liz chattered on, "after all my eavesdropping, we got to talking on the way out of the store, and you're not going to believe this, but he's a chef of sorts...and he's looking for a job."

"You're kidding," Nora said.

"I swear I'm not," she beamed. "He moved down from somewhere up north, where he was an assistant to some private chef. Like a sous-chef, I guess."

Nora lifted her eyebrows.

"And the best part is that when I told him your situation and about the inn, it totally sparked his interest."

"Really?"

Liz nodded, a continuous smile pulling her lips up. "I took his number down and told him I'd give it to you."

"Liz, that's wonderful. Thank you."

"Wait until it works out, then you can thank me with another evening of wine and girl talk."

Nora laughed. "You're on, even if this guy doesn't work out."

Liz handed her the slip of paper. "His name is Adam. And not that it matters since you and Ben are together now, but to tell you the truth, he's gorgeous."

"Poor Scott," Nora said with a laugh.

"Hey, now, a girl can still have a little fun. I've been married a long time," she added, winking at Nora. "At least allow me a few harmless fantasies."

"Your secret's safe with me," Nora said, tapping the door to the truck. "And hey, thanks again. I can't tell you how much I appreciate your help with all of this."

Liz started the engine. "No problem. Let me know how it turns out."

"I will. I'll call you as soon as I know anything."

Liz pulled away slowly. "Talk to you later then. Tell Ben hi for me whenever you talk to him again."

"Will do," she said.

She looked down at the slip of paper and let out a breath of pent-up air. "Here's hoping."

CHARMING. That would be the one word she would use to describe Adam Hill.

Nora hadn't wasted time in calling him. And he, in turn, had been eager to come out and see the place, which set a good tone to the meeting.

As she'd opened the front door, he'd been talkative right away, instantly putting her at ease. And Liz had been right. He was handsome, in what Nora would call an *intelligent* sort of way, with striking hazel eyes and a warm, comfortable smile that held a small mole just above his lip on the left side. A great sense of humor, and a touch of awkwardness—which Nora found oddly endearing—made him down-to-earth, likable. It hadn't taken her long to feel as if she'd known him for years. To top it off, he'd blown her away with his culinary knowledge, making him a perfect fit for the job.

As they neared the end of the house tour, Nora led him down the back servant stairs to the kitchen.

"I saved the best for last," she said. "I have a feeling this final room is the one that will interest you the most."

"Ah, the main event," Adam said as he walked inside. "This is really something. What a great space. All I need is some cookware and a few fresh ingredients, and I could do some serious damage in here."

She laughed. "Feel free to look around, this would be your domain."

He took his time walking the perimeter, checking out the double oven, the six-burner gas stovetop, the pantry space and cabinets. "It's a dream kitchen," he finally said. "In fact, the whole place you've got here—the guest suites, the house, the property, it's the perfect setup for an inn. It really is. People are going to flip for this place."

"So I've been told. Let's hope you're right, for all our sakes," she said, grabbing a cup from the counter. "Coffee?"

"I thought you'd never ask. I'd absolutely kill for some."

Nora grinned. "No need to commit any felonies. This is what I like to call the endless pot." She lifted the carafe from the burner. "All of us here are addicted, so this poor thing takes a beating all day, every day."

Adam ran a hand through his hair, smiling at her as he took another look around the kitchen.

"So," Nora said, filling one cup and reaching for another. "From what you've told me, it sounds like you have plenty of experience. And I hate to be so business-like, but can you get me references at some point? I mean, provided you're even interested in the job."

"I am," he said. "And no problem at all with the references. I could get you a letter of recommendation from my latest boss by the end of the week. Might take just a tad longer to round up the rest."

Nora nodded. With Ben away, it was a dire necessity to have another strong back and an extra set of hands around, sooner rather than later. References could follow, she decided, refusing to lose him over a few days' wait on the info.

She handed him the coffee. "That should be fine. Whenever you can get them to me."

"Perfect," he said, taking a long drink. "This is good coffee. Really hits the spot. Thank you."

"You know, I'm not gonna lie to you," Nora said, blowing the steam away from her cup before sneaking a sip, "it's going to be a lot of work if you accept the job, but plenty of fun, too, I'd like to think. I do hate to take you away from the hotel that wanted you, but since you said you'd prefer to be closer to Marietta anyway, I—"

"So…is this a formal offer, then?" he asked, lifting a brow.

She was desperate, and he seemed honest enough, up front anyway. Clearly quite capable and knew his way around the kitchen. "I guess it is."

The expression on Adam's face sealed the deal. "Well, then, that would be a firm and resolute *yes*. I can't thank you enough. I'll do my best to make sure you won't regret it."

"Sounds good. I'm going to hold you to that," she said with a smile.

He took one last drink of his coffee and set the cup on the counter. "I hate to run, but I really need to go find some temporary housing," he said. "Wish me luck. I hope I can find someone who will sublease to me for a month until my cousin gets here. We're looking at going in together on an old loft downtown. It's got a ton of space and we both sort of dabble in renovation. We're planning to section it off. An apartment for each of us and another for extra income."

"What a great idea," she said, following him into the hallway.

Adam turned back briefly. "It's too bad you don't have a garage apartment or something here. We could have bartered a little for a place to hang my hat until I can get the loft deal signed."

"I'm so sorry, wish I did," she said. "If I hear of anything for rent out this way, I'll sure let you know." She reached around him to open the front door, but as she did, a large stack of metal scaffolding crashed to the floor behind. Nora screamed as she whirled around, smacking directly into Adam.

"My bad," Carlos hollered from around the corner. "Sorry about that, Nora."

"You're killing me, Carlos," she answered back, attempting to laugh, but still trembling.

"You okay?" Adam asked.

"Yes. Just exhausted, and apparently a little jumpy." She took a second to command her heart to exit her throat, unable to stop recalling the numerous reasons the house had given her to be on edge as of late. "You know," she quickly added, "I actually have plenty of empty guest rooms here, until the opening, that is. It would help you for at least a couple of weeks or so."

Once the words were out, she was surprised at herself for being so hasty in saying them, not having taken any kind of time to think it through. But her mouth had opened and the offer had flown right out. She couldn't very well take it back now. And if she were to be quite honest with herself, the thought of having another human around until Ben returned held undeniable appeal. Besides, what was she racing to the finish for anyway? It was, of course, to welcome an endless string of strangers into the halls of Black Willow, into her new home. So what was the harm in a little practice beforehand? A win-win, she convinced herself.

"You're serious?" he asked. "I'd be willing to pay you something in addition to the barter, of course. Or better yet, how about I cook for you each night? Dinner's on me, while I stay here. Whatever you're hungry for."

Another bonus, Nora mused.

He shook her hand. "I'm glad you called, Nora. And please tell your friend I said thanks for approaching me at the market this morning."

"I will," she said. "I think you're a perfect fit. Funny how things have a way of working out."

"Yeah, for sure," he said, stepping outside. "Well then, I guess I'm off. A buddy of mine in Lancaster has been nice enough to let me hang out at his place until I figured things out, so I'm going to head over there and pack up, let him know my new plans. Okay if I come back out tomorrow, then? Unless you need me for anything this evening."

"No, no. Tomorrow is fine." She followed him down the front steps.

"Well, call me if that changes," he said.

As he reached his car, Adam stopped and looked up at the front of the house for a long moment. "If those old walls could talk, I bet they'd have a lot to say."

"No doubt about that," Nora agreed. "This place has been around for a while."

He pulled the car door open, hesitated. "You know, it's really beautiful," he said staring up at the third floor. "But the longer you look, there's an eeriness about it, too. Kinda reminds me of a house you would see in a horror movie. Like the sort of place you wouldn't be at all surprised to find out is haunted."

A nervous laugh erupted from Nora. "Wow, that's quite an observation," she said. "Are you sure you want to move in here for the next couple of weeks? After hearing that, I may just move out, myself."

Adam turned toward her, a sheepish look on his face as he realized how his comments had come across. "Oh man, Nora, I hope I didn't offend you. I'm so sorry, I wasn't meaning to suggest that your house is *actually* haunted, or that it's creepy in any way..." He sighed. "*Damn.* I really have a way with words, don't I? Open mouth, insert foot. Again, my apologies. And yes, I definitely want to move in."

Nora smiled. "I knew what you meant, I was just giving you a hard time."

He chuckled. "Okay, I'm gonna go now, before I say anything else stupid." He climbed into the car. "See you tomorrow...if I still have a job by then, that is."

"Oh, your job is safe. You're not getting out of this gig that easy," Nora teased, tapping the car door. "Besides, I have to admit it's refreshing to meet someone who has the potential to be as awkward as I've been known to be on occasion."

He grinned. "It was really nice meeting you, Nora."

"Likewise," she said with a nod. "See you at some point tomorrow."

She waved as he pulled away, relief washing over her at the idea of having found her first employee, as well as a temporary roommate.

Nora reached for her phone. The next thing on her agenda was to try Ben again, tell him the good news. She only hoped he would agree she'd made the right decision with the short-term living arrangement.

"Ms. Bassett?"

She turned around to find a large, burly man in a tool belt and florescent orange hard hat behind her. "That's me. Can I help you?"

"Yes. I'm from the cable company. One of your construction crew let me into the house earlier. Hope that's okay. He said I could go ahead and have a look, and to find you when I finished."

"Sure. Thank you so much for coming out."

He nodded. "I wanted to let you know your Internet is back

up. Signal is good, router is good. Shouldn't give you any more problems."

"Oh, thank God," she said. "I was starting to feel like I was living on a homestead."

He smiled. "Welcome back to the modern world."

"So, I'm curious, what was wrong?"

"Well, the signal wasn't making it to your router, so I back-tracked the Internet supply line to the coax distribution hub and noticed it had been disconnected."

"Ah, so maybe someone just bumped it then?"

He shook his head. "No, those connectors are screwed on pretty tight. Someone would've had to physically unscrew it."

Nora raised an eyebrow. "Why would someone do that?"

"That, I don't have the answer to. Sorry. But things like this happen once in a while, especially during remodels. Looks like your guys have been running new lines to what I'm assuming are your guest rooms. It could be that one of them got mixed up and disconnected the wrong thing. I marked it with a tag so hopefully it won't happen again."

"Super. Thank you for coming out. I appreciate it."

"No problem," he said as he headed toward his truck. "Glad to help. Give us a call if you have any more issues."

"I sure will," she hollered, climbing the steps up onto the front porch.

She watched him drive down the hill and then walked inside the house to find Mitch and Carlos packing up their tools in the entryway.

"We're finished for the evening," Mitch announced. "Guess we'll head on out."

"Okay, thanks for your hard work," Nora said taking off her coat. "By the way, the Internet's back on now, so my work for the night has just begun."

"Bummer about the work," Mitch said with a chuckle. "But glad it's fixed. I know you've been worried about it." He tossed his tool belt over his shoulder, grabbed his bag. "Oh, hey, if you talk to Ben tonight, will you have him call me sometime tomorrow?"

She nodded. "Sure. I tried to call him a couple of times today with no luck, but I'm gonna try again later tonight."

"No big deal, I just have a quick electrical question for him."

Carlos opened the front door, motioning for Mitch to go first, then tipped his ball cap toward Nora and smiled. "Don't work too hard this evening, Miss Nora."

"I'll try not to. Good night, guys."

Nora closed the door behind them, anxious to find her laptop and get started, but a low rumble in her stomach moved her toward the kitchen first. She threw together a sandwich and poured a glass of wine, then made a beeline up to the bedroom.

The house was quiet around her, a stark contrast to all the action it had seen earlier in the day. She dropped onto the bed, stretching her legs out as she turned on the computer. Just as expected, there was a long list of unopened emails. Nora dealt with the important messages first, then stole a moment to type *Black Willow Farm* into the browser.

She scrolled through the better part of a dozen pages until finally, she came across a news story highlighting Pennsylvania's oldest Underground Railroad hubs. She sat up and leaned in toward the screen as the farm's name appeared with a photo link attached, listing it as one of the homes that had helped save dozens of lives during the war. "Now we're getting somewhere," she whispered.

She clicked on the link and a picture of the house in its glory days appeared. Nora smiled. It was gorgeous. Tall and mighty against the willow trees, which were much shorter then. Its lawn and grounds manicured to perfection. She stared at it for a long moment, then redirected her search to the fire that had nearly destroyed it.

Again, nothing of much consequence popped up right away.

She took a few sips of wine and tried again, digging deeper

until she found an article attributing the death of the owner's daughter to the horrible blaze, as well as a brief mention of the damage to Black Willow's structure. But that was it. There were still endless blanks that needed to be filled in. Nora sighed, rubbed her eyes. *That*, she reminded herself, was where Mrs. Krenshaw was hopefully going to come in handy. She would call her again tomorrow.

She reached over to the plate for a nibble of her sandwich, but stopped halfway there as a sound drifted into the room from the hallway. She slid off the bed and gingerly walked out into the hall, hoping against all hope that it was just the pipes rattling or the heater kicking on and she could go back to her research. Just enjoy a normal evening, like a normal person. But as she leaned over the banister, Nora's eyes widened at the sound of a chair being dragged across the hardwood floor downstairs, followed by the soft click of a door closing.

Not again.

"Who's there?" she called, unable to hold her voice steady.

She inched down the stairs and into the front hallway. At first glance everything looked untouched. The house was dark and quiet. But as she stepped to the credenza to flip on the lamp, the basement door swung open behind. Nora screamed and spun around to see a man striding down the hallway toward her. She clamped a hand to her mouth trying to mute the sound as she braced for whatever was about to happen.

And then he stepped into the light.

"Ethan," she stammered, clutching her chest. "You almost scared the life out of me. How in the world did you get in?"

"Back was open," he said in the cool tone Nora had come to expect from him.

"Oh. I could swear I locked all the doors earlier. Guess I must have missed that one." She tried to relax her shoulders. "Sorry I screamed when I saw you. It's just that I thought I was alone in the house, and—"

"Wouldn't have expected you to scare that easy. I must have really frightened you."

"You just startled me, that's all. Mitch said you'd left town for your grandmother's funeral."

"Yeah, turns out there was something I needed to take care of out here before I left. I knocked but I guess you didn't hear me."

"I see," she said, the look on Ethan's face—the way his eyes seemed to stare right through her—making her skin crawl a little. She scrambled for a reason to excuse herself so he would leave. "I don't mean to be rude, but I have a lot of work I need to catch up on, so..."

He stayed where he was.

Nora opened her mouth to try again, but as she did, her cell rang. Relief washed over her as she pulled it from her pocket.

"Ethan, I should take this. I'm so sorry about your grandmother, and again, I hope I'm not coming across as rude, but—" She gripped the phone tight, hating that his presence had caught her so off guard, unnerved her so. "If you're done, can you go ahead and let yourself out?"

He hesitated, and Nora felt sure he had something on his mind, something he wanted to say to her. But no words came.

The phone stopped ringing, then immediately started up again. "I really do need to grab this. It might be important."

"I was finished anyway," he finally said.

Nora watched him leave, never before so glad to be alone in the house. Once he was out, she trailed behind and quickly locked the door, then answered the phone.

"Sorry about that. How can I help you?" she asked.

"I'm trying to reach Nora Bassett. That wouldn't happen to be you, would it?"

"Yes, that's me."

"Oh, good. My name's Robert Krenshaw, but I'm actually calling for my mother, as strange as that may seem. Evelyn Krenshaw."

"Oh, of course, I've been trying to reach her."

"Well, that's the thing. She hasn't been feeling well lately, and we admitted her to the hospital a few days ago for chest pain."

"Oh, no. Is she okay?"

"She will be. They had to put in a pacemaker and a couple of stents, but she came home today." He paused. "My mom's mentioned you several times and has been worried that you might think she'd either, A, forgotten about you...or, B, dropped dead." He laughed. "Her words, not mine. I swear. My mother is a real spitfire."

Nora returned the laughter. "Well, this explains a lot. Please tell her not to worry about me right now and to focus on getting better."

"I will. She asked me to let you know that as soon as she's up to it, she'll have someone get the packet together for you, and that you should feel free to call her any time after you pick it up."

"Super. Thank you for letting me know. Please give her my best."

Nora ended the call, but before she had a chance to set her cell down, it rang again. She looked at the screen, her heart beating a little faster as Ben's name flashed across the front. "This day just got a whole lot better," she whispered. She walked into the library, a warm smile spreading across her face as she swiped the phone on and lifted it to her ear.

CHAPTER SEVENTEEN

The better part of a week flashed by as a string of various people made their way in and out of Black Willow.

The landscaping crew Carlos had recommended worked like Trojans, giving the border of the house, front yard and grounds a much needed facelift. And a reporter for the *Marietta Tribune* had come out to meet with Nora about a press release for the paper, in addition to the chamber members who'd stopped by to set a date for the upcoming ribbon cutting.

Nora snuck into her room to lie down for a minute, catch her breath. She looked over at the empty pillow next to her and sighed. With all the craziness, it had become increasingly difficult to connect with Ben for more than five minutes at a time and she ached to see him.

Thankfully, his dad continued to improve each day and would be out of the hospital soon, which would mean Ben's return to her. He would finally be home. She smiled at the thought. And, she reminded herself, he would have a chance to meet Adam, who'd stepped up far beyond expectation.

She'd been relieved at Ben's support of her decision to have Adam move into the house with her. He'd encouraged her to do what she felt was best. Even so, Nora had been unable to ignore the concern that bled though the edges of his voice the night she'd told him. She was certain Ben would approve of Adam, though, once he'd spent a few minutes with him. In fact, knowing Ben the way she did, she would wager a bet that the two of them would be like old friends by the end of the first day.

Adam had begun to feel like an old friend to Nora, too. He'd moved his things into one of the guest rooms on the third floor the night after they'd met, and had delivered a shining letter of recommendation from the man he had recently been a chef for.

She'd decided to contact the previous employer herself, just to be absolutely certain, but once they'd connected, his message back to her simply confirmed what she already knew—that Adam was a keeper. And the best part was that he was great in the kitchen, as promised.

A tap on the door pushed Nora up and to the side of the bed.

"Nora?" Mitch said through the door. "I hate to bother you, but there's someone downstairs to meet you."

She scooted off the edge of the mattress. "Thanks, Mitch. I'll be down in a sec."

She put her shoes back on and made her way downstairs.

Laughter wafted from the kitchen.

"Hey, Nora," Adam said as she walked in the door.

She stopped abruptly, her eyes darting to the attractive woman with a head full of loose auburn curls and a beaming smile, seated across from him at the island.

Adam stood. "This is Jessica."

"Hi, there," Nora said, wondering who the woman was.

Jessica stuck her hand out to shake Nora's, flashing her another beautiful smile.

"I'm sorry to just pop in like this," she chattered, "but I'm Bella's niece. She said you were looking for some last-minute help? I don't have any experience working at an inn, but I love the idea." A stray curl slipped out from behind her ear, and she reached to tuck it back. "I just moved here and would be happy to work for you if you still need someone."

Nora's confusion changed into recognition. "Oh, my goodness, of course. I remember Bella mentioning you. I'm so glad you stopped by. And yes, I do need someone to help out with house-keeping and check-ins, maybe some errands."

Jessica nodded eagerly.

"Can you stay for a few minutes?" Nora asked. "Adam and I will give you the cook's tour."

"Sure, I'd love to," she said. "And my schedule is open right now. I could even come in tomorrow for a while if you need the extra help."

"Oh, we do," Nora answered. "We absolutely do."

NORA PLOPPED down on the sofa in the library, thrilled to have such an obvious bright spirit sign on to work at Black Willow. Jessica had fallen in love with the house sixty seconds into the tour, and Nora could tell she was going to be a huge help and a good friend, as well. She let out a long sigh. The employee situation was handled.

She closed her eyes. The longer she sat, the more alluring the idea of re-attempting a nap became, but then she remembered she needed to ask Adam where Jessica had left her contact information before any of the crew inadvertently tossed it out.

She pushed herself off the sofa and walked down the back hallway to the servant stairs, fairly sure she'd seen him head up that way out of the corner of her eye as she'd walked Jessica out.

There was no sign of him on the second floor, but as she climbed to the third, she heard voices. Not clear enough to make out, but more of a low murmur. And she'd swear she heard her name.

"Adam?" she called. "Are you up here? I had a quick question for you."

No answer. No sign of anyone at all.

She walked farther down the hallway.

"Hello?"

The door to a guest room near the end of the hall swung open and Adam appeared. "Oh, hey. What's up?" he asked, scooting a stepladder through the doorway.

"I was looking for you," she said. "Is Mitch up here with you?"

"What?" He gave her a strange look. "Not that I know of."

She glanced toward the room he'd just come from. "I heard voices."

"Voices? Hmm, I hate to disappoint, but I didn't hear anything, and the last time I checked, it was just me up here."

"That's bizarre," she said peering inside the room, only to find it empty. "I could have sworn I heard my name."

Adam shrugged. "I honestly didn't hear anything. Sorry."

"Well, I've lost it."

"Lost what?"

"My mind," she said, with a sigh. "I've lost my mind."

Adam frowned. "Don't be too hard on yourself. Maybe it was coming from downstairs."

"Yeah, maybe," she said, trying to convince herself. "Just so you know, I really am a sane person. Well...*mostly*."

Adam juggled the stepladder to the other hand as he squeezed by her. "That makes one of us," he said back with a wink.

Nora followed him down the hall.

"Oh," she said, snapping her fingers. "Do you know where Jessica put her info? I almost forgot what I came up here to ask you."

"Dining room table, I'm pretty sure. So, what did you think of her?"

"She's great," Nora said. "I think I'm lucky to have both of you."

"Good. Glad to hear that," Adam replied. "So, I'm finished with my work and I don't have anywhere to be. Anything else I can do for you?"

She thought for a moment. "Yes, actually. There are a bunch of Christmas decorations that need to be brought up from the basement. I was going to go through the boxes and organize them later tonight, put them in categories to make it easier. Decorating this place is going to be a several day process, and we're getting so close to opening."

"I know exactly where the boxes are. Consider it done."

Nora sat at the desk in the library, finishing up the last of her paperwork as Adam wandered in.

"Christmas decorations brought up, labeled and stacked along the back hallway, by category," he said. "I also checked all the strands of lights to make sure they work. And, I'm happy to report, they do."

"Wow. You are a lifesaver. Thank you so much," she said.

"Pretty sure I should be the one thanking you for allowing me to be here."

"How about we call it even, then."

"Sounds good," he said with a smile. "So, you hungry at all?"

Nora noted the burn in her stomach. "Starved would be more accurate."

"You like Italian?"

She tossed her pen on the desk. "As a matter of fact, besides my well-known addiction to caffeine, Italian food is my second love. Please tell me that was not a hypothetical question."

Adam laughed. "Not hypothetical."

Nora stood, her interest piqued. "Keep talking. You have my undivided attention."

"I was thinking I might run into town and try a new little

place on the square. I read about it in the paper, and it's getting rave reviews. Figured I should head over and see if they know what they're doing."

"Count me in," she said.

"Okay, that was much easier than I thought it would be. I assumed you'd say no. Even had a rebuttal prepared, just in case."

Nora laughed. "Like I said, you had me at Italian."

She flipped off the light and followed him into the entryway, grabbing her coat and purse from the hall tree.

～

Serafina's Vineyard was packed. A little out-of-the-way kind of place draped in warm colors, dim lighting and the golden glow of candlelight.

As Nora walked in, the soft, subtle undertones of an Italian mandolin instantly transported her from a bitter cold night on the small town square of Marietta, Pennsylvania, to the old-world cobblestone streets of Tuscany on a warm summer's evening. She followed the maître d' back to a quiet corner table, her gaze wandering up to the lush vineyard above, where clusters of plump, ripe grapes dangled from their vines, just out of reach. Nora smiled, soaking in the scene. She loved the Italian-inspired architecture. The arched doorways covered in ivy, the worn brick and mortar pillars. The soothing fountain that bubbled softly in the background. Serafina's oozed romance and charm.

"Thank you so much," she said as they reached the table.

"My pleasure," the maître d' chimed back, pulling out the chair for her. "Nathaniel will be waiting on you this evening. He'll be with you shortly." He gave Nora and Adam a small nod and turned to leave. "You two enjoy your meal."

"I have a feeling we will," Nora said. She breathed in the tantalizing blend of vine-ripened tomatoes and garlic and wine, her senses engulfed as she leaned back in her seat. The sprint to the finish of Black Willow's grand opening, and the emptiness of Ben's absence, rolled off of her for the moment. "This place is amazing, Adam."

"What did I tell you?" He smiled. "Rave reviews. People have been coming from all around."

"Well, if the food is half as good as it smells," she said, "then I want to live here. *Literally*, right here, in this restaurant, in this booth. I'm not leaving...ever."

Adam laughed. "Somehow I think management might frown on that."

"I'm not above fighting them," she said flatly.

He tossed his head back, laughed again. "Just don't get us kicked out of here before I've gotten to sample the veal scaloppini, please, Nora."

"Pushy, pushy," she quipped, grinning as she opened her menu and began to peruse its mouthwatering contents.

BEN STRUMMED his fingers on his parents' kitchen counter as he waited for Nora to answer. Again, her voicemail sounded in his ear. Disappointed, he sent a quick text and walked down the hall to his parents' bedroom to tell them good-bye.

"Mom," he whispered, motioning her to the doorway. "Truck's packed. Just wanted to let you know I'm heading out."

His mother rose from the chair beside the bed. "Did you get ahold of Nora?"

"No, I've tried several times. Still no answer. Guess she'll find out I'm coming, when I land on her doorstep. Might be more fun to surprise her anyway."

His mother hugged him tight. "I wish you would hold off until daylight to go, but I know the heart has a hard time waiting."

He smiled and pulled her in tight. "Love you."

"I love you, too, Benjamin. You are such a good man and a

sweeter son than I could have ever hoped for. Thank you for coming and for going through this with us. I don't know what I would have done without you. I hope Nora knows how lucky she is."

He smiled. "I'm the lucky one, trust me. Just wait until you meet her." He looked toward his father, the smile fading. "I thought the police would have come up with a solid lead by now. A part of me hates to go back not knowing who did this, and why."

"I understand, but you can't wait here forever. They still think there's a good chance it was a mugging. We'll just have to trust that they'll do their job, even if it takes time."

"Something keeps bothering me, though," he said. "There hasn't been any crime to speak of in that area at all. No previous muggings, no robberies. And this asshole pulled it off so flawlessly. I don't know, it just feels...*predatory*. Like Dad was the specific target." Ben rubbed his eyes. "It's not sitting well with me. I should probably put in another call to the detective before I go. In fact, maybe I'll stay here in town until they"

"No," his mother said firmly. "I will call the police station first thing tomorrow. Check in with them, reiterate our concerns. You, my dear, are going back home to get caught up on all that you've missed while you've been up here tending to us, and more importantly, to be there for Nora. She's got her hands full. Your father and I are going to be okay. I will call you the minute they tell us anything about his case."

He hugged her again and kissed her cheek, then knelt down to his father's bedside. "You take care of yourself, Pop. I'll be back in a week or so, to check in on you. Promise me you'll have mom call if you need me for anything at all."

His father reached for his hand, squeezed it tight. "Thank you for everything, Ben."

Ben's eyes dampened. "You're very welcome. I'll see you soon."

He tossed his father one last wave and walked into the hall, his mother following close behind.

He turned back to her briefly, his eyes dark. "You'll call 911 if you see anything unusual? Or if anyone comes around that you don't know? I'm serious, mom."

She hooked her arm in his and squeezed. "I will, you have my word. We'll be fine."

He gave her a nod, but the unease lingered. "Lock the door behind me," he said as he stepped out onto the porch. "Deadbolt, too. I'll call you tomorrow."

He hopped up into the truck and started the ignition, turning toward Marietta.

HE MOVED FREELY through the house now that Nora was gone. He touched her things. The power of knowing he was in control, intoxicating.

In the kitchen, he ran a hand over the smooth granite counter. Changes had been made to his house. But most were fixable, with only a very few worthy of remaining once he returned. He strolled toward the bay window, Nora's phone beginning to vibrate on the counter behind. He ignored it. It vibrated again.

Irritated, more than curious, he walked over and picked it up, reading the message on the screen.

Hey, babe. They discharged my dad this afternoon. I can't spend another night away from you. Already on the road. Be there around midnight. Can't wait to show you how much I've missed you...

"Shit." He gripped the cell hard.

His little jaunt to Connecticut to handle Ben's parents hadn't bought enough time. He cursed himself for not finishing the job before the wife showed up. He should have taken care of her, too. That would have given him plenty of time to settle things with Nora before Ben was back.

How could he have let this happen? Irritation pulsed like a river through him, but he soothed himself with visions of the endgame —entertaining ideas he knew he shouldn't. Not yet, anyway. He looked down at his watch, weighed the options. Angry that things had to be thrown into fast forward, but relieved that he had all the tools necessary, ready and waiting. He commended himself for that.

He rolled the phone over and over in his hand. Success would rest in the timing, as well as Nora keeping to her usual routine— that particular factor would be key. But expediting things *was* possible, and was by far the most viable option. A grin slowly spread across his lips as he paced the kitchen. Yes, everything would still play out as intended, simply faster. Perhaps more of an obstacle now, less of one later.

Nora's cell jolted to life again. Another call from *lover boy*. He took one last look at the phone and dropped it onto the floor— hating Ben as he did—ready to be rid of him and have that particular *problem* on a short road to resolution. He lifted the heel of his foot high as the phone rang out in vain, bringing his boot down hard and fast, crushing it with one swift blow.

CHAPTER EIGHTEEN

"You know, it really should be illegal to eat that much food," Nora said as she pushed her empty plate to the side and pulled her coffee cup in.

"True, but totally worth it, right?" Adam asked.

"Yes. A thousand times, yes. That was some of the best manicotti that has ever crossed my lips."

The waiter removed their dinner plates, offered more coffee.

"So," Adam said, lowering his voice. "Can I ask you something?"

Nora sat up, unable to ignore the serious undertone moving in. "Of course, go ahead."

"The thing is..." He paused for a moment. "It's an odd question and I don't want to make you uneasy or upset you at all."

"Hmm, might be a little late for that," she joked. "The uneasy part, anyway. Better hurry up and ask before I change my mind." She couldn't imagine where the conversation was going, and was starting to feel as if she might not want to.

"Okay, well, here goes." He looked at her squarely. "I'm just going to throw it out there. Has anything strange ever happened to you at the house?"

"At Black Willow?" Nora's stomach twisted. "Like what, exactly?"

She watched Adam search for the right words.

"I'm not sure, but I could swear—and this is going to sound crazy—I've been hearing someone walk around up in the attic at night. Moving things around. And I mean, like, *late* at night. Usually somewhere between two and four a.m., or so."

Nora stared at him, the twist of her stomach now causing actual pain.

"Any chance it was you?" he added.

Heat rushed to her cheeks. The urge to blurt out all of the strange things that had happened in the house lately, nearly unbearable. She wanted to tell someone. Needed to. But something held her back. "Adam, I—"

His cell buzzed, breaking the tension. He looked down at the number. "Do you mind if I grab this? I'll be right back, I promise." He excused himself, dropping his dinner napkin on the table in front of him as he left.

Dear God, she thought, allowing herself to crumble in his absence. *It wasn't my imagination.* Someone else had experienced it, too. Which should have brought her some sense of comfort, she knew. But what did that mean for the inn? Nora hadn't been ready to face that notion. She couldn't have guests lying in bed at night hearing strange noises. *And just how did a person get rid of a ghost, anyway?* She was way out of her field of knowledge. Way out.

She looked up to see Adam return, his face clouded.

"I am so sorry, but I'm going to have to cut our evening short. My friend in Lancaster was in a car accident."

"Oh, no."

"Yeah, his wife said it could have been a lot worse, but she sounds pretty shaken, so if it's okay with you, I'll run you home and then head on over to meet her at the hospital."

"Of course." Nora stood. "Go. I can call a cab if you need to hurry."

He motioned for the waiter. "No, it's fine. I'll drop you off first."

He handed the bill along with the payment to the waiter, as Nora grabbed her purse.

"Thank you for dinner," she said as they turned to leave. "I didn't mean for you to pay for mine. My treat next time. And I'm so sorry about your friend, I hope he'll be okay."

"Thanks. Me, too."

THUNDER RUMBLED in the distance as Nora kicked off her shoes and walked into the kitchen. Her earlier conversation with Adam weighed heavily on her mind. *Nice timing,* she thought to herself. *Tell me you've been hearing creepy sounds in the attic and then get called away for the rest of the night. Super.*

She reached into the fridge. There was less than half a bottle of wine left, and she planned to drink every drop. Wished for more. But maybe if she could squeeze one full glass out, it would at least be enough to take the edge off. Help her settle down and be able to sleep, in what was rapidly becoming her house of horror.

Ben. She needed to call Ben. Now that someone else had experienced the same craziness she had, she felt much better spilling all the details to him. She felt a pang of guilt for not telling him sooner. He would have believed her, of course he would have. At the very least, he'd have humored her.

She glanced around the room. Where had she left her phone?

She hurried into the library, looked on the desk and checked all the outlets. Nothing. Then she remembered. It should have been in the kitchen, that's where she'd plugged it in after Jessica had left. But as she walked back in, no phone. Just the charger dangling from the wall.

Irritated, she continued her search, knowing if she didn't find it, she couldn't contact Ben—or anyone for that matter. Installing a landline in the house hadn't been on the top of her to-do list, since the answering service had been handling all reservations and guest inquiries for the time being. A mistake, she quickly decided.

Minutes passed, every room she'd stepped foot in earlier in the day, scoured. Again, no phone.

Giving up, she took the glass of wine and the very last of the bottle and trudged up the stairs to her bedroom.

Lightning flashed closer, beautiful hot colors jumping from cloud to cloud, in near perfect unison with the thunder. She took a long sip of wine and crossed to her window, not wanting to miss the incredible show that had begun to web across the sky above the willows.

She felt her body begin to relax. Maybe sleep would come after all. She changed into one of Ben's shirts, not bothering to button it but instead pulling it in close around her. She returned to the window and curled up in the chair, covering her legs with a throw blanket as she drained the last of the wine from the glass.

Before long, her head began to feel heavy, as if she couldn't hold it up. She leaned back, wondering why the wine was kicking in so much stronger than usual. Nora blinked once, and again, trying to focus as her eyelids drooped.

She reached out to set the empty glass on the side table next to the chair but missed, sending it spiraling down onto the hardwood floor, where it shattered.

Why did she suddenly feel as if she'd had the whole bottle?

Another clap of thunder shook the house. Nora gripped the arm of the chair and pressed her eyes tightly shut, trying to clear the cobwebs from them, desperate to concentrate, to snap herself back. But the harder she tried, the more the haze pulled her in.

A sound from the hallway drew what little focus she had left. "Is someone there?" she rasped, her throat as dry as the desert, her words slurring.

The sound came again.

Were those footsteps?

That was the last fragment of a thought that would drift through Nora's mind as she slipped away into the darkness.

HE PULLED Nora from the chair, cradling her in his arms. As he did, the shirt fell away from her shoulder, revealing one of her perfect breasts. His body hardened, began to throb. He carried her down into the library and laid her on the sofa, then turned to build a fire.

He watched as the flames climbed high, before he walked into the kitchen to get a pair of wine glasses, snapping his fingers as he remembered he'd seen the empty bottle up in her room.

He pulled up his sleeves and checked his watch, reminding himself to monitor the time carefully. He climbed up to the second floor and retrieved the bottle, as well as her bra and panties. Another crucial part of the equation.

On the way back down, he glanced out the stairwell window. Rain had begun to sheet, the house groaning against the wind. A perfect night to curl up with a warm woman by a fire, he thought. *Lucky me.*

He finished his work and turned the lights off before rejoining Nora on the sofa, sinking his fingers gently into the flesh of her shoulders. She let out a tiny sound, her back arching as she tightened up against his touch.

He waited. Then eased a hand up to smooth a wave of silky brown hair away from her face. He studied her as she sank deeper and deeper into the dimness, her breathing heavier, the movement of her eyes slowing beneath their lids.

His gaze moved down over her body. "So very tempting," he whispered.

He traced a hand across her cheek and on down to the soft skin of her neck. No more movement. She was completely out.

"That's a good girl, Nora. Just let go." He checked the time again, then leaned her on her side to slip Ben's shirt all the way off her body, tossing it on the floor in front of the sofa along with the bra and panties. He walked to the front door and unlocked it, shedding his own clothes as he returned. He slid in beneath the warmth of her body, his eyes closing as he savored the sensual feel of her bare skin against his. "You sleep," he whispered, running a finger down the length of her arm. "And I'll take care of everything else."

~

BEN TURNED OFF THE IGNITION. He sat for a minute and looked up at the house. It was massive against the horizon. Even in the darkness, everything about it was awe-inspiring. And the woman he loved waited inside. It was good to be home. And this was, without question, *home*.

He swung the truck door open and jumped out, his legs feeling the long drive.

The air was frigid, as the storms he'd encountered had brought a trace of sleet along with the buckets of icy-cold rain they'd dumped on him all the way from Connecticut.

Reaching back in to the console for his phone, he gave one more quick check to see if Nora had ever responded to his messages. Still nothing, which wasn't like her at all. He pushed the truck door shut behind him and checked the time. Twelve forty-five a.m. The weather had slowed him down a little, but he'd made it there and that was all that mattered.

As he headed up the front walk toward the house, Nora's car was the only vehicle he could see. He wondered where Adam was, but hoped that maybe he was away for the night. Ben understood that Nora needed to hire help, of course she did, and he trusted her completely, but he couldn't deny the sting he'd felt when she had told him that Adam was moving in with her. It was just too much, too fast. Especially when he'd never met the guy. Still, he'd chosen to be supportive, because he loved her.

Ben stepped to the front door, greeted by the familiar smell of a fire burning in the fireplace. Within a few minutes, he hoped to be pulling Nora into his arms in front of it. He gave a quick study of the entryway through the glass. The house was dark inside, with the exception of the fire's faint glow oozing in from the door to the library.

He knocked.

The whole way home, he'd expected to see radiance pour from Nora's face, her breath catching in her throat at the sight of him. He'd imagined how she would slip into his arms. Their lips would meet, and soft words would be spoken between them, kicking off the celebration.

But Nora was nowhere in sight.

He knocked again, his heart sinking with every passing minute. She had to be there.

Finally, after giving her several minutes to wake up and come down, he reached into his pocket for the key she'd given him long ago. He hadn't intended to let himself in, had pictured the scene differently. But desperation left him no choice. At this point he had to make sure that she was all right. It would still be a surprise, he decided, since she obviously didn't know he was there, maybe didn't even know he was coming at all.

Ben frowned as his pocket came up empty. He checked the opposite pocket. No key. He knew the only other place it could be was in the truck and he started to turn back, but stopped. He looked down at the door handle. Surely she would have locked the door before she went up to bed, but at least it was worth a shot.

He reached for the handle, surprised when the door easily opened. An instant pang of worry shot through him. Why would she be so careless? It wasn't like Nora at all.

"Hello?" He kept his voice low. "Nora?"

No sound returned other than the distant crackle coming from the fireplace.

He turned toward the library. The fire was down to glowing coals, making it difficult to see. He took a step farther inside the room, his eyes straining to focus in the dark.

"Nora?" he whispered again.

He could make out a shape on the sofa but couldn't see the face...or *faces,* rather. He suddenly realized that it looked more like two people.

Who in the world? He leaned in closer, then froze, his eyes refusing to accept the image.

There in front of him, Nora lay on the sofa, entwined in the arms of another man. A stranger to Ben, but very obviously *not* a stranger to her.

All the air rushed from his lungs.

He blinked hard, his eyes finally coming into full focus.

It was her, all right. There with the stranger. *His Nora.* The woman he'd hoped to spend the rest of his life with. Her body lay limp and relaxed, draped over the man, as if there had been a familiarity, a shared intimacy, there for ages.

Her head was nuzzled into the stranger's bare chest while, in return, his arms held her close, a single light blanket draped across the lower half of their bodies.

Heat rose in Ben's throat. He couldn't look away, his eyes locked on the two. It didn't make sense. The way Nora's hand rested gently up under the man's chin. The way she appeared so casual and content, her bare breasts glowing in the firelight.

He looked down at the coffee table. Two long-stem glasses and an empty wine bottle sat across from them. Ben stood motionless, a statue of cold, solid stone. The stench of disgust, of disappointment, suffocating him. He took a step back, forcing himself to look away from Nora.

His heart pounded. Shock melted into hurt, hurt into anger. Anger into rage.

He stared at the stranger. Despising him. Wanting nothing more than to knock the satisfied look off his face with one of the two-by-fours out back.

He'd seen enough.

He had to leave at that very moment, before he did something he would later regret. No amount of dramatic and tearful explanations on Nora's part would undo the damage that had been done, and he couldn't help but curse himself for somehow allowing it to happen. Was it because he'd had to leave? Because he'd gone to help his parents during an unthinkable crisis? She'd been so supportive. Had even offered to go with him. Ben had known her to be different than this. At least, he thought he had.

In the darkness of the front foyer, confusion and disbelief swelled inside him. How could he have misjudged her on such a huge level? Something felt off about the whole situation, something besides the fact that she'd slept with someone else. He needed to think, needed some distance. Otherwise, Ben knew he'd kill or, at the very least, hospitalize the inconsiderate asshole who had moved in on Nora, taken advantage of her while he'd been gone. Who was this bastard anyway?

Ben landed back in the front seat of the truck. He slammed the door, a combination of anger and sadness tearing a gaping hole in his heart as the stranger's face flashed through his mind again. And then it hit him. *Adam*. It must have been Adam. It was the only thing that made any scrap of sense.

Ben jammed the key into the ignition and started the engine, blinking back hot, bitter tears. He pointed his truck away from Black Willow, not knowing where he would end up. But *anywhere* was better than there.

CHAPTER NINETEEN

Head pounding, Nora shielded her eyes against the sunlight. She was still in the chair she'd gone to sleep in.

She tried to stand, the room threatening to spin as she massaged the throb that had taken up residence in her temples. If she didn't know better, she would swear she had a first-class textbook hangover. But of course that wasn't possible from a single glass of wine. Leaving her to assume she'd picked up some sort of strange twenty-four-hour bug and would prayerfully be on the mend by late afternoon.

A look toward the hallway produced no sign of anyone. She reached for her phone to check the time, cursing as she recalled she'd misplaced it.

Pain reliever. God bless the genius who invented it, she thought as she remembered the bottle she'd tossed on the dresser a few days ago. She braced herself and took a few steps, putting her hand to her head again. The farther she walked, the more it felt like an overripe melon, teetering on her shoulders. She unscrewed the bottle cap and swallowed a double dose of pills not wasting time to search for liquid to wash them down, then slowly made her way downstairs to the kitchen.

As Nora walked through the doorway, Jessica looked up from unloading the dishwasher.

"Oh, gosh," Jessica said, clamping a hand over her chest. "You startled me."

Nora looked at her curiously.

"I hope it's okay that I'm here. I stopped by this morning like you'd suggested and one of your construction guys answered the door. Mitch, I believe. He said he hadn't seen you yet today, but it would be okay for me to help out in here while I waited."

"Oh. Of course," Nora said, steadying herself against the island as another wave of dizziness hit her. "What time is it, anyway?"

"A little past eleven."

Nora's mouth dropped open. "It can't be that late," she stammered. "I swear it's not like me to sleep the day away like this. How embarrassing. I must have picked up a virus or maybe I ate something last night that didn't agree with me. I'm still queasy as we speak."

Jessica poured a glass of juice and slid it across the counter.

Nora held a hand up, stopping her. She felt positively green. "I'm not sure I'm ready for juice quite yet. And you'd better keep your distance, just to be on the safe side."

"I'm not afraid of you," she chattered. "I come from a family of seven. Growing up, I was exposed to enough germs to wipe out a small village. I built up so much resistance that I never get sick anymore. Don't worry about me." She pulled the coffeepot from the burner and lifted it toward Nora. "A shot of this, maybe?"

Nora managed a smile, but not even coffee sounded good, and that spoke volumes in her world. "Thanks, but all I want is a hot shower. That'll help, I'm sure. I already loaded up with pain meds."

"Okay," Jessica said. "But I'll help you in any way I can. All you have to do is holler."

"You're very sweet. Everything looks great in here. I can tell you've tidied quite a bit. Glad you're with us."

"Well, I'm thrilled to be here. Now, why don't you go on up and start that shower. If you change your mind on a little break-fast, I'd be glad to make you some toast when you're finished. Sometimes it helps."

"I'll see how I do with the shower first. If I survive that, we'll go from there." Nora forced another smile, her stomach lurching at the idea of a single bite of anything. "Thanks so much for the offer."

Jessica nodded. "Okay to keep myself busy in here for a while? I still see plenty of things I can handle."

"Absolutely." Nora headed toward the door, turned back. "Oh, have you seen Adam anywhere? He went to Lancaster last night, to help a friend, and I was just wondering if he'd made it in yet."

"No, I guess not. I've been here quite a while and haven't seen him at all."

"Okay, then. I'm off to shower. Wish me luck."

Nora made it to the staircase and looked up. It felt like a mile to the top, and her first step was almost enough to send her to her knees. She cradled her stomach.

What on God's green earth is going on with me?

⤳

BEN DIALED LIZ. He was tired, he was angry and he needed someone to keep him from ending up in jail.

He'd spent the remainder of the previous night pacing, curs-ing, pacing some more. And now, by the light of day, he wanted some answers. Not from Nora, though. He wasn't even close to ready for that yet. But Liz might know something. And he knew that he could trust her. She'd be honest with him, no matter what.

"Hello?" Liz said over the sound of kids playing in the background.

"Liz, it's Ben."

Her voice brightened. "Ben, I'm so glad you called. How's your dad?"

"Yeah, better. He's back home now. My mom's taking care of him."

"Oh, thank God. I know you were so worried about him. Does that mean you'll be back in town soon? Because I know someone who's going to be happy to hear those words. Thrilled to hear them is more like it."

He couldn't hide his anguish. "That's why I'm calling," he said. "To find out if you know what the hell has been going on with Nora while I've been gone."

She hesitated. "What do you mean? Nothing's going on that I know of. She's been missing you like crazy, but that's all I"

He stopped her, diving straight into the previous night's events, sparing no detail.

"No way," she insisted, once he'd finally finished. "Ben, I've been over there many times in the last couple weeks and I'm telling you the woman is nuts about you. She would never—"

"Well, she did. I saw the two of them myself."

"I don't know what to say then. She only talks about you, never anyone else."

"What about her new chef?"

"Adam? I've met him. Actually, I'm the one who told him about Nora and the job. He was polite, genuine. I can't believe she would do that with him...or anyone else, for that matter. This is insane. You need to go over there. Somehow you've misinterpreted something."

"No, that's just it. I didn't misinterpret anything. I was there... and so was she. And I'm telling you, Liz, she was wrapped around this guy, like they'd been at it for hours." He stopped to collect himself. "I'm sorry. I hate thinking this way about her. But I saw what I saw."

"Go talk to her," Liz said bluntly. "You need to go today. Go now."

Ben closed his eyes. "That's not going to happen. I can't think of anything she could say to me that would undo what she's done. I keep seeing her in his arms, like..." His voice dropped off.

"Something doesn't add up here," Liz pressed. "She wouldn't do that to you. I don't believe it. Not for one minute. And I don't think you do, either."

"I love her, Liz. I do. More than I knew I could ever love anyone. But I think it's pretty clear I can't trust her."

"If you're not going to talk to her, then I will," she warned.

"No," he said, his voice unwavering. "I need to sort this out. She didn't see me. Doesn't even know I'm in town. Please, I'm asking you to give me a day or two to get this anger under control first. Then we'll see."

"Fine. But I still believe this is all a misunderstanding of some kind. So, give yourself a day to cool down, and then after that, either you go talk to her about it...or I will."

NORA GRIPPED the handrail as she climbed the stairs to the attic. The combination of pain pills and hot shower had helped, but the wooziness still snuck up on occasion, taking her breath away. Food poisoning was the culprit she'd settled on. It had to be. And though she'd decided not to make Adam feel bad, she knew it must have been her dinner at Serafina's.

But the growing list of things that had to be done was not going to magically disappear, so she'd given Jessica some things to work on and had jumped in herself, too. She couldn't afford to lose more than the morning she'd already slept through.

She reached the top step and slowed, glancing toward the brick doorway Ben had found hidden behind the wall. Luckily, she hadn't had to make any explanations to the crew yet, since there had been no reason for them to go up to the attic since Ben had gone.

Her heart warmed at the thought of Ben. She missed his smile, his kiss, his touch. The way he made her feel whole. Once she'd realized she had misplaced her phone, she'd sent him an email, but he obviously hadn't gotten it yet since she hadn't heard back.

More than anything, though, she just needed to hear his voice, talk to him. And if she didn't find her phone soon, Nora had decided to beg, borrow or steal someone's phone later to call him.

Her thoughts of Ben lingered as she dug through a pile of boxes, looking for the new curtains for the parlor. She sifted through odds and ends of décor and greenery and books, about to give up, when she came across an unmarked box near the bottom of the pile. She opened it and peered inside, rifling through more books and magazines until she came to a small leather-bound journal. Her heart lunged in her chest.

Lucy's journal.

She would have recognized it anywhere. Nora had bought it for her sister and mailed it to her the day she'd signed the papers on Black Willow. A simple housewarming gift.

"Oh, God, Lucy," she whispered, gripping the journal with both hands. "I miss you more than there are words."

Nora's legs wobbled beneath her. She lowered herself to the floor, remembering the day Lucy had embarked on her dream of opening the inn, and the excitement she'd shown over the book. *Something to keep track of your journey,* Nora had told her over the phone that night. And Lucy had promised to use it often.

A tear escaped, falling onto the front cover. Nora wiped it away and traced a hand across the nicks and scratches in the leather, bracing herself as she cracked open its pages.

She began to read, drinking in her sister's last days, hanging on each word as if what lay scribbled in front of her was a direct connection to Lucy.

And in a way, it was.

As she moved through the pages, Nora came across names that would have meant nothing to her months ago but now had become a large part of her life. Ben, of course, was front and center. Followed closely by Mitch and Carlos, as well as Liz and numerous others.

She was surprised to see her own name make as many appearances as it did, and was haunted by the fact that she hadn't been there for Lucy as much as she should have, during her last days.

If only she could go back, make things right.

She turned another page and stared at the first word, written at the top. *Lilacs.* Her sister had noticed the heavy, sweet scent of lilacs in the house, too. Just as she herself had numerous times. But what did that mean? Where was it coming from?

Nora read on, captivated. She found an entry mentioning Bella's Antiques, where Lucy had picked up the surprise painting she'd found for Nora. And then, of course, there was the less appealing entry that recounted the ongoing issues she'd had with the house's previous owner.

Why hadn't Lucy mentioned him to her?

He hadn't bothered to come around since Nora had moved in. For that she was grateful. She knew she would have nothing good to say to him if he did.

The only name in the journal she didn't recognize was a man by the name of Richard. Nora found the name more and more toward the end. Her sister had shared meals with the man, met him for drinks. The romantic undertone was undeniable as she flipped through the pages. Nora found it strange that her sister had spent so much time with someone but never mentioned him to her. Not once. Why would Lucy leave out these things when they'd talked? Had Nora really been that absent from her twin's inner circle? She would never know.

As she turned to the final entry, she stopped, giving her mind a moment to wrap around the words that would begin to change her perception of all things Black Willow, forever.

AUGUST 30

The strangest things have been happening lately. I've tried to rationalize them, to explain them away, but I don't know what's going on. Doors slamming. I could swear things are moving around. Last night, as I was falling asleep, I would have bet my life that I heard a man's voice coming from downstairs. But when I went down to check, the house was still locked and no one was there.

One of the weirdest things is, that I keep smelling cigar smoke. It's driving me batty. And there have been moments, too, when I've felt I wasn't alone—even though I know, of course, that sounds completely paranoid. Seems like absolute nonsense to see these words on paper, even as I write them.

I haven't mentioned this to anyone. And if I did, what would I say? That I bought this big, lovely old house to rent out to guests, but now I'm finding that I may be keeping the company of ghosts? Absurd. I've always been intrigued by that type of thing, but not so much anymore. I know it would definitely be better for business, not to make a big deal of it. I'm leaning toward at least calling Nora, though. Getting her take on all of this. I know she'll be a hard-sell, even I think it sounds nuts. But nuts or not, something is going on here and I'm starting to feel that I should talk to someone about it.

As crazy as it may seem, I still couldn't possibly love this house any more than I do, and even though I've been scared out of my mind quite a few times lately, I am not leaving. No matter what. So, I guess for now, I'll just keep sleeping with the door locked and one eye open...

Nora closed the journal, in utter disbelief. Her body numb. What did all of this mean? And more importantly, why had Lucy waited so long to tell her about all of the odd...no...*downright scary* things that had been happening to her at the farm?

She thought of the many times unexplainable things had happened to her, as well. She, just like Lucy, was guilty of writing them all off. Explaining them away, not wanting to believe that something was amiss inside such a beautiful place, one that brimmed with so much promise.

She pushed up from the floor and tucked the journal beneath her arm as she headed for the stairs. She had to find some answers. A phone call to the library was as good a place to start as any. Maybe the packet from Mrs. Krenshaw was finally ready.

She remembered her missing cell.

"Damn it," she whispered under her breath.

The time had come to make the trip into town to get a temporary phone until she laid hands on the one she'd misplaced. A dozen people were likely trying to get ahold of her. And Ben was at the top of that list, she was certain. Oh, how she'd love for him to walk through the front door right about now.

She went back down to the entryway to look for her purse and car keys, hoping they hadn't disappeared along with her phone.

Jessica stepped into the hall from the kitchen. "Feeling better?"

"Starting to," Nora said.

"Oh, good. Well, I'm about finished and ready to head home, unless you need me for anything else."

"No, no. Today has been a really off day for me, and I appreciate you coming and pitching in. Go whenever you like." She glanced around the entry for Adam's coat. "Did Adam ever get back? I was going to borrow his phone to make a couple of quick calls."

Jessica shook her head. "No, I don't think so. It's been pretty quiet here except for your two workman. And they finished up and left a few minutes ago."

She scooted past Nora to the coatrack by the front door. "Here," Jessica said, pulling her cell from her jacket pocket. "Feel free to use mine."

"That would actually be great," Nora said. "I'll get it right back to you. By the way, since you worked so many extra hours today, you can have tomorrow off if you'd like."

"Sure, whatever works for you. I appreciate it."

Once Jessica had disappeared into the kitchen again, Nora dropped onto the staircase and dialed the library. The busy signal echoed in her ear, and she tried a second time. Busy again.

Next, she tried Ben, but his voicemail kicked on.

"Hi, it's me," she said, deflated. "Call me when you get a chance, I—" She stopped. "Well, actually, scratch that. I've lost my phone and have to run into Marietta and grab a temp. I'll call you with my new number when I get back. Anyway, I have a lot to tell you. Talk to you soon."

She stood up and started to walk back to Jessica in the kitchen, but decided at the last minute to call Liz and ask her to relay a message to Ben.

Liz answered on the first ring.

"Hey, Liz. It's Nora."

"Oh, Nora. I didn't recognize the number."

"Yeah, I can't find my phone and had to borrow one. I swear I've looked everywhere. I'm so scattered lately I must have let it slip between cushions somewhere, or maybe it's lodged under the seat in my car. Anyway, the crazy thing seems to have vanished."

Liz hesitated. "So, while I've got you, what's been going on over there? I haven't talked to you in a few days. Everything...all right?"

"I think so," Nora replied. "I've been sick, but other than that I'm—"

"That's it," Liz scoffed. "I can't do this."

Nora stood silent, shocked at the bite in Liz's tone.

"He asked me not to say anything, and like an idiot, I agreed. But this is ridiculous. What is it that happened over there that's made Ben so upset?"

"Ben's in Connecticut, Liz. What are you talking about?"

Liz slowed her words. "Ben isn't in Connecticut, Nora. He's here. He was at your house last night."

"What?" Nora's heart leapt in her chest. "He's here? Why didn't he come in? I don't understand."

"I can't say anything more. He'd be beyond upset with me if he knew I'd said this much. But I consider you a close friend, and I couldn't just let you wonder. I'm telling you, though, you need to talk to him right away. I've known Ben a long time and I've never seen him this angry."

There was a long pause while Nora tried to process what she'd heard. "I think there's been some confusion, I"

"Just call and talk to him. And if you need anything later or need to hear a friendly voice, I'm here."

"Okay," Nora said. "I really can't imagine what's going on, but I'll call him right now."

She hung up with Liz and dialed Ben again, knowing that Liz must be wrong. He couldn't be back in town. He would have told her he was coming.

No answer.

Nora's brow creased as she tried once more.

When his voicemail kicked on again, she hung up and pasted on a smile long enough to return Jessica's phone. Then collected her purse and keys and climbed in her car, aiming it toward Ben's.

CHAPTER TWENTY

Ben heard Nora's car pull into the drive and walked to the window, watching as she climbed out. He closed his eyes as the image of her body, bare in the firelight, nuzzled close to her *mystery guest*, filled his mind, threatened to bring him to his knees. He couldn't handle this right now.

The doorbell rang. Rang again.

"Ben? I know you're here. Please open the door, we need to talk."

The sound of her voice softened him. How could she have done it? Deep inside he wanted to believe that she hadn't—that she couldn't. He raked a hand through his hair, contemplating, but finally opened the door.

She stared at him through the screen for a long moment, then spoke. "What are you doing here?" she asked. "I thought you were still with your dad."

"He's better," Ben said, feeling the chill roll off his own voice.

"I'm so glad to hear that," she said, then hesitated. "Don't be upset with Liz, but she said I should come talk to you. She said she's never seen you so angry. Please tell me what's going on."

Ben didn't speak. He knew that if he opened his mouth, he couldn't control what might come out.

Nora leaned closer to the screen door. "I didn't do whatever it is that you think I've done," she insisted. "I didn't even know you were in town—"

"Yeah, that was pretty obvious," he said quietly.

"What?" She stared at him, shock washing out her features. "You clearly think I've done something wrong. At least tell me what it is."

"Nora," he said with almost no emotion. "I can't get into this right now. I need some time."

She pulled the screen door open, leaving nothing between them. "Get into what, exactly?"

He took a step back. "I think you know what I'm talking about. *You just didn't know that I knew.*"

NORA FORCED IN A DEEP BREATH. The sight of him made her heart ache. She'd longed to see him for over two and a half weeks. And now she wanted nothing more than to fall into the comfort of his arms, letting him hold her close.

An awkward silence wedged between them. This was no game. Something had happened, even though she had no idea what. She could feel the invisible wall he'd created. His words, his demeanor shocked her. His face clouded with not only anger but a deep-seated pain. He looked like he hadn't slept in days. But what surprised her the most was the darkness in his eyes...and it scared her to her core.

She opened her mouth to speak, tears of confusion and disappointment, filling her eyes as she did. "Talk to me, Ben," she pleaded. "Will you please tell me what this is? I love you with all of my heart and I don't have any idea what has happened. Please explain it."

She couldn't take it any longer and reached for him. If she touched him, he would realize that this was all a mistake. He had to. But as she reached out, he withdrew. He slid a hand into his pocket and pulled something shiny from it. Nora felt her throat close as she realized it was the key she'd given him to her home—to her heart—that was being handed back to her. "You can't be serious—"

He held up a hand to stop her. "I don't know what to say to you. I fell in love with you and believed that you felt the same. I couldn't wait to spend the rest of my life with you."

"Me, too," she rasped. "That's all I want. I love you more than I—"

"Where I come from, Nora," he said, facing her eye to eye, "faithfulness and loyalty accompany that kind of love."

"I'm telling you, Ben, I have never done anything wrong toward you."

Ben shook his head. "Don't waste your time." He looked out over the yard and to the street beyond before looking back at her matter-of-factly. "*I saw you.*"

His words fell like boulders, settling to the bottom of the unseen and impenetrable ravine that gaped between them.

Nora searched for a response, anything at all, to contest his accusation—an accusation she still didn't even understand. But nothing came. Instead, anger rose up inside her. She'd done nothing even remotely questionable. And the idea that he would condemn her like this, was more than she was willing to take lying down.

"Saw me *what,* exactly?" she shot back.

Ben shook his head again. "Don't, Nora."

"Tell me, damn it. I have done nothing wrong. I don't know what you think you saw, but you are way out of line here."

"I'm out of line?" He choked back laughter, laced with disgust. "You and Adam were the ones out of line. At least that's who I'm assuming it was. And let me be very clear. I was at the farm and I saw the two of you, myself. There is nothing you can say or do to erase it from my mind."

"Saw us what? Are you kidding me?" Nora said, wide-eyed. "Adam and I did exactly *nothing* inappropriate together. Ever." She gripped her car keys, twisting them in her hand. "So, let me get this straight. You were out at the farm and thought you saw something going on—some sort of betrayal, I guess—but it never occurred to you to go inside the house to talk to me about it? To make sure you hadn't completely misunderstood something? Made a terrible mistake, maybe?"

"I did."

"You did what?"

"Go inside," he said. "But you were clearly very...*busy*. Way too busy to notice, apparently."

Words escaped her. What could he have misinterpreted to this extent? And how in the world had she missed him walking into the house?

"I thought you knew me better than this," she snapped. "I guess I was wrong."

Ben's jaw rippled, his eyes flashing as he shut down the conversation. "Like I said earlier, I can't do this right now. You should go, Nora. I'll call you when I'm ready to talk."

Nora hadn't been angry when she'd arrived, but she was now. She turned and stormed down the steps.

Before she knew it, she was inside the car, jamming the key into the ignition.

The car's engine cranked to life and she threw it into drive.

BEN CLOSED THE DOOR, an even bigger hole torn in his heart. Even through his raging disappointment, his anguish, he still loved her.

He was painfully aware of that now.

He'd felt the warmth of her breath on his face as she'd tried so hard to convince him that she loved him, that she would never do anything to betray him. The hurt and disbelief gushing from every part of her. It had been almost enough to break him. And the strangest thing was that some part of him believed her. Even though he'd seen her with Adam. Had witnessed it with his own eyes. It made no sense.

So, why did he feel that way?

Because something just doesn't add up, a voice in the back of his mind warned.

Ben walked into the living room, plagued by the thought. He dropped onto the sofa, leaning his head back. *God, he loved her.* There was no denying it. And the more he thought about it, the less convinced he was that she was capable of sleeping with Adam after all. Ben had put enough trust in what he'd thought he'd seen, that he had closed off his mind, never giving Nora a fair shake to even attempt to offer any kind of explanation. His anger had led him to a single conclusion. One where she was the villain and Ben the victim.

But what now? He'd ordered Nora to leave, and had made her angry enough that she'd been more than happy to oblige.

What had he done?

He sat in silence for a long moment. Time was the best solution, he decided. He needed time to clear his head, figure things out. And Nora—after the way she'd stormed out—needed time to cool off. Of that, he was certain.

CHAPTER TWENTY-ONE

Nora veered onto the farm road that would take her back to
Black Willow, her eyes swollen from the torrent of angry
tears streaming down both cheeks.

The cold stranger she'd just stood in front of was not the man
she knew.

The man she'd fallen in love with had been gentle, compas-
sionate, trusting. He'd single-handedly pulled her through the
horrifying days after Lucy's death and had continued to care about
her, to support her every day since.

Every day until this one.

She made it to the covered bridge, but stopped halfway across,
gripping the steering wheel. No matter how hard she tried, she
couldn't escape the look on Ben's face as he'd accused her. The
very idea that she would be capable of something like that was
inconceivable to Nora.

She sat in the car for a long time, watching the river race
beneath her. The shock and anger she'd felt only moments ago,
now shifting to a sadness so deep it threatened to swallow
her whole.

The moment she'd seen Ben, she had forgotten about the

phone and the journal and the strange things that had happened lately. All of it had simply slipped away. What mattered was him.

Nora pulled up the hill and parked in front of the house, new tears erupting. She wanted nothing more than to turn the car around and go back to him, find some way to make him listen. But he wouldn't allow it. He'd made that clear. And that left her very little choice.

She grabbed her purse and pushed the car door open. She was spent. Emotionally, mentally, physically. She made her way onto the porch as the front door swung open.

Adam smiled. "I was wondering what had become of you. I got back from Lancaster earlier and you were gone."

"Yeah," she said softly. She walked inside the house, took off her coat. "I had to take care of some things. How is your friend?"

"Looks like he's going to pull through. Thank God. A couple more days in the hospital, but that certainly beats the alternative."

"For sure," Nora said, trying her best to keep it together. "I'm glad he's going to be all right. I could see how worried you were."

Adam reached for her arm, looked her in the face. "Hey, you okay?"

She forced a smile even though he was the *last* person she was ready to see at the moment. "I will be," she said.

"You don't sound so sure. Anything I can do? You hungry?"

"No, but thanks."

"A glass of wine, then?"

Her stomach lurched. The mere mention of wine left her needing to sit down. "No…I don't think so. I'm just gonna make some hot tea and head up. Sorry to be a bore. It's been a very long day."

"No big deal. I really should finish changing out the rest of the old light switch cover plates, anyway. Needs to be done." He paused. "Just thought hearing about someone else's day, might be a nice distraction from my own grueling afternoon of waiting rooms and beeping machines and of course, my favorite, the gourmet hospital food." He smiled at her. "The murky green gelatin they tried to pass off as dessert in the cafeteria was truly tempting. Let me tell you."

Nora smiled back. This time it was genuine. Ben's mistake was not Adam's fault, she reminded herself. And she could really use a friend.

"Join me in the tea?" she asked.

"I will," he said. "And I'll even up the ante. I'll throw in some double chocolate chip cookies, how about that?"

Nora felt a tiny laugh escape. "Now we're talking."

Adam followed her into the kitchen and pulled out the container of cookies as Nora heated up water. "So, none of my business," he said, "but the look on your face when you first came in was pretty awful. Is everything really okay?"

The microwave beeped and Nora dunked a tea bag into her cup, sliding Adam's over toward him. She pulled out a barstool and eased down onto it. "Ben and I had a pretty nasty disagreement today."

"Something with the house?" He offered her a cookie, climbed onto the stool next to her.

"No, no. Everything's good here, as far as I know. Mitch said all we have left now are little things. Installing the rest of the trim, paint touch-up in a few places and...well, the heating and air guys have to come out once more at some point. But Mitch and Carlos have worked really hard these past couple weeks to be sure we're ready. And you," she quickly added. "You've been a big help, as well."

"Glad to do it. It's been fun to play a part in this. Can't think of anywhere I'd rather be."

He lifted his cup and drank. "Oh, I almost forgot to tell you. When I called Mitch earlier to ask where he'd stashed the new switch cover plates, he mentioned that he and Carlos won't be here tomorrow, and maybe the next day."

Nora raised a brow. "Really?"

"That's what he said. Some kind of emergency construction job. I told him I'd pass the info on to you."

"Okay, thanks for letting me know."

Adam twisted on his stool to face her directly. "You know, Nora, we didn't get to finish our conversation the other night. The house, the weird things I've been hearing. Do you remember what I'm talking about?"

She remembered, all right. How could she forget? "Yeah, I guess you're right, we never did."

"I hope I didn't make you uneasy. Just wondered if you'd had anything odd happen, that's all."

His statement almost made her laugh out loud. She'd had enough crazy things happen to her since she'd moved in, to fill an entire trilogy.

She thought of Lucy's journal.

Nora met Adam's gaze, held it. She had intended to tell Ben about the journal as well as her suspicions involving the house... but that had all changed in a matter of minutes earlier. She opened her mouth to speak, deciding to tell Adam instead. And she wouldn't stop herself this time, like she had at the restaurant. It would be a monumental relief to talk with someone who had similar concerns—had experienced it himself.

But almost as soon as Nora started, one of Lucy's comments toward the end of the journal planted itself front and center in her mind. The fear her sister had explicitly expressed of not wanting to share her secret with anyone because the knowledge could be bad for the upcoming business...*very bad*.

"Nora?" he said, leaning toward her.

"Hmm?"

"You were a million miles away there for a minute."

"So sorry. Like I said, I have so much on my mind tonight. You were saying?"

"I was wondering," Adam continued, "if you've noticed any

strange things going on here. I know I joked with you the day we met about the house looking haunted, but I guess the joke's on me because I keep hearing bizarre sounds at night. They haven't stopped. In fact, they're worse."

Nora swallowed back the discomfort his words caused her. "I'm so sorry," she said, keeping her voice steady. "These old houses can really play tricks on the mind. If it's bothering you enough that you want to move out, I completely understand."

"No, I'm good. I don't want you to think I don't appreciate being here or that I'm some kind of coward. It's just that I've always bought in to that kind of thing. You know, purgatory and all. People caught between worlds, so to speak." He attempted a laugh. "I'm just saying there's an unusual feeling here. I notice it more the longer I stay."

"Well, on the off-chance that noises tend to carry more in your room, or it's draftier than the others, maybe you'd rather try a different one. I say have at it, whatever makes you comfortable. And for the record, I don't think you're a coward. Not at all."

Adam hesitated. "One other thing, and I know this is odd, but I keep smelling smoke. So much so, that I've gotten up in the middle of the night to check it out several times, afraid something in the house was on fire. But it's really more like the smoke from a pipe or a cigar. Something like that." He shrugged. "Crazy, I'm telling you..."

Nora stiffened. He'd smelled the cigar smoke. And that made it all the more real. The temptation to tell him everything she knew taunted her once more. She thought of the lilacs. Had he experienced that, as well? She decided it wouldn't raise too much of a red flag to mention it. "It's the flowers I can't figure out," she said.

"Flowers?" he asked, his interest spiked to the point she would have to offer some type of answer.

"Yeah, it's no big deal, but I've smelled the strong fragrance of lilacs up on the third floor several times. A few other places, too.

But mostly up there. And don't get me wrong," she added, "it's a beautiful smell. I've always loved lilacs. We used to have a bush in our yard growing up. It's just that it comes on strong all of a sudden, and then it's gone. I always wonder where it's coming from."

The color drained from Adam's face. "*Lilacs?* Are you sure?" he asked.

"There's no mistaking it," Nora said, surprised by the reaction her comment had evoked. "Is something wrong?"

"No," he mumbled. "It's just strange, that's all."

He stood up from the stool abruptly. "You know, Nora, I hate to cut out on you, but the long day has finally caught up with me. Think I'm going to call it a night."

"Oh," she replied. She wondered what she'd done wrong. "Okay, then. Well, I hope you can get some sleep. Thanks for hanging out with me."

He nodded and quickly carried his cup to the sink. "Thanks for the tea. Good night then."

"Good night."

Nora watched him disappear around the corner before standing. She had no idea what had just happened, but somehow she felt even more unsettled now, than she did when she'd walked in the front door earlier.

She wiped off the counter and headed upstairs, beyond ready to throw in the towel on the whole day.

As Nora climbed into bed, her mind spun with thoughts of Ben.

What had he seen—*had he misinterpreted*—that turned him against her? She'd searched her memory over and over for any possible causes, coming up empty.

Her head hurt again. Between the final remnants of her

illness, and now the insanity of being accused of sleeping with Adam. She needed to close her eyes and shut her mind off. Maybe a day or two would bring answers, as well as an apology from Ben. At least she hoped so.

She shifted to her stomach and fluffed the pillow, tried to sleep. But a new myriad of thoughts swam at her, including the notion that she had to address all of the terrifying occurrences with the house, and fix them, before the fifteenth of December. Even if it meant finding a priest or an agency or *whoever a person hired* to come figure it out and put an end to the madness.

～

HE STOOD over Nora with a growing boldness, her eyelids fluttering as she dreamed. He hadn't intended to stay long. But the need to see her, to study her—to be in control of what seemingly would not be controlled—had invited him to linger.

She slept peacefully before him, her body relaxed, vulnerable. Oblivious to what was in store. He could strike at any moment, and she wouldn't know what hit her. Soon, he reminded himself. *Very soon.*

The time had finally come to set things in motion. The victory would be in the end result, of course, still he couldn't help but salivate over the coming game that would take them there.

He looked at the clock on the dresser and stepped closer to her, brushing a thumb across the silk of her nightshirt and down the edge of her arm until she moved slightly against his touch. Once he was satisfied that she'd taken the bait, he drew his hand away and melted back into the house once again.

～

SLEEP HAD PULLED her in so deep that Nora barely noticed the soft caress at first. She rolled over and traced a hand across the pillow opposite her, reaching for Ben, wanting more. Still lost somewhere between the webbing of dreams and reality.

But reality quickly sunk its teeth in.

Ben was not there. And someone had touched her. Briefly, yes, but still a touch. Nora's eyes shot open, searching the black expanse of the bedroom.

"*Nora...*"

The whisper of her name made her blood seize in her veins. She jerked her head toward the hallway.

"Adam?" she called. "Is that you?" She waited, her words hanging in the air. "Adam?"

She hadn't imagined it. Not only had she heard someone call to her, but someone or something had touched her.

Had actually *touched* her.

And that changed everything. It was playing with her, and she was suddenly, terrifyingly aware of the potential for it to be a very dangerous game.

A crash from upstairs thundered through the house.

Nora stifled a scream and plunged a hand through the antique fringe of the bedside lamp. Twisted it on. Nothing. She twisted it again and again, getting the same result.

The crash came once more. She looked at the ceiling, worried about Adam. She had to get upstairs to check on him. But just as Nora aimed her attention to the third floor, a slamming sound shot up from the first floor below her.

The kitchen.

It sounded as if the cabinets were being slammed shut one after another, each bang bulleting up through the house like gunshots.

Her focus torn between the first and third floor, Nora tried to breathe, tried to make sense of anything that was happening. This wasn't a dream. She could feel, she could hear, she could see. She was excruciatingly aware of everything going on around her.

She fumbled for the flashlight she'd made a habit of keeping on the nightstand, but it was nowhere to be found. She shoved a hand out farther to sweep the area again, cursing out loud as she knocked the lamp backward and down behind.

Nora stopped. Footsteps approached in the distance, and it sounded as if they were coming down the hallway toward her room. "Adam," she cried. Desperate for the steps to be his. But they were heavy, slow. Not the sound of someone rushing to answer her pleas.

She called out once more, her voice bolder this time. But again, no answer. Just the continued banging downstairs in maddening harmony with the approach of whatever was coming down the hallway.

Her heart springing forward in her chest, she made a split-second decision. She would fight. But as she leapt out of bed, not knowing yet where she was leaping to, she caught her ankle on the side rail and fell hard, cracking her head on the edge of the nightstand.

A rush of wet warmth raced across the right side of her temple. The room now a twirling and twisting merry-go-round. It spun around Nora as her focus began to drift further and further away. She reached up to her head, overcome by the sensation that it was just out of reach.

She tried to come up with a new plan, but the agonizing sound of the bedroom door creaking open stopped her cold. *Please let it be someone to help me*, her mind begged.

But it wasn't help.

Instead, it was what she'd feared most. The shadow loomed in the darkness, waiting. She could sense it as much as see it.

Nora couldn't move.

She blinked her eyes once and then again, her mind beginning to set adrift out over a dark and quiet sea. It was then that she realized she must have hit her head much harder than she'd thought.

She blinked her eyes one last time, and as the room began to fade out of sight, the shadow moved across the threshold. Slowly, purposefully.

Somewhere in the distance, in the very outskirts of her mind, her conscious pleaded with her to get up, try to fight, scream, do *something*. But it was no use. The concussion wove its spell around her, pulling her down and down into the darkness. Slowly spinning her into its web, until there was nothing.

CHAPTER TWENTY-TWO

"Nora!"

Her eyes fluttered open.

Adam knelt over her, a frantic look on his face. "Are you okay?"

"I'm not sure," she mumbled. She winced as she lifted a hand to her head, pulling back a blood-tinged finger.

"You're bleeding," he said as he helped her to a sitting position.

She steadied herself. "What about you? Are you all right?"

"Yeah, I'm fine," he said. "It's you that has me worried. What's going on here?"

Fragments of what had just happened danced in her mind and she struggled to piece them together, her mouth gaping as she remembered. "Something touched me," she blurted. She quickly scanned the room. "I remember now. I was asleep, but it felt so real it woke me." She stopped for a moment, her heart still banging in her chest. "And then I saw something. At least I thought I did—"

"I saw it, too."

Nora locked eyes with Adam. "What do you mean?"

"It was dark, but it was almost like something was hovering over you."

Nora swallowed hard. "What do you mean by *hovering*?"

"I know it sounds unreal, but to tell you the truth, it looked unreal. I swear I've never seen anything like that before. Ever."

"I tried to get your attention," she said, taking the hand he offered, to pull herself up from the floor. "I called out your name as soon as I heard footsteps."

"I know. I was in my room and I tried to get to you, but my door was jammed—like it was locked, *but from the outside*. It was crazy, Nora. I finally took a chair and knocked it against the handle. Afraid I may owe you a new one."

Nora looked up, suddenly aware the lights were back on. "I swear a few minutes ago these lights weren't working."

"They weren't," Adam echoed. "When I got down here the whole second floor was dark. Power finally came back on a couple minutes after I found you."

"I have no idea what to even say right now. I don't understand what just happened."

A steady stream of blood made its way down Nora's cheek. Adam brushed her hair back enough to get a better look. "Oh, man, it looks like you sprang a pretty good leak."

"Yeah," she said, the pain of the laceration starting to sink in.

"I'm sure it hurts, but I'm hoping it's more of a superficial wound. Let's get that bleeding stopped before we do anything else."

He helped her downstairs, where she sat at the bay window seat in the kitchen while he went for the first-aid kit. She looked at the clock on the wall. It was just after five a.m., and there was zero chance she would be sleeping any more now.

Coffee. It might at least help.

Nora's hands shook as she reached into the cabinet above the sink for the container of coffee. She couldn't stop entertaining the idea that something had made these very same cabinets slam wildly only moments ago. "Stop. Just stop," she commanded. She was angry with herself, angry with everything.

"Were you talking to someone?"

Nora jumped as she noticed Adam behind her.

"Just myself," she said, unable to even attempt a smile. "Think I'm probably about ready for a padded room somewhere."

NORA NURSED a second cup of strong black coffee and popped in another round of pain relievers. She'd tried to lay back down, rest a while, but finally decided to get up and get dressed. Moving on with the day was the only thing that was going to keep her from completely losing it. She opened the closet door and rummaged through her clothes, but as she stepped into the edge of the darkness to reach for a sweater, she remembered the night before. She froze as images of herself on the floor, desperate and bleeding, played through her mind like a movie. How she'd cried for help. How whatever had been there with her in the darkness had been in control. *And when would it decide to strike again?* Fear reached down inside Nora, twisting her in its bony grip. She spun around to scan the room behind. But there was nothing there. Only the warm splash of sunlight spilling onto the hardwood floor from the bedroom window.

Another thought forced its way into her mind, pushing everything else out. The journal. The unimagined connection to Lucy. The last words from her sweet sister.

Nora wiped a tear away and pulled on her jeans, a barrage of questions demanding answers shifting in her mind like an insane puzzle.

Lucy had experienced many of the exact same things that she had, which meant Nora was not crazy. That was good. But it also meant that *something* was in a cutthroat battle against her and her sister, and Nora was the only one left standing. Her head pounded. Oh, how she wanted to wipe all of this away. Start with a clean slate. She was tired of footsteps and voices, slamming doors and the scent of lilacs. Tired of being wedged between the urge to say to hell with it all, running as fast as she could in the opposite direction and, equally, the desire to stay and answer the unanswerable. The *need* to see all of this through.

She looked over at the bed, her skin crawling as she recalled the feeling of being touched while she'd slept there the night before. She quickly turned away and walked to the dresser, worry creasing her features. How could she go up against something like this all alone? But then her eyes came to rest on the bible her grandmother had given her. Nora smoothed a finger over the front cover, the pages frayed at the edges from her habitual reading of it at night when she couldn't sleep. She picked it up, the story of David and Goliath entering her mind. Nora stood there for a long moment, thinking. The realization that even a giant of epic proportions could be taken down by a single person armed with only a tiny pebble—*given enough determination*—shifted something inside her.

She laid the bible back down and looked toward the bed again. Anger battled fear. She'd been harassed enough. She was finished being afraid. There was no way in hell she planned on living the rest of her days like this.

"*Enough*," she said out loud, an inner strength rising up. She was ready to fight. To end this. She would do it not only for herself, but for Lucy, too. She'd never been more determined. All she needed...*was to find the right pebble*. And she planned to do exactly that.

She finished getting dressed and turned to leave. She wanted answers about the house. Wanted them now.

She hurried down the stairs and snatched up her keys.

"Are you going somewhere?" Adam hollered, rushing down the stairs behind her.

"Yes," she said. "I'm going to end this."

He looked at her as if she'd lost her mind.

"The library is my first stop. I won't rest until I know the complete history of this house. From the moment the foundation was poured until the day I walked in the door. Every person who's lived here, died here, everything that's ever happened here. *Everything*."

Nora yanked her coat on. "My next stop?" she scoffed. "Probably a church. I have a feeling we're going to need a priest."

"Do you really think you should be doing all of that in your condition? You took a bad fall last night. I'll go for you. Just let me grab my wallet."

"I'm fine, Adam. This can't wait a minute longer. And if I don't get anywhere with the library or the priest, I'm going to the police." She paused. "I owe you an apology, by the way. I had decided not to tell you, but actually there have been quite a few odd things happening around here for a while. Pretty much off and on since I moved in. I found out yesterday that it happened to my sister, too. But now it's escalating. Last night was by far the worst. I should have made you aware, I see that now. I'm very sorry."

"Oh, man. How can you want to live here like this?" he asked. "That was some crazy shit last night. No one in their right mind would blame you if you were trolling the yellow pages for a Realtor this morning."

She planted her feet. "I'm not going anywhere, but whatever has been preying on this place, preying on my sister and me, *will be* when I'm finished."

He moved closer. "I understand that you're upset, but you were out cold just a few hours ago. Should you even be driving? Maybe we should take you over to the hospital to get checked out first."

"Not going to happen, but thank you." She reached for the front door handle, stopping for a moment to look at him. "And I'll completely understand if you're gone when I get back. If things were different I'd probably race you to the door, myself. But this house was my sister's whole life, and now it's become mine, too. I've made my decision and nothing will chase me away. Still, I can't open this place up to the public until this is over and done. So, even if I have to cancel a dozen reservations in the process. This stops now. Period."

"Understood. But let me do the running for you. You need rest. It's the least I can do to help after you've let me stay here."

She opened her mouth to object, but a tap on the door drew her attention. She looked through the glass to see Liz.

Nora swung the door open.

"Good morning," Liz said brightly, her tone changing as she noticed Nora's head. "What in the world happened to you?"

"I'm all right, just a bump," Nora answered, wanting to leave for town sooner than later. "Hey, I'd love to talk to you, but I'm on my way out. Can I come by your house later? I know we have a lot to catch up on."

"Of course you can, but first you have to at least tell me what happened to you. You look terrible. I came over to check on you and see if you'd talked to Ben, but now you have me worried. Is everything okay?"

Nora sighed. Who was she kidding? She wanted to let Liz in on everything, needed her support. "No, it's really not. Nothing's okay anymore." She felt tears form, denied them.

Liz peeked over Nora's shoulder. "Oh, Adam. I didn't see you back there."

Adam tossed her a wave, then slid his hands into his front pockets and edged out of the conversation. "Nora, I'll give you a minute. But talk to me before you leave."

Liz grabbed her arm as Adam disappeared. "Okay, now spill. What happened to your head? And why do you look like hell?"

"I'll explain more when I have a chance to sit down with you, but I will say that something's not right here. There've been some things happening in the house that—" Nora stopped. If she went any further, Liz would press her for more details, and she couldn't take the time for that before she'd gotten some answers herself.

"What things? I can tell by the look on your face that you're upset. Can I help? Does this have anything to do with Ben?"

Nora stepped out onto the front porch, pulling the door closed behind her. "I think it's over with him."

Liz's eyebrows shot up.

"But I can't talk about it right now, or I'll lose it again. I was out-of-my-mind upset last night. It was all I could think about, until something horrible happened and I ended up hitting my head and blacking out and—"

"You passed out?" Liz asked, startled. "And what horrible thing happened? What is going on here?"

Desperate to keep the momentum she'd found, the last thing Nora wanted to do was talk any longer. But she'd already said too much. Liz was in too far now, and she knew she'd have to give her something before she'd let Nora leave. "Ben doesn't even know this, but there have been some *occurrences* over the last few weeks that..." She honestly didn't know how to make it sound any less absurd. "First, let me say I know this sounds unbelievable, but things have been moving around in the house. And there've been bizarre noises, slamming doors in the night, with no obvious explanation. And last night, someone or something..."

"What?" Liz gaped. "Someone or something what?"

"Touched me."

Liz grasped Nora's hand. "Are you kidding me? What are you saying? That you think Black Willow is haunted?"

"I don't know what I'm saying. There are too many things I can't explain, and last night sealed the deal. My first instinct was to leave. To move away now that Ben..." She trailed off. "But my life is here; I feel close to Lucy here. It's what I want. And that's enough to make me stay. But I have to put a stop to this insanity before it goes any further. I mean, the little things have been bad enough, but when it actually touched me, I—"

"The dead don't touch people, Nora...*the living do*. You should call the police."

"I did consider it, and I may still contact them, but what would I say? That someone nudged me while I slept? And then banged a few kitchen cabinets around before they left...leaving the doors locked from the inside on their way out? No, I don't think the police are the ones to call for this kind of thing. Not yet, anyway. Although, I'm sure it would make for some great laughs around the water cooler at the station."

Nora dropped her hands to her sides. "I don't know, Liz," she added, "if the Underground Railroad entrance wasn't blocked off, maybe I would be more inclined to think it was a person. That would make some kind of terrifying sense, but it's—"

"Wait, what? Underground Railroad?"

Liz's mouth hung open.

"I haven't had a chance to tell you yet," Nora explained, "but yes, this house was a part of the Underground Railroad. I know it sounds unreal. But the access was in the attic and it's sealed up tight. I saw it myself, so I don't think that has anything to do with this."

"You have to tell Ben all of this today," Liz commanded. "Immediately."

"He gave his key back to me yesterday," Nora said, her voice low. "And that speaks volumes about how much he would not want me to call him right now." She looked at her watch. "I really have to go, Liz. But don't worry. Everything will be okay. I'm not giving up until I figure this out and beat it. I'll stop by your house later tonight, to talk more, if that's all right."

Liz hugged her tight. "I'm counting on it. There is a lot to say."

"There is," Nora agreed, thinking of Ben again. "There definitely is."

CHAPTER TWENTY-THREE

Ben threw his bag into the back seat and climbed behind the wheel of the truck, flipping the headlights on. He'd worn the floor thin all day, thinking about Nora, tormented by the uncertainty of how to undo what he'd done. Eventually, he'd decided to head back to Connecticut for a day or two while he sorted things out. But now, as his foot hovered over the accelerator...he wasn't so sure. The strange feeling he'd been unable to shake since he'd gotten back into town, had blossomed into an unbearable case of unease, of worry. And though he didn't understand why, the sensation had grown strong enough to keep him from leaving Marietta.

He reached to turn off the ignition, hesitating as his cell phone rang. He leaned over to see Liz's name, then swiped it on and lifted it to his ear.

"Oh, Ben, thank God I got you," she said. "I've been trying to call you for hours."

"Liz, I—"

"I know you may be angry with me for talking to Nora, but don't hang up. I really need to talk to you about something."

"I'm not," he managed to slip in. "Angry with you, I mean. You were right, I should have gone and talked to her, let her have a chance to explain. I'm sorry for—"

"We can do the apologies later. I need to tell you something."

"What's wrong?" he asked.

Liz's tone was ice cold. "I think Nora's in trouble."

"What do you mean? What kind of trouble?"

"From what she told me, something is very, very wrong at Black Willow. Someone has been in the house wreaking all kinds of havoc. Terrorizing her. I don't know, but she's convinced the place is haunted. Which I can see how easy it would be to think that about the house, as spooky as it is. But when I saw her this morning, she told me that something was in her room last night and she felt it touch her. *Touch her.* Then she fell and hit her head and God knows what else."

"What?"

"Yes. I'm telling you she looked awful. Her temple was bandaged up. She looked like she hadn't slept in days. I got a terrible vibe about the whole thing and I told her I thought she should call the police, but I couldn't convince her. And I know you broke it off, she told me that much. But I'm telling you, if you love her, or have ever loved her, Ben, put whatever has happened between you two on the back burner and check on her so—"

"Where is she?" he cut in. "*Where is Nora now?*"

"I honestly don't know. Several hours ago, she said she had some things to take care of, but I haven't talked to her since. And her phone is missing, so I can't call her."

"I'm on my way."

Ben jabbed at the end button, tires squealing as he backed out of the drive. He aimed for the farm, clutching the steering wheel with such force that his knuckles turned white. He'd known something was off. *Damn.* Why hadn't he followed his gut?

Thoughts barreled at him. The cornfield at the Halloween party, the footprints in the snow, Nora's belief that she'd heard someone lurking time and again. What if she'd been right?

Guilt washed over him, seeping into every pore.

Ben didn't believe in ghosts or hauntings or spirits...but he believed in bad people. And as his mind raced to uncover who might want to frighten Nora—to terrorize her—a new thought struck him. He remembered back to Lucy's string of nasty run-ins with Black Willow's previous owner. Ben hadn't thought about it for a long time because the guy had been quiet ever since Nora had moved in.

Maybe too quiet.

But if it *was* the previous owner, how had he been getting in and out of the house unnoticed by anyone? Then it hit Ben—and the thought made his blood run cold. When he'd suggested to Nora that there might be more tunnels...had he been right? Tunnels that only someone who'd lived there for years might know of? It was a long shot, but Ben had to check it out.

After what Liz had just told him, he was convinced there was a very real possibility that this psychopath was stalking Nora like prey. And if he was right, which he hoped to God he wasn't, she was likely in grave danger.

NORA PACED across the library foyer, focused, driven. She was beyond ready to get the packet that Mrs. Krenshaw had said she'd have someone set aside for her. She couldn't wait to dive in, get to work.

She looked up at the giant antique clock on the wall. It was now minutes until closing time.

She'd gone straight there from Black Willow hours ago, but when she'd arrived the teenage girl behind the counter had cheerfully—a little too cheerfully for Nora's mood—asked her to come back later, once she'd been able to get in touch with Mrs. Krenshaw regarding the whereabouts of the packet.

A good opportunity, Nora had decided, to find a store where

she could pick up a temp phone. But she'd had to drive all the way into Lancaster, which had eaten up the remainder of the afternoon. Dusk was falling fast now.

The longer she stood there waiting for someone to return to the front desk, the longer she had to wonder if Adam had been hurt when he realized that she'd slipped out earlier. She regretted it now, and hoped she hadn't come across too rude, but he'd been so persistent in his notion that she should take the day to rest. And that just wasn't going to happen.

She looked up as the same girl from earlier walked toward her.

"Hi, there," she greeted. "I hope you weren't waiting too long. I am so sorry. I had to run to the back for what I thought was only going to be a second, and then someone asked me how to use the copy machine, but I'd forgotten to change out the ink and then I couldn't find the refill and..."

She stopped, drew in a long, slow breath and smiled sheepishly at Nora. "My Grandma Evelyn says sometimes I tend to ramble. Sorry."

"Evelyn is your grandmother?" Nora asked.

The girl nodded.

"So, did you happen to get ahold of her about the packet?"

"Oh," she said with a giggle. "Yes, I did."

Nora watched her rummage through some papers on a shelf.

"Here you go," she said, pushing a thick manila envelope toward Nora. "Grandma said she figured you'd want to talk to her in person at some point, once you'd gone over things. Her cell number is there for you."

Nora smiled. "Thank you very much. And please tell Evelyn I appreciate her getting all of this together for me. More than she knows."

～

THE SUV SLOWED to a crawl across from the library. He drew

Nora into his sights. Her incredible figure and long legs made her easy to spot among the small-town scene.

"*Son of a bitch.*" He slammed his fist down on the console with a strength that nearly dented it. His eyes narrowing as he realized what this meant.

"Now look what you've done," he whispered as he watched her unlock her car door. "You had to go and make it hard, make more work for me. Well, guess what, whore? I'm still one step ahead of you."

He searched the jacket in the seat next to him for his phone. "Guess it's time for plan B. Good thing I took the time to make one."

He eased the SUV farther up the street, where Nora pulled her car into a gas station. He stole one last glance at her as she climbed out of the car and lifted the pump.

"You know," he said. "I had a feeling you might be more of a problem than your sister was, and as usual, I was right. You'll be sorry, though. Trust me on that."

He sped away from the curb, dialing the phone as he did.

BEN'S TRUCK flew up the hill to Black Willow, a trail of dust and gravel spraying behind him. He didn't know what to expect. He just wanted to find Nora, get her the hell away from there and then go for the police.

He skidded to a stop in front of the house, his heart sinking as he noticed Nora's car wasn't there. He pulled around back, finding a car he'd never seen before. *Adam*, he assumed. Ben's chest hurt.

To hell with it. He yanked the gearshift up, parking right where he was. He walked around the side of the house and up onto the front porch. Since the jackass was there, maybe he would at least know where Nora had gone.

Ben knocked on the door.

No answer.

He peered through the window, scanning the parlor, then the library. A flash of movement caught his eye. Someone was definitely there. He wrapped his hand around the door handle and twisted, but it was locked tight. He knocked again.

"Hello?" he yelled. "I'm looking for Nora. It's Ben Whitfield. Come on, open up!"

Something wasn't right. He balled up his fist and pounded this time, hating himself for giving his key back to Nora.

He circled back around the side of the house again, looking in every window he came to. A sick feeling crept into his bones. He'd seen someone inside, so why the hell wasn't that person coming to the door? He decided to try the front door once more and break it down if he had to. He raced back up the front steps and reached to knock, his hand freezing in midair. The front door was now cracked open a tiny bit.

"Hello?" Ben called as he pushed it farther open. He yelled Nora's name, already knowing full well she wouldn't answer.

"Down here," a male voice called in the distance.

Ben moved quickly toward the cellar door, which stood ajar. He leaned into the darkness. "Who's there?"

"You're looking for Nora?"

Ethan. Ben recognized the voice now. But why was he here? He was supposed to be away at the funeral. He shoved the question aside for the time being, focusing on finding Nora. That was all that mattered.

"Yes. I need to talk to her right now," Ben said, his feet nearly tripping beneath him as he moved down the cellar stairs two at a time. "It's really important. I don't know what's going on, but I think the previous owner of this place may be causing some issues. I have a feeling the son of a bitch is off his rocker."

Ben blinked several times, trying to let his eyes adjust to the darkness. He stepped toward the wall, feeling for the light switch. Once he found it he flipped it several times, but nothing happened. "What's up with the lights? It's pitch black down here. Ethan?"

A figure appeared in the far corner of the cellar.

"Oh, good, you are here," Ben said. "I thought I was losing it there for a second. So, do you know where she is, or not? I'm in a huge hurry."

The figure made no sound or movement.

"Ethan? What is going on?"

Again, there was only an eerie silence.

"Answer me," Ben demanded, a surge of caution washing over him like a tidal wave.

It was then that Ethan's voice broke the silence, but to Ben's surprise, it didn't come from the figure standing in front of him. *It came from behind*. Ben whirled around, completely caught off guard.

"See, I told you he would eventually come down here," Ethan stated proudly.

"I guess you were right," a second man's voice chimed in from across the cellar—where Ben had originally thought Ethan was standing. "I underestimated his stupidity. My mistake."

"What the hell?" Ben whispered, his mind racing to catch up.

The strike of a match cut through the darkness, the second man lighting a kerosene lantern.

Ben tried to get a look at the face, but before he could turn— before he could even form his next thought—Ethan lunged toward him with an iron fireplace poker, crashing it down on Ben's skull.

Ben tumbled down, pain seizing his whole body as his face greeted the rough cement floor. He struggled to get up, but any hope of that was shattered as the poker came down on him once more, twice more, until he felt a river of blood rushing from his head. He drew in all of the breath his lungs would allow and tried his best to swing at Ethan. Missed, tried again.

Ethan chuckled, delivering a swift kick to Ben's stomach. He crouched down beside him. "I'm guessing by now you're regretting your decision to come out here tonight. And to be honest, dealing with you wasn't on my agenda. But this is the kind of thing that happens when you can't keep your nose out of other people's business. See?" Ethan shrugged. "Now I can't let you live."

Ben moaned in pain as he struggled to move. In the flicker of the lantern light, he could see a void in the wall just beyond him, where he'd known there used to be a set of shelves. *A tunnel*, he realized.

Ethan cleared his throat. "Thanks for hiring me, by the way. It's been great being in such close proximity to Nora. Very helpful."

Through the agonizing throb in his skull, Ben thought of her. "Oh, God," he whispered. "*Nora.*"

"Oh, don't worry about her, lover boy. We'll take good care of her. That's a promise. I hope she doesn't take too long getting back here, though. Don't want her to be late for the party."

Ethan's mystery guest stepped out of the shadows and walked toward Ben.

"Oh, I'm so sorry," Ethan said with a smile. "Where are my manners? This is my brother, Adam."

Ben's head swam. The figure across the room had been Adam? And Adam was Ethan's *brother?* He cursed himself for not realizing sooner that Ethan was dangerous.

"Anyway," Ethan continued, "where was I?" He snapped his fingers. "Ah, yes, I was about to tell you how much I've enjoyed the time alone with Nora these past two weeks. I believe Adam here would agree with me. Many thanks for that." He checked the time. "She should be joining us soon. Quite soon, actually, so we need to finish this up."

Ben tried to piece it together in his mind, the entire picture beginning to make some sort of sick and twisted sense. The two brothers, the hidden tunnels, all of the terrifying things that had been happening to Nora. And to Lucy. There had been no accident in the icehouse that day six months ago. Ethan and Adam had killed her in cold blood. He'd bet his life on it.

Ben pushed himself up onto his haunches. "You'll never get away with all of this."

Ethan's face twisted into a grin. "You mean like I *didn't get away* with beating the hell out of your father in Connecticut a few weeks ago?"

Ben froze.

"Surprised?" Ethan asked. "Thought you might be. No hard feelings, though. Just something that needed to be done to keep you busy for a while. And as you can see now, you should have stayed gone."

Ben struggled to stand, fully prepared to kill Ethan with his bare hands, but the room spun wildly in and out of reach. "What did you say?"

Ethan clucked his tongue. "Pretty sure you heard me the first time, but if you need me to repeat it, I'd certainly be glad to." He paused. "And since we're on the topic, just how is dear old Dad holding up? He must have been in pretty bad shape."

"You son of a bitch, I'll kill you!" Ben shouted, using every last bit of strength to grasp for any part of Ethan's body.

But Ethan anticipated it and leapt out of the way, kicking Ben hard in the small of his back.

"Ethan, enough, okay?" Adam yelled. "Nora's going to be back any minute. We need to move on."

"Don't be a coward, Adam. You're the one who wanted him out of the picture so you could have your chance with her."

"Yes. A chance to convince her to leave, which I would have done. We agreed that you wouldn't get rid of her, like you did Lucy." He stared at Ethan. "You know Nora would have eventually left. She practically had one foot out the door. I just needed a little more time. But you had to screw with her, play your damn games."

"She wasn't leaving, and you know it," Ethan shot back. He took a step toward Adam. "Now it's time to finish, and we'll do it my way."

~

ADAM KNEW what Ethan was capable of. His brother was a poison he could neither control nor abandon. There was very little hope of saving Nora.

He looked at Ben, who lay motionless, even as Ethan kicked him again. "What are we going to do with him now?" Adam asked.

"Get rid of him," Ethan said, eyeing Adam. "What did you think we were going to do with him, little brother? Huh? Let him go so he could call in a stream of red and blue lights blazing up the drive?"

Adam knew Ethan was right. "Then what's the plan?"

"Please..." Ben rasped as he lay in the fetal position between them. "Just don't hurt Nora—"

Ethan dug the poker into Ben's back, grinding down on his shoulder blade. "Nora is no longer your concern."

Adam watched as Ethan leaned over Ben's body, the iron poker poised for one last life-ending thrust, but the distant sound of a car pulling up outside jerked him to a halt.

"She's here," Adam choked out.

"Shit," Ethan said looking down at Ben. "His truck is still up there."

Adam started toward the stairs. He hadn't wanted it to go like this. "I'll find a way to get her out of here for a few minutes while you—"

"No," Ethan hissed with enough voltage to stop Adam dead in his tracks. "You stay down here. I'll take the south passage to the river and come back around to the front. I'll handle things from there. I told you, we'll do it my way now. Do you understand me?

We don't have much time." He turned toward the tunnel. "Just shut Ben up and get rid of him for now. I'll finish it later if you don't have the balls."

"What are you going to do? With Nora, I mean," Adam asked.

"You'll see."

"But—"

"Shut your face and do what I tell you."

Adam glared at Ethan, but did as his older brother ordered. *Just like he always had.*

CHAPTER TWENTY -FOUR

Nora's breath caught in her throat as she spotted the corner of Ben's truck parked out back. Her heart flooded with equal parts of joy and concern.

Why had he come?

Was it to make amends? She hoped with all her heart that was the case. To hold her and cover her in kisses, tell her how wrong he'd been. Her bitterness had faded. Whatever he thought he'd seen, he'd believed himself justified. They could work it out, if given the chance. She knew they could.

She turned off the ignition and grabbed the packet from the seat next to her, surprised to find the house completely dark. Where was Ben?

She walked around back only to find his truck empty. Cringing as she noticed Adam's car next to it. Ben had come to talk to her, but had found Adam there instead. She prayed that hadn't made things worse.

Nora looked around the yard, straining to see what she could by the light of the moon. There was absolutely no sign of Ben. She climbed the front steps and headed into the house, confused when she found no trace of anyone at all.

The first floor was eerily quiet. "Ben?" she called, slipping her car keys into her pocket and tossing the library packet onto the kitchen counter. She began a room-to-room sweep of the downstairs. "Adam?" She leaned against the stairway banister and looked up. "Anyone? Hello?"

It dawned on her that she had a phone again. She pulled it out and dialed Ben. No answer. She tried Adam. Again, no answer.

Bewildered, she walked back into the kitchen, saw the packet. Nora opened it and slid out the contents.

The top page was a note from Mrs. Krenshaw with her phone number scratched on the upper right-hand corner. Nora pulled out a barstool and began to read.

> **Nora,**
>
>   *I'm sorry to have dropped the ball a bit with this, but I'm finally feeling better now and ready to help.*
>
>   *This envelope has everything I could lay hands on, but I do remember some things I think you'll find of considerable interest that didn't make it into the newspapers. I haven't thought about any of this for years, until you called. What a sad leap back in time.*
>
>   *Again, please feel free to contact me.*

Nora laid the note aside and skimmed through the clippings. "Bingo," she said. The first news article was regarding the fire. She quickly read it and then shuffled through the stack of papers to the next headline.

> **Tragedy strikes Black Willow Farm again as we lose yet two more of our own**

She clutched the edge of the newspaper, shocked at the dynamic the long awaited packet was setting, right off the bat. No wonder strange things were taking place.

She pulled out her phone and dialed Mrs. Krenshaw.

"Hello?"

"Mrs. Krenshaw, it's Nora Bassett."

"Nora, dear, hello."

"I'm so glad you're doing better now," Nora said. "Thank you for the information and for leaving me your number."

"Oh, sure. I'm just sorry it took this long to get it to you, but I'm glad we are finally able to connect."

"Me, too. I haven't read all of it yet. I decided maybe it would be better to talk to you first."

"Not easy stuff to read through, is it? That property of yours caused quite a buzz in the community years back. Made the headlines several times. Mostly for terrible reasons, just terrible. But you know, not many people around here would even know anything of it this many years later. Most folks have either long since moved out of town or passed away. There are only a few of us scattered around who would even know your farm's history unless they had a reason to look."

"I'm sure you're right," Nora said.

"And the two surviving brothers, of course," Mrs. Krenshaw added. "They knew everything that happened out there, and still do, undoubtedly."

"Brothers?" Nora pressed the phone closer.

"Yes, they were still around Marietta somewhere, last I knew. The oldest boy inherited the property by default after both grandparents died." She paused. "Another two notches in that property's belt."

"The grandparents died on the property, too?"

"Afraid so."

"How?" Nora asked.

"Both fell into bad health. No one ever knew exactly what illness they died of, but they passed within months of each other. The older boy couldn't have been much past nineteen or so, but he was named custodian of his younger brother. He raised him.

Just the two of them out there alone on all that property, until they'd whittled away any money that had been left." She paused. "Then it went up for auction. Pretty much common knowledge the bank took it over."

"What happened to the boys?"

"They were forced out, and that big, old house sat vacant up there on the hill forever. Literally years. It was a shame. Pity the two of them couldn't have at least stayed there until it sold."

Nora hung on every word.

"Strange ones they were, but I haven't actually seen them much since they were kids, so who knows now. If you ask me, the poor things never had a chance to know what normal was." She sighed. "And the tragedies out there just continued. I was so sorry to hear about what happened to the poor girl who bought the property before you."

The comment made Nora twinge, but she decided not to muddy the waters by mentioning the connection. There was no reason to. She thought of the tunnels. "Is there anything you can tell me about the Underground Railroad aspect?"

"Oh, yes, of course," Mrs. Krenshaw replied. "After the first time you and I talked, I was so intrigued that I did a little reading. I discovered that back even before my time, Black Willow Farm was regarded with the highest of standards. Godly people, good crops. Pillars of the community, I guess you might say. Not many people even knew or talked about the fact that it had been used quite frequently to hide slaves, helping them to safety during the late 1800s."

Nora cut in. "My contractor found the entrance you mentioned. It was sealed up tight."

"Actually, dear," Mrs. Krenshaw wavered, "I found it recorded —and I highlighted it somewhere in your information there— that somewhere under that giant house, and likely throughout, there's a honeycomb of tunnels and passageways. A good bit more extensive than I first told you."

"What?" Nora couldn't breathe.

"I was just as shocked as you to learn that," Mrs. Krenshaw said. "But like I told you earlier, at one time Black Willow Farm was a main hub on the railroad. One of those tunnels used to lead all the way back toward the Susquehanna River, offering a perfect way for the slaves to travel unseen." She cleared her throat, took a sip of something. "Once they got to the river, they were nearly home free."

"How could I live here and not know any of this?"

"Well, how would you know, if it's all been blocked off and sealed up for countless years? Probably been that way since they remodeled after the fire."

"I guess so," Nora mumbled. "Speaking of the fire, do you know any other details about it?"

"Not too much. But it was the first of the *happenings,* as I've come to call them. There's a news clipping among your papers that gives some explanation."

Nora flipped through the pages until she came to an article from thirty years before. She scanned the first few lines, her heart aching as it recounted the gruesome details of an accidental fire caused by a six-year-old boy. A fire in which he was found solely responsible for the death of his own mother.

The article went on to say that the dead mother left behind the six-year-old boy and his brother, who were placed in the custody of their grandparents, James and Nola Rutherford, the proprietors of Black Willow Farm.

"It was such a shame," Mrs. Krenshaw said, making Nora jump. "My husband and I knew of the Rutherfords early on. We knew they'd been estranged from their daughter for years, furious with her over the way she'd gotten pregnant by some ne'er-do-well when she was a junior in high school. Back then, that was a pretty big blow to a family. Especially one like theirs."

She paused for a moment. "You know, it was obvious to anyone who paid attention that James Rutherford was a hard man, cold. Terribly strict on his daughter's two illegitimate boys when she finally brought them back home with her. But before those babies came along, he was close with his daughter. It just killed him to find out she'd gotten pregnant at sixteen."

"I'm sure," Nora agreed.

"When she found out she was going to have that first child, she ran off. And you know what made her death even more unbearable for her parents? She'd finally come back home after years away, to reunite with them, reclaim some of what they'd lost. By that time, she'd had a second little boy, brought them both with her. Next thing you know, she burned up in that fire."

"Wow," Nora said, shaken. "I can't imagine. How did the fire start?"

"The older of the boys was playing with matches."

"Oh, that poor child," Nora murmured. She thought of the scratches on the bricks in the attic, the single word *mother* repeated over and over. She shuddered. "The mark that kind of thing would leave on a person," she added. "Especially a small child. Being responsible for the death of his mother."

"Oh, honey, I wish I could say that was the end of it, but there's more. The grandfather had a mental breakdown, went crazy. He turned on those boys something terrible. The farm had a few hired hands, and they heard things, saw things. You know how people talk. Word gets around." She let out a low sigh. "I heard that the grandfather made a practice of beating the older boy and locked him away in the attic for days at a time, without food or water, while the grandmother did nothing to stop it. People just didn't intervene back then the way they do now, so those poor children had no choice but to endure."

Nora's heart hurt. "Did the boys go to school?"

"No. They were never allowed."

"How terrible," Nora said. "It's amazing those children even survived—the mental scars that must have left on them."

"I couldn't agree with you more."

"Mrs. Krenshaw," Nora said, "you have shed an unbelievable amount of light on all of this for me. Thank you for your help."

"I'm sorry it wasn't the happy history you might have hoped for. It must be disconcerting for you to find out the property has claimed so many lives. It's almost as if it was built on bad ground, as odd as that sounds."

"Well, thank you again and I hope you continue to feel better."

"You're very welcome. Good luck, Nora."

Nora hung up the phone, a shiver moving through her as she thought of the labyrinth of dark, silent passages beneath and around her. Sealed off like a tomb from the outside world. She thumbed through the next several pages looking for the high-lighted section Mrs. Krenshaw had told her about, but something at the bottom of the third page caught Nora's eye. She blinked her eyes hard, looked again. There, in front of her, was a faded black-and-white photo showing two young boys standing in front of Black Willow. And as she glanced at the first child's face... *she recognized it.*

"No. It can't be," she stammered. But it was. The child on the left was *Ethan.*

She leaned in closer, desperate to be wrong, to have imagined it. He was much younger, yes. And frail, sickly almost. But it was definitely him.

Her mind raced to come up with a benign, logical reason why he would be in a photo in front of her house as a child. But there was none.

Her eyes shifted over to the other child—a younger boy. A brother of Ethan's. And to her disbelief...*it was Adam.* There was no doubt in her mind. If the strong curve of his chin didn't give it away, the small speck of a mole just above the top left corner of his lip did.

She stared down at the pair of names beneath the faces:

Ethan J. Rutherford and James Adam Rutherford, Jr.

The room tilted, spun. *She'd trusted them.* Dear God, how could she have been so stupid—so dangerously naive? All of the times she'd been alone with each of them in the house. The idea of it made her want to scream.

Nora stood and backed away from the counter, thoughts firing at her like red-hot flares.

She yanked her phone up and dialed Ben, commanding him to pick up this time. But he didn't. She bit the edge of her lip until it bled. Where could he be? What if Adam or Ethan had done something to him before she'd arrived? What if he was hurt? *Or worse...*

She rushed up to the second floor, the third and then the attic, checking every place she could think of until she ended up back downstairs in front of the cellar door. It was the only place she had yet to look.

Her pulse racing, Nora pulled the door open and flipped on the light switch, but nothing happened. She grabbed a flashlight from the kitchen and started down the stairs, calling out Ben's name as she went.

Halfway down into the darkness, she decided to dial him one last time. But as soon as Ben's phone rang in her ear, somewhere in the distance another phone began to ring, simultaneously. Nora froze. It was Ben's ringtone.

But it was coming from behind the wall.

She ran down the remainder of the stairs, Ben's voicemail kicking on in her ear. The ringing behind the wall stopped. Nora dialed him again, it immediately started back up. It was his phone all right. She yelled his name again and again, with the cell phone still plastered to her ear. But no answer came. Panic took over. Each time his voicemail kicked on, she tried again, her fingers racing across the dial pad.

Then the line went silent. Her heart dropped into her

stomach as she watched the phone battery blink out. "Damn it," she shrieked, hurling the cell phone toward a stack of boxes. She should have called the police. Now it was too late.

Nora paced back and forth frantically. She knew there must be a hidden passage somewhere. She aimed the flashlight toward the long row of wooden shelves that butted up against the wall. She'd never had any reason to look at them under any kind of scrutiny before. But as she studied them now, she questioned why the far left section was slightly set apart from the rest.

She bolted over to it and pushed against the side, adrenaline surging through her. No luck. She repositioned and pushed again until she was sure the bones in her arms would shatter. But then it occurred to her that maybe she should *pull*.

She stepped back, locked her fingers around the front and pulled as hard as she could, her eyes widening as the wall attached to the section of shelves swung open.

The stench of earth and must rushed past her as it came to a stop.

Nora stared at the black abyss before her, swallowing hard at the unsavory prospect of what might lie in wait in the darkness beyond. But even though every rational part of her screamed to run the opposite direction, the determination to find Ben drove her forward. She gripped the flashlight and moved into the tunnel, sweeping the beam of light back and forth, stopping periodically to call Ben's name.

The farther she walked, the more the realization that she'd been living smack in the middle of a real-life house of horrors, hit home. And her sister had done the same.

Was Black Willow haunted? No. She would bet her life against that notion now. As her mind raced to place each piece of the puzzle, Nora grew more certain that Ethan or Adam, or perhaps both, had contributed to Lucy's death. She knew it in her heart, and once she found Ben and got him safely away, she would see to it that they paid for their crimes. Her sister would have justice.

A noise ahead stopped her dead in her tracks. The heavy rasp of someone breathing. Nora shut off the flashlight and held her own breath, listened.

No other sound accompanied it. Just the labored but steady struggle for air coming from somewhere low to the ground ahead of her. It was Ben. She knew it was. But it was obvious by the sound of it, that he was hurt—at the very least unconscious. And she feared it was much worse than that.

She flipped the flashlight back on and made a mad push farther down the tunnel.

Less than twenty feet ahead and off to the right was another passage. Nora stifled a cry as she found Ben covered in blood and dirt. Breathing, but barely.

CHAPTER TWENTY-FIVE

"Come on, wake up. Wake up, Ben," Nora pleaded. She knelt over him and flashed the light across his body, finding the blood was coming from a wound on his head. Tears of anger and fright spilled down her cheeks. "Please. I need you to open your eyes. Wake up, for God's sake."

Ben stirred slightly, but didn't open his eyes.

"I'm here now," she said close to his ear. "Everything's going to be okay. Do you hear me?" Her voice cracked. The magnitude of the situation threatened to break what was left of her spirit.

She felt his hand touch hers. One eye blinked open.

A warm surge of joy and hope rushed through her. "Ben, thank God. I thought you were—"

"Nora," he whispered, pulling in a shallow breath, and then another. He struggled to focus.

"Did Adam do this to you?" she asked.

"It was Ethan," he said, his voice a little steadier. "Nora, listen to me. He and Adam are—"

"I know they're brothers," she blurted. "I know everything."

Ben squeezed her hand, pulled her closer to him. "They're still here. And they're dangerous."

"They're here now? Both of them?" she asked, panic rising up inside her again. She knew one of them would have been bad enough, but if both of them were on the property at the same time, Nora realized the chances of her and Ben getting away unnoticed had just been slashed in half. "Do you know where they are?"

"No. But they're out for blood."

"Where's your phone?" she asked, searching the adjacent ground. "I heard it ringing, through the wall. It must be close by. If I can find it, I can call for help."

Ben grimaced as he tried to sit up. "I have no idea, but you have to get out of here, Nora. Right now. Do you hear me?"

"Not a chance." She wouldn't leave him. Period. She scanned the darkness ahead and behind. "Can you walk at all?" She offered her hand.

Ben pulled himself up briefly, only to collapse back against the side of the tunnel. "Something's wrong," he whispered, his hand shooting to his temple. "*Really wrong*. Everything's spinning..."

Nora watched in horror as he went into a seizure. "Oh, God, Ben. You're going to be okay." She said the words over and over, as much to herself as to him, until his body calmed and he came back to her.

Ben looked up at her, despair derailing him. "I can't make it. You have to go without me."

"I already told you, I won't leave you."

He squeezed her hand with what little strength he had left.

"Nora," he pleaded. "It's your only hope of surviving this."

"I don't care, Ben. Do you hear me?"

"Okay, then it's *our* only hope of surviving this," he said. "Get to safety and send help back. Ethan and Adam could be here any minute, and we both know it. So, please...go."

He was right. With his head injury, he could have another seizure at any moment. She had to go find help, and fast, if they were to have any hope at all.

She leaned down and pressed a soft kiss on the side of his mouth, her own tears mingling with his. "I'll go, then," she whispered. "But only to bring back help." She grabbed his hands, cupped them firmly in hers. "I'm coming back, I swear." She kissed him again and turned to go.

As she left, Nora breathed a quick prayer that God would keep Ben hidden and safe until she returned with help. Where the help was going to come from, she had no idea. But she would find it, or die trying.

She rushed down the tunnel, hoping that each new arm of the maze, would lead her out of the darkness that had become her worst nightmare.

As she approached an alcove that looked different than the others, Nora slowed. She stepped inside to check for an exit, jerking to a stop as a voice sounded in the main passage behind. Ethan's face flashed through her mind, an army of tiny knives stabbing their way up and down her spine.

"Nora," he called out, with a gentleness that chilled her to the bone.

"Come out, come out, wherever you are. We need to talk."

Nora's eyes darted to a ladder on the back wall. She had no idea where it went, but there was no other choice. She gripped the first rung and bolted up to the top. A flash of her light revealed a tattered wooden hatch above. To her surprise, it pushed easily upward, and within seconds, she'd slipped inside a quiet cramped space.

The ceiling slanted at a sharp angle, forcing her to hunch forward. Cobwebs clinging to every part of her. To her left, Nora noticed tiny pinholes of light shooting through a small section of the wall. *Where was she?* And to her right, another ladder led up. She took several steps over to what appeared to be a strange narrow door. She leaned her ear to the wood. All was quiet. There was no handle to grasp or turn, but with a little shove, it opened.

"Dear God," she whispered. She was staring at the hallway

leading to the kitchen in Black Willow. *She was back inside the house.* Another push of the door quickly put it in place again, and she watched it dissolve back into the ornate wood paneling on the side of the staircase.

The tiny pinhole lights, she realized, had been the hallway light shining through the vintage vent cover attached to the lower part of the wall. Her horror mounted—the hallway and kitchen could easily be seen and heard through the intricate design of the vent, yet the darkness inside the staircase ensured that no one from the outside could see in.

Nora's legs betrayed her, refusing to move.

Snap out of it, her mind pushed.

She raced toward the front door, but stopped dead. It had been bashed in, the lock dangling, ripped from the trim. Someone had come in that way when she was in the tunnel. She made a run for the back door, but heavy footsteps on the basement stairs whipped her attention toward the cellar.

She screamed as she leapt for the door, shoving the slide lock into place.

"Nora!" Ethan growled from the other side. He yanked the handle back and forth, throwing his weight against the door.

Choking back wild fear, she grabbed hold of the sign-in credenza and shoved it with all her might. Ethan exploded into another violent attack against the door.

"*Nora!*" he yelled again over and over as he banged against it.

She scrambled backwards, her eyes wide as she stared at the door, watching in terror as its heavy wooden frame shook against Ethan's strength. She turned and made a run for the back door, tearing at the locks as quickly as her fingers would go. She bolted out into the night. The bite of the cold air dove deep in her lungs, but her adrenaline pumped so hard and fast she barely noticed.

Nora ran. She ran faster than she knew she was even capable of, but all at once a dark figure appeared from the side of the porch and tackled her to the ground.

"No!" Nora screamed, arching backward hard against him. Strong arms closed in around her, clenching her in a vise, pinning her to the ground. She bucked and kicked with all her might, all the while screaming at him to release her.

A hand groped at her mouth attempting to cover it.

"Let me go!" she screamed. She fought blindly against him, the darkness swallowing them both.

He turned, and she saw a glimpse of his face in the moonlight. It was Adam. Nora's breath caught in her throat. Even though she now knew he was the enemy, it seemed impossible that someone she'd shared so much with could be in on her demise.

He grabbed both of her wrists. "Calm down. Please. I'm not going to hurt you."

Adam's grip was firm but not painful, and Nora felt a faint glimmer of hope that maybe, just maybe, he could be reasoned with. She looked up into his face, forcing herself to loosen, knowing that her only hope was to try and connect with him.

Her breathing slowed, and as nauseous as it made her, she allowed him to hold her close for a moment and relaxed in his arms. Her gaze met his, and she softened her voice as much as her fear would allow.

"Adam," she breathed. "I don't understand—"

"*Shh*..." He pressed his finger to her lips. "Just calm down. Let's get you back inside. It's freezing out here." He hoisted her to her feet, hooking his arm under hers in such a way that she knew better than to try to break free.

Dread filled her every pore as she dragged one foot in front of the other back up the stairs and inside the house—led by a madman she'd once called her friend.

She was terrified, furious, utterly violated.

Adam ushered her upstairs to her bedroom, locking it behind them, careful to keep a watchful eye on her every second.

Nora wondered what had become of Ethan. And desperately hoped he hadn't found Ben.

She looked at Adam, but for a long moment, neither said anything.

It was Adam who broke the silence between them. "Nora, I want you to know—"

"*How could you?*" she demanded, her original plan to reason with the enemy momentarily derailed.

Adam walked toward her. "There's a lot you don't know. That you couldn't possibly understand."

"Try me." She failed to hide the bitterness in her voice.

He slid a hand up her forearm to her elbow, his grip once again firm but not painful. He escorted her to the chair, lowered her into it.

"I need you to quiet down and listen. I mean it." He rubbed a hand back and forth across his jaw. "There are circumstances here that you don't know anything about."

Nora was half listening, half searching for a foolproof path of escape from her new prison.

"No matter what has happened...or will happen," he continued, "I want you to know that I do care about you."

Her mouth went dry. What *will* happen? Oh God, what did that mean?

She focused on his face, pushing the what-ifs to the back of her mind for the time being, allowing anger to lead her.

"Care about me?" She laughed. "You could have fooled the hell out of me."

His eyes shifted toward the doorway, brimming with unease. "I want to tell you something," he said, "and I want you to open your mind and listen. Please."

Nora was confused. It was obvious by the sound of his voice, that Adam was afraid of something. But what?

His phone rang. He drew it from his pocket with reluctance and backed up toward the door, keeping a close eye on her as he did. "Be quiet," he warned her.

The darkness in his eyes told her that he meant what he'd said.

"Where are you?" Adam's voice all but shook as he spoke into the phone. He looked at Nora and then back at the bedroom door again, pacing back and forth like a caged animal.

"No, Ethan," he said firmly. "I haven't seen any sign of Nora. She's probably headed up the road by now."

Nora sat up. Why did he just tell Ethan he hadn't seen her? *Was he protecting her?*

Adam's eyes locked with Nora's. And for one strange moment, there was some sort of connection between them, although she didn't understand it.

He turned his attention back to the phone. "Just let her go, forget about her—forget about the whole thing. We need to get out of here. Right now. Before it's too late. It's not worth it anymore."

Nora could hear Ethan's voice boom in the receiver, as he responded. She watched Adam's hand tighten around the cell.

"No," Adam argued.

He listened and paced for another moment, then stopped abruptly. His body stiffened. "I'm telling you...*I won't do it.*"

A new wave of fear hit Nora. *Do what exactly?*

Adam slowed his words, choosing them carefully. "Listen to me when I tell you this, Ethan. I have done all you have ever told me to do, even when I knew it wasn't right. Even when everything—*everything*—inside me told me not to. I did it because you're my brother. Because you raised me." He hesitated. "And to tell you the God's honest truth, Ethan...because I was scared as shit of you. But, now," he said, bearing down on the phone, his volume climbing fast, "now I want you to listen to what *I'm telling you,* and know that I mean it. I'm done. It's over. I won't allow it to happen. *Not. This.*"

Adam listened to Ethan's response, the blood draining from his face. He pulled the phone away from his ear and slammed it against the wall with a fury that sent fragments of glass across the room. He looked at Nora, a new raw intensity sparking in his eyes. "Do you have the keys to your car?"

"Adam, what are—"

"Just answer me."

"Yes, I have them."

He reached for her, pulling her up off the chair.

"We don't have much time. Ethan is coming and he will kill you, *trust me.*"

"I don't understand," she said. "Why are you helping me?"

Adam took her hand in his. "In the beginning, I agreed to help Ethan get you out of this house, Nora. But I can't do this anymore." He hesitated. "The longer I spent with you, the more my feelings changed. Getting to know you, being with you. At dinner the other night, the way we laughed, the way we enjoyed each other, I—"

She stared at him blankly.

"I'm telling you that I care about you."

"Then why the hell have you been doing all of this to me?"

He squeezed her hand hard. "You don't understand. This house belongs to Ethan, and to me."

Nora jerked her hand away from his. "All of this over the title to some damn property?" she stammered. "Do you even hear what you're saying?"

"That's just it. It's not just a piece of property. How can I make you understand? To make you see what I've come to see?" He swallowed hard, his voice dropping to just above a whisper. "Nora...my mother is here."

Nora couldn't believe her ears. "Adam, I read the newspaper articles. Your mother died a long time ago. You can't actually believe that."

He took her by the shoulders, held her there. "Listen to me. Please. My mother is here. I'm telling you the truth. I—" His words tumbled out of control. "I know how it sounds, I do, but I swear it's real. Ethan believes she's here, and I feel her here, too."

He looked across the room. Nora shuddered at the odd way he appeared to disengage for a long moment before he spoke again.

"My mother, she..." Adam paused, his eyes shifting back to Nora's. "She talks to Ethan, Nora. *Touches him.* Has ever since the night she died in the fire."

He watched her closely, continued.

"Ethan started the fire but it was an accident, honest to God, it was. And after the house was engulfed, no one could find him anywhere. My mother went crazy, pushing through everyone to go back in to search for him, but—" Adam's face turned ashen. "She never came back out."

Nora balanced the urgency to bolt with the need to understand. "So let me get this straight. Your mother died in the fire, but you and Ethan believe she's still here in the house somehow. And the goal was to scare the hell out of me, so that I would leave the *three* of you alone...and you would all live happily ever after. Is that what you're telling me, Adam? Seriously?"

"I'd hoped that maybe you would have more of an open mind toward the situation. This is what I was afraid would happen. You have to understand that Ethan just wanted what was his. That's all."

"*His?*" she gaped. "This place was my sister's! Not your psychotic brother's, not yours, and not your dead—"

"Careful," Adam warned. "Don't go there. You can be angry at my brother. And you can hate me if that makes you feel better. But don't disrespect my mother like that."

"Listen to me, Adam. This is insane. Your mother is not here. She's dead, and that's tragic and terrible, but if Ethan has you believing that she's not—"

"But even you smelled the lilacs."

"What?"

"That was her perfume. She wore it every single day of her life, and that's not something any of us could have imagined."

"Maybe Ethan had something to do with it," she yelled. "Maybe he was attempting to keep you here. Did you ever consider that?"

"Stop!" Adam pressed a hand over her mouth. "Just stop. Ethan will be back any minute. If he hears us, it's over. Do you hear me? *Over.*"

Nora tasted the salt of his sweat on her lips. She wanted to wipe it away but knew better.

Adam slowly removed his hand. "I don't want anything to happen to you. I want you to get out of here alive."

He moved to the closet and pulled the door open. From behind, Nora watched in shock as he reached high above the built-in shelving and pulled out a small section of the brick and mortar work. The edge of her floor-to-ceiling shoe rack jutted open, revealing a narrow stairway leading down.

The same stale air from earlier crawled across her skin. Her thoughts exploding as she realized the passageways inside the house were far more invasive than she'd dared imagine.

"Listen to me," Adam said. "Take these stairs down and follow the tunnel. It comes out beneath a bluff back toward the river, so you'll have to come back around to your car. Go as fast as you can, do you hear me? This is your only chance to get out of here. I will handle Ethan."

"Adam, you have to listen to me," Nora said. "Ben is hurt. He may be dying for all I know." The thought terrified her. "I have to get him out, too. I'm not leaving without him."

Adam shook his head. "No. There isn't time."

"Then I'll die here with him."

"Damn it, Nora, Ethan is—"

A sound from beyond the door stopped him. He turned to Nora.

"*He's here.*"

CHAPTER TWENTY-SIX

Ethan pulled the revolver from his pocket. His hatred for Nora growing by tenfold as he came to realize the true depth of the hold she somehow had over Adam. His brother was weak. He'd always known it. Ethan had been the one to lead, to take control, get things done. Always. It had been the only way they'd survived their childhood.

He thought back to the years of torture their grandfather had forced them to endure, the beatings, the seclusion. Ethan had been the one to finally step in and end it.

His body tightened as the image of his grandparents skirted through his mind. Getting rid of them hadn't been as difficult as he'd imagined, once he'd stumbled across the rat poison in the barn. Both of them had gobbled it down day after day in their coffee without a clue. It had been a long process, watching them slowly waste away, but fruitful in the end.

They'd been the first lives he'd taken, and it had surprised him how good it felt. How liberating. He'd felt that way with Lucy, too. Victory was indeed sweet.

And now the time had come to finish things with Nora. He simply needed to find her and drag her from beneath the protective wing of his brother. She was just another obstacle, like all the other women in his life had been, with one exception—his mother.

Her face flooded his mind. She had been the only one to ever really love him. *And had given her life as proof.*

The thought threatened to bring him to his knees.

He closed his eyes, remembering the night of the fire. How she'd appeared in the window after she'd died, calling him back inside. How she'd drawn him into her arms, held him close. How she'd forgiven him and promised she'd always be there with him in the house, that she would never leave. And she'd kept her promise. He could feel her with him as he roamed the halls, feel it in every fiber of his being. She was there, just as sure as the blood pulsing through his veins.

He opened his eyes and cocked the revolver. No one was going to take that away from him.

No one.

He climbed the stairs, following the murmur of voices. Going over the plan in his mind. He had to succeed in pulling this one off without any hitches. Red flags would pop up to the highest degree if Nora turned up dead here in the house so soon after her sister. But he'd come up with a plan that would work. And Adam was going to help him, even if his coward of a brother didn't know it yet.

Ethan smiled as he heard the spike of Nora's voice from the other side of the bedroom door, the desperation in her voice whetting his appetite for the finish.

THE DOORKNOB CLICKED as it twisted back and forth in Ethan's hand.

Nora had seen Adam lock it earlier, but she knew Ethan would be inside the room within a matter of seconds, regardless.

"You should have gone when I told you, Nora," Adam snapped.

"Come on, now," Ethan cooed through the door.

Nora wanted to scream.

"Seriously. Open up, you two, so we can have a little...*staff meeting*." He laughed out loud, then stopped. "I mean it, now. We've got some business to finish up. Let's get this over with."

Adam locked eyes with Nora, and for a split second, both of them seemed to clearly understand that the worst kind of trouble, the devil himself, was only a door's width away.

Nora looked at the closet.

"Go," Adam ordered her.

"Don't let her go!" Ethan yelled, slamming a shoulder against the door. "I mean it, Adam," he roared, practically on top of them now, a fury of angry flesh pounding on wood.

Adam shoved Nora toward the closet and raced over to the bedroom door to hold his brother off.

She ducked inside, just ready to scramble down the stairs as the blast of the revolver rocked the house.

Time stopped.

Shards of woods exploded through the room as Adam dropped to the floor, blood flooding through the front of his shirt in a giant crimson stain.

Nora stared at him. This man she'd once cared about—but now knew she should despise—unable to tear her eyes away as he struggled to hold on to the last fragment of his life. He was conscious, but just barely, and with blood pouring from his chest, she didn't have to be a doctor to see that the damage was likely irreparable.

Nora edged across the floor to where he lay calling for her.

"I'm so sorry," Adam whispered as he looked up at her. "Please forgive me..."

He struggled to swallow as a gurgling sound bubbled up in his throat.

Nora couldn't move. She watched as the color slowly drained from his face, his eyes.

He was almost gone. There was nothing she could do.

Ethan's screams on the other side of what was left of the door jolted Nora from her paralysis. She stumbled backwards, her feet nearly toppling her over as she took one last look at Adam. The image would stay with her for the rest of her life. Assuming there was going to be any of her life left after Ethan broke into the room.

Adam coughed, blood streaming from the side of his mouth as he whispered one last word to her.

"Go."

She hesitated, blinking back terrified tears, but the sound of Ethan barreling against the door lit a fire beneath her.

She made it back to the closet and sprinted down the stairs.

Behind her, Ethan screamed out in agony.

He'd found Adam.

ETHAN KNELT over the lifeless remains of the only family he'd had left.

She'd made him kill his own brother. *His own flesh and blood.* And Nora would die a painful death for it.

His screams of pure raw hatred pounded through the house.

He was going to kill her slowly, and with any luck, he would find Ben first and use him as the pre-show entertainment. Yes, he would see to it that Nora paid for what she'd done. Paid in full.

DARKNESS BECAME her enemy as she raced down the remainder of the stairs as fast as she could. Her flashlight was long gone, and without it, she tripped, tumbling hard to the bottom.

Pain splintered through her ankle. *Get back up*, her mind demanded. But as she struggled to stand, a monstrous hand reached out and yanked her up by the hair, then slammed her back down again.

"Get back here, bitch," Ethan hissed.

He dragged her back up the stairs, her body raking against the jagged walls as she went. Before she realized it, they were in her bedroom again. Adam's body lying between them.

"*Do you understand what you've done?* You killed my brother!" He shoved her down to the floor. "You're nothing but a useless whore just like your sister was. And you will die now just like she did." He lifted the barrel of the revolver and pressed it painfully into her leg. "Only slower."

He cocked the trigger, aimed it toward her thigh. "Let's start here, shall we?"

"Please," Nora begged, hating the frail, helpless sound of her voice as she did. "Please, just listen to me."

"Shut your mouth."

One hand gripping her hair and the other wrapped around the revolver, he dug it in deeper. "Since you're the big-time writer, Nora, got a question for you. Just how would you kill off your lovely heroine? We've already done *slippery stairs on a dark and stormy night*, so that's out."

Nora thought of Lucy and instantly wanted to kill Ethan with her bare hands. She lunged up into him, her knee slamming into his groin.

Ethan howled, grabbing her once more. He shoved her face down, smashing her teeth against the hardwood. "Hope you enjoyed that, because it's the last thing you'll ever do," he snarled, his weight choking her.

She tried to scream for help as he drew back the gun and smashed it down onto her left cheekbone.

God, help me, please help me somehow. The words tumbled and twirled wildly, around and around in Nora's head as death roared toward her like a freight train racing down the tracks.

But just as Ethan aimed the barrel of the gun toward her temple, he screamed and arched backward, writhing in pain.

What was happening?

He cried out again, twisting to face the unknown assailant, just in time to receive a second and much harder blow.

His body dropped down onto Nora like a rock. She froze as everything suddenly stopped.

Was Adam alive? No, it couldn't be. She'd seen him die.

Shock pinned her under Ethan's weight. Then suddenly arms struggled to pull her from beneath his body, dragging her out.

"Nora!"

She looked up into Ben's badly bruised and swollen face, the realization that he was her saving grace—*that he was alive* —igniting her.

"You're here. You're all right," she cried, pulling herself to her feet as Ethan slumped to the floor beside her.

Ben labored under his pain as he eased her into him. "I was so afraid I'd be too late," he choked, his voice crumbling as he buried his face in Nora's hair.

"No. I'm okay, I'm okay," she whispered. "When I left you in the tunnel, you couldn't walk, you couldn't even stand. I can't believe you're here."

Nora looked down at Ethan's body. He lay motionless, blood spilling from the back of his head.

She looked back at Ben. "How did you—"

"With this." Ben held up the fireplace poker. "The bastard used it on me earlier and was stupid enough to leave it behind."

Sirens blared toward them in the distance.

Nora's eyes brimmed, beginning to spill. "How did they know to come? My phone battery died. I couldn't call for help—"

"Ben? Nora?" Liz's frantic voice floated up from downstairs.

"We can thank Liz for that," Ben said, attempting to smile.

"She was standing at what's left of the front door when I came up."

Ben's body swayed, his strength finally starting to give way. Nora reached to steady him. "We need to get you to a hospital," she said.

"Can't really argue with that," he replied. "But first, all I really need is this." He grasped her hand, pulled her closer.

Nora blinked back a fresh round of tears and fell into him, held him tight. Losing herself in the strong arms of the man who had saved her life, the man she loved with all her heart. She would never let go.

EPILOGUE

"You ready, Mrs. Whitfield?"

Nora laughed lightly as Ben wrapped his arms around her. "I'll never get tired of hearing you call me that, just so you know."

"I was kind of hoping you wouldn't," he said, pulling her close. "You know," he added, kissing her neck softly, "we should probably head downstairs to the parlor for the reception so we can smear each other with cake and then get the heck out of Dodge. We have a honeymoon to begin."

"Yes, we do. I'm really looking forward to having you all to myself for a couple of weeks."

"Me, too. More than you know," he said. He lifted Nora's suitcase off the bed and took it to the door. "So, do you think Liz will be able to handle running the inn while we're gone? Now that we're finally open, reservations are flooding in."

"I think she'll do great. She has Scott and Jessica to help her, as well as our secret weapon." Nora smiled as the face of the new chef she'd hired flashed through her mind.

"You're right," he nodded. "I guess she's used to wrangling two kids *and Scott*, on a regular basis anyway, so I'm sure she'll be fine. And we'll be back home soon enough."

Nora smiled at Ben. Hearing him call Black Willow his home, warmed her. She looked forward to running the inn together with him when they returned from their trip—beginning their new life side by side, continuing on with a dream that had meant so much to her sister, and now to Nora, too. Her heart overflowed.

Ben leaned in and planted a kiss on her lips. "I'm going to take our bags downstairs and come back up for you in a minute."

She watched him leave, then walked to the window. Beyond the pane of glass, spring was in full bloom. The grounds were bursting with bright flowers against the rich green backdrop of the willows and woods beyond.

She looked down at the brilliant sparkle of her wedding ring, wrapped seamlessly around her finger. In the months since the fateful night she'd almost lost Ben—almost lost everything—Ben had remained by her side, loving her every moment. He'd shown her that not only would life go on but that their days and nights from now on would be filled with the kind of love fairy tales are spun from.

Nora let her mind wander back through the ceremony that had just taken place. It had been perfect. A small wedding, but everyone that she and Ben cared about had been there. His parents, Nora's parents, their closest friends—everyone except Lucy. But Nora had felt her presence. She'd felt it as she'd walked down the aisle and continued to feel it every time she moved through the halls of Black Willow. Her sister was at peace now, she was certain.

Nora was at peace, too. It was as if all of the turmoil in the house, the unrest, had faded away the night Adam and Ethan had died. Nothing any longer went bump in the night. No more footsteps or cigar smoke or slamming doors. *No more lilacs.* The house itself had taken on a new feeling. One of courage and redemption, of pride.

She and Ben had decided to embrace the house's historic connection to the Underground Railroad. To highlight the *good* Black Willow had done in the past—the lives it had helped to save. By now, Nora had come across dozens of stories, documenting how the property had helped to bring safety and salvation to countless souls throughout the years. And she'd been pleasantly surprised when Ben had suggested the idea to open up a few of the hidden passages, allowing guests to tour them, share in those stories, those triumphs.

Nora turned around as Ben walked through the door.

"Did you miss me?" he asked, collecting her into his arms again.

"Maybe a little."

He gently pushed her hair aside, tracing his fingers across her bare shoulders.

"Don't stop," she murmured.

Ben leaned his forehead against hers. "Believe me, I don't want to, but I have to. At this rate, by the time we're done with the reception, we're going to get a really late start. We'll be driving all night."

"I'll drive," she offered. "All I need is a cup of steaming hot coffee in my hand when I climb behind the wheel."

Ben cocked his head to the side and chuckled.

Nora stopped, pulled back a little. "What's so funny?"

"Oh, nothing," he said, grinning. "Just thinking back to another time, not too long ago, when you climbed behind the wheel of a vehicle with a cup of steaming hot coffee in your hand —and how my truck landed in a ditch as a result of it." He winked at her. "Isn't that how we got here in the first place?"

Nora's mind darted back to her first visit to Black Willow. How she'd spilled scalding hot coffee down her leg and lost control of her car, running Ben off the road and how she'd nearly died of embarrassment as he strode in the front door of the house moments later, announcing he was Black Willow's contractor. It felt like a lifetime ago.

She tossed her head back and laughed—trying, but failing, to scowl at him. "I'd really hoped you'd forgotten about that by now."

"Not a chance," Ben said, planting a quick, firm kiss on her lips. "Why would I ever want to forget? That was the very best day of my life—*the day I met you*." He smiled and slipped his hand in hers pulling her toward the doorway. "Okay now, we really do need to get downstairs. It's cake smearing time. Liz and Scott are taking bets on which one of us has better aim."

Nora laughed again. She followed Ben downstairs, hanging back just long enough to take a good look at the house as she did.

Where once there had been darkness, secrets, fear, there was now strength and perseverance. There was hope and the promise of happiness. She could imagine the laughter of their children as they raced up and down the halls. Imagine birthdays and holidays bursting with joy and warmth.

Nora caught up with Ben and squeezed his hand tight. "I love you," she whispered as they made their way into the sea of smiling faces below.

"I love you back," he answered. "I plan to spend the rest of my life showing you just how much."

And Nora knew that he would. *Always*.

Made in United States
North Haven, CT
13 March 2023

33998973R00164